Droughtbringer
Volume One

DESOLATE DAWN

Kristen Kail Roberts

Copyright © 2025 Kristen Kail Roberts

All rights reserved.

ISBN: 979-8-9922042-0-9

Cover designed by Getcovers

This book is dedicated to my partner Sam.
Thank you for teaching me how to use a sword,
and for never letting me give up on using the pen.

Author's Note

Droughtbringer Volume One: Desolate Dawn is the novelized adaptation of the first season of Droughtbringer, previously available in serial format on Kindle Vella. While the overall story is essentially the same, adjustments have been made with regard to format and overall clarity. *Desolate Dawn* also contains added scenes and world building details not included in the original episodes thanks to the questions and suggestions of my beta readers.

If you enjoyed Draya's adventures the first time around, I think you'll still find reading − or at least skimming − this new edition worth your effort. There are things you definitely do not want to miss (especially Chapter 11).

1

The loud crunch of shattered bone echoed off the stone walls of the narrow tunnel. Draya stomped her heel into the brittle skull for good measure before turning towards her second attacker. The undead guardian advanced, the bones of its fleshless digits inexplicably wrapped around the haft of a rusted battle axe. If the skeleton mourned the loss of its companion, there was no way to tell as it stepped over the spine of the ruined corpse in a jerking, unbalanced gait. Its empty eye sockets seemed to absorb what little light escaped the fallen lantern nearby, making the darkness inside them all the more complete. Draya pulled her attention away from its sightless gaze, searching for a weakness. She found it in the deep red ruby hanging like a pendulum from its throat.

Unlike freshly turned undead, no clothing hung from its ivory frame. Presumably, anything it might have been wearing had long ago disintegrated, leaving a rusted iron circlet and the pendant as its only adornments. She hazarded a glance at the severed vertebrae of her first attacker. Sure enough, she spotted an identical glint of red a few feet away. *Lucky shot,* she realized. *That explains it.*

She narrowed her eyes as her focus shifted to the crude work of some long-dead necromancer. The tunnel traveled beneath the Radiant Sea, and the fathoms of fresh water that surrounded them should have been more than enough to keep any mundane undead pacified. Unless, of course, they carried a blood token. She breathed a sigh. Judging by their speed, it may have taken the pair the better part of the last decade to make it this far from the palace. Draya might have felt some remorse if the things were capable of appreciating the emotion.

The skeleton lifted its axe high over its head, but she was prepared. With practiced ease, she struck out with her boot, the flat of her foot connecting hard against its bare breastbone. The kick would have knocked the wind out of a living opponent, but in this case, the dead thing only staggered backward. The weight of the axe head threw it off balance, and the skeleton teetered awkwardly. The exposed bones of its feet found no traction on the slick stone, but eventually, it managed to right itself.

The fragile state of the circlet gave her an idea.

Seeing an opening, Draya spun the thin blade of her rapier in an upward arc, catching the chain of the pendant in a loop. With the flick of her wrist, the ancient iron chain snapped clean. She smiled triumphantly, but instead of toppling over, the skeleton lunged. Its weapon came down towards her like a hammer, and she barely managed to drop and roll out of its wake. The axe blade struck the ground with a spray of sparks, metal grinding against the well-worn rock.

Draya looked up in confusion and groaned. The blood token had lodged itself between the skeleton's broken ribs, allowing the magic to maintain its hold on the corpse.

"Not fair." She spat out some blood and wiped her mouth with the back of her sleeve. "That has to be cheating." She got back on her feet, careful not to lose her footing on the loose fragments that littered the floor. Pain blossomed from a spot in her hip where one of the rocks had broken her fall.

The skeleton gave her no respite. It swept the axe upwards in an attempt to catch the tender flesh below Draya's chin. Rather than retreat, she sidestepped and lunged, grabbing the blood token with her open hand. As it came free, the axe dropped to the ground with a dull thud. The skeleton swayed for only a moment, then dropped beside the remains of its companion. Its frame collapsed, leaving nothing more than a pile of bones.

Not wanting to take any chances, she stomped down on the skull as she did with the first, sending dust and fragments in every direction. Slipping her rapier back into its sheath, she snatched up her fallen lantern and continued forward. She couldn't hear any shuffling ahead and suspected the way was clear. She was fiddling with the iron casement of the lantern when she felt the ground squelch beneath her foot.

"You have got to be kidding me." Draya scrunched her nose up in disgust as she lifted her ankle boot out of the muck. The fetid water had splashed upwards, soaking the hem of her pants as it leeched into her socks. She lowered her lantern and the firelight reflected off the stagnant surface that coated the floor of the ancient tunnel. Up until now, she'd been surprised at how dry the secret entrance into the palace was, but it was clear she'd celebrated too soon. She continued onward, her eyes surveying the gradual increase in moss growing along cracks in the wall. As a trickle of water seeped from a particularly large crevice, she couldn't help but second guess accepting this contract. That stone was all that stood between the treasure hunter and the crushing weight of lake water pressing down from above. Her employers had said it was safe, but between the ancient undead sentries and the level of disuse she could see with her own eyes, she doubted they'd scouted out the location enough to know that for sure.

And why would they bother? she thought to herself. *I'm the one with their neck on the line, after all.* She shook her head. She knew it wasn't her expendability that got her hired. Clients paid her significant coin for a reason. She could find the things no one else could find. Some would have said it was a Calling, but Draya rolled her eyes at the suggestion. She just had a knack for puzzles, a studied knowledge of maps and schematics, and the perseverance to keep going where others might retreat.

She was also incredibly stubborn.

The silence of the underground tunnel was a presence in and of itself. Everything was muffled so far below the surface, insulated from the abundance of life that existed above. Draya was considering whether she should start singing a sea shanty to pass the time when the trickle of water ended and the floor began angling upward. Abandoning any regard for further skeletons, she picked up speed, eager to reach the tunnel's end. It took longer than she would have liked, but finally, the passageway opened up into a small antechamber. There was a short pedestal in the center, but whatever artifact it once showcased was long ago taken by looters. Beyond stood three archways, the furthest one to the left half-concealed with rotting wooden boards. Luckily, that wasn't the way to her prize. She looked to the top of the archway on the far right. Assuming her clients had any idea what they were talking about, she'd found the next path she needed to take. Dismissing the other options, she strode forward, encouraged by the continuous ascent the path seemed to take toward the surface.

Past the threshold, the right wall was lined with a series of identical heavy doors. She counted them as she went - Nine. Ten. Eleven. She paused at the twelfth door and looked it up and down. This had to be it. Draya hung her lantern on the iron hook to the right of the door and examined the ring that hung from the latch. The old brass was dull and tarnished, and it didn't look like it was coated in anything. Nevertheless, it was impossible to know what kinds of defenses had survived the test of time.

Better safe than sorry, she reminded herself.

She pulled a pair of new leather gloves from her belt and dutifully slipped her hands inside each one. She flexed her fingers and grimaced. They were completely identical to her former pair, custom-made from the same soft hide and sewn by the same tailor. They should feel no different, and yet Draya couldn't help but miss her old pair. She repressed a shudder as she remembered the slight tingle of the acid gel as it burned through the calfskin. The gloves had provided protection just long enough for her to strip them off before they were completely eaten through. Prepared for whatever might be awaiting her, she tugged at the ring that served as a latch.

It didn't budge.

She rolled her eyes, then braced her feet against the stone floor and wrapped both her hands around the ring. Throwing all her weight backward, she felt the bloated wooden door resist for a moment, finally breaking free of its rusted hinges. The momentum threw Draya backward against the far tunnel wall as the door fell with an echoing thud. Beyond was exactly what Draya had been seeking – a staircase out of the deplorable tunnel she'd been stuck in for over an hour. Dusting herself off, Draya took back her lantern and propelled herself forward, scaling the spiral steps two at a time.

Her exuberance had waned by the time she reached the small landing at the top, and she found herself breathing heavier than she'd normally expect. The tunnel must have been even deeper under the lake than she had imagined for the flight of stairs to go on for so long.

"This better be the right room," she mumbled. No more than a hand's breadth away stood a sliding door with only a small handle on one side. Tentatively, she pulled at the latch. After a brief hitch, the pocket door slid easily on its tracks. The humidity must have had far less of an impact this close to the lake's surface.

Past the threshold, lantern light reflected off a cascade of tattered cloth that had once hidden the secret door from view. Draya held her breath and gingerly pushed it aside. It may have been a tapestry, but whatever it once depicted had long since faded. Rather than dwell on its potential provenance, she turned her small light towards the center of the pitch-black space, checking the floor for any hazards or loose tiles. Finding none, she lifted the lantern to eye level.

Ivory fangs as long as daggers greeted Draya from the absolute darkness.

2

Draya flung herself backward, her adrenaline racing as her free hand dropped to the hilt of her rapier. She sank into a defensive stance as she prepared to deflect the beast's snapping jaws.

She froze.

The creature hadn't moved. It hadn't even made a sound.

The tension in her muscles melted. Draya swung the lantern in an arc, illuminating a plethora of similarly pointed teeth, beaks, and even a few pincers. Their owners each stood stock still, the flame reflecting off their glassy black eyes.

Taxidermy, she realized. She was in some kind of curio or trophy room.

Thankful no one had witnessed her embarrassing overreaction, Draya searched the room in further detail. A set of broad double doors served as the room's main entrance, and on closer examination it was clear that the lock had been broken at some point. She weighed the ramifications against the profitability of her mission, but decided the previous looters were of no immediate concern. The layers of dust proved that the burglary had happened a long time ago, and it seemed unlikely her clients would have hired her if they weren't absolutely sure the artifact was still unaccounted for. She waved her lantern over one of a pair of braziers flanking the threshold. As she assumed, the charcoal within was enchanted with old magic. The contents immediately caught fire, casting warm light throughout the crowded space. She let out a low whistle.

There had to be at least twenty large taxidermied creatures arranged artistically around the room, and a countless number of smaller specimens peered out from shelves and glass-enclosed cabinets. Heavy sets of dark velvet curtains punctuated the walls at regular intervals, presumably hiding the windows of spell-worked glass that protected the interior of the palace from the elements outside. She turned her attention back to the long-dead beasts. The skills of the taxidermist were evident. The creatures were perfectly preserved despite the passage of time, with not even an errant whisker or razor-sharp claw out of place. Draya tried to decipher their species but came up empty. As far as she could tell, they were amalgams – seamless combinations of various animals that made a final whole. She may have thought they were merely a hoax – some flim-flam art project of an eccentric nobleman – if not for the first-hand accounts she had read in her pre-Deluge studies. She reached out and patted the shoulder of a hulking beast with the body of a bear and the head of a lowland elk. A cloud of dust erupted from its pelt, and before she could stop herself, Draya let out a bellowing sneeze.

For the second time since she'd entered the room, she froze and held her breath. After a beat, she rolled her eyes. "Who do you think will hear you?" she asked aloud. "The ghosts of curators' past?" Her incredulous reflection stared back at her from the glass door of a specimen cabinet. *Aside from the glorified groundskeepers at the main entrance, there isn't a living soul for at least a league,* she reminded herself. *And no squatter would brave the superstitions that haunt this sunken deathtrap.* She considered the security patrol stationed on the floors above the sea's surface but shook her head. According to the most recent intelligence, not even priests of the Cresting Tide were allowed inside the submerged levels of the palace, let alone any soldiers left in their stead.

She returned her attention to the room. Even if she was assuredly alone within the bowels of the monolith, she had work to get done. Narrowing her eyes, she concentrated on the objects around the room, one by one. She'd been given a rudimentary description of her quarry, but even her clients seemed unsure of its exact appearance. It didn't matter. Draya was sure she'd know the object when she saw it – or she hoped she would anyway. She circled the perimeter of the room with methodical care. It was unlikely the item would be in plain sight, but it didn't hurt to check. On her second circuit, she began knocking on walls and checking the depth and height of each drawer for secret compartments. Twice she discovered false bottoms to drawers and thought she had succeeded in her search only to be disappointed. One was empty, the other filled with a handful of smudged and faded charcoal drawings. She gave the latter a cursory look, but all they contained were blurry shadows of faces. She shoved them back into the compartment and slammed it shut.

That left the interior of the room.

Draya side-stepped between a pair of particularly vicious wolf-lion hybrids poised to attack one another. After her initial survey, she realized the placement of the stuffed monstrosities wasn't random. The collection was almost imperceptibly divided into four clusters, each arranged into a rudimentary triangle with their points converging on one central sculpture. It was one of the largest, second only to the elk-bear she'd encountered upon her arrival. If not for its size, she may have mistaken it for a muscular ram, but there was more to it than that. Its heavy horns spiraled forward from the center of its skull, the twisting surface opalescent in the firelight, and its muzzle was long and flat, bearing a pair of tusks on each side. Its deep-set eyes were obscured by a permanent scowl.

"Don't you look pleasant." Draya examined the strange creature. It was the nightmarish offspring of a goat, a warthog, and a water buffalo with the charm and warmth of a crocodile. Its long legs ended in cloven hooves, and it was perched on a massive pedestal of carved black marble. Her eyes were drawn to a small bronze plate affixed to one side. She knelt down and wiped away the accumulated grime with her sleeve, expecting to find some words of identification – or at least some maudlin quote about the wonders of the wilderness. Instead, she found a few words written in the Loatrin tongue. The shapes of the triangular logograms were vaguely familiar to the treasure hunter, but her skills in deciphering them were rusty at best. The palace was a long way from the southern continent, and while it wasn't impossible, it was incredibly odd to see the language north of the Mahdjor Steppes. "A proper name, not a species," she mused aloud. She almost recognized the epithet etched beneath it. "Beloved? No — loyal?" It was some iteration of that, she was sure. Curious, she pulled out her graphite and journal from a sealskin pouch on her hip and made a quick rubbing to translate later. As she slipped both back into her hip pouch, she met the thing's strange opal eyes looming over her. "You were somebody's pet, weren't you?"

From this vantage point, she could see beneath the thick, coarse hair that fell almost like a beard from its chin. She was about to start checking the base for compartments when something glinted from its throat. She cocked her head to one side and reached up to find a tiny metal triangle. Intrigued, she found the charm was hooked to a thin leather collar buried in the hair of its neck. She followed it, but there were no other adornments. She traced the point downwards, her finger trailing toward the creature's sternum.

Suddenly, the translation clicked into place.

"Heart-Keeper," she breathed. She'd been right. The word did mean 'beloved' or 'treasured' in the Loatrin language, but that wasn't the literal definition of the composite word.

Her own heart began to pound with the realization. Stretching to her maximum height over the marble base, she managed to press her fingers up and under the heavy breastbone. As she hoped, the fur gave way to her touch and her gloved fingers met with an object enveloped in soft cloth.

"Jackpot."

Eager to finally see her prize, she pulled the bundle out from its hiding place and gingerly peeled away the layers of decayed velvet. Inside was a casement of burnished gold a little larger than her palm, with more Loatrin script delicately carved into the soft metal. A glass teardrop hung inside, suspended by what looked to be strands of gossamer thread. Even through her gloves, she could feel its cold temperature rising to match her body heat. She pressed her fingertips against the glass vessel at its center. It seemed to hum in response to her touch.

She shook her head in disbelief. "I should have doubled my fee."

When her client's request cited the retrieval of a Vivication Sarcophilum, Draya never considered they were referring to a genuine specimen. The reliquary in her hands might have been an elaborate forgery, but the green-tinged gold used in its construction gave her pause. Natural veins of the silver-infused alloy had dried up long ago, and if it was real, the material predated the palace by more than a century. The ancient legends surrounding such relics were absurd, but even if they were remotely true, the ritual practices were as lost as any other remnant of old magic. Countless religious sects had appropriated the Pre-Deluge term for more mundane objects of veneration, and she'd assumed the Fellowship of the Sun had done the same. The mere possession of a true Sarcophilum might lend weight to any challenges the Fellowship made against the supremacy of the Order of the Cresting Tide.

All the more reason to collect their coin before the Coronet collects their heads.

She shrugged her knapsack off her shoulders and slipped the ornate item into a specially made hidden pocket. She then proceeded to ransack the rest of the room, grabbing hold of any palm-sized items the previous looters had left behind. What were mere decorative items even half a century ago could be sold on the black market for their age alone. She could make a minor fortune with a few well-placed auctions. Finished rummaging through the shelves at last, she took a final look at the disturbing array of creatures before extinguishing the burning braziers with ladles of provided sand. She'd spent enough time in this sunken tomb. It was high time she found her way back out.

Descending the staircase was only mildly less strenuous than the ascent. She eagerly made her way down the sloping hallway and back to the tunnel junction she'd passed through earlier. Draya was midstride towards the exit when her head swiveled to the far right. Unlike the other tunnel entrances, this one had been boarded up with planks. The raw wood looked out of place in comparison to the age and quality of everything else she'd seen, and the bottom few feet were so dark with rot that it was a miracle they hadn't already dissolved.

Draya had what she'd come looking for. She'd done all she'd been paid to do. She had no reason to investigate further. She looked back to the tunnel she'd come in through but found herself frozen in place. The trophy room hadn't even been protected by a simple lock. On the contrary, this particular corridor had been hastily blocked off sometime after the Great Flood, presumably by the Cresting Tide when it assumed possession of the palace. Why agents of the religious order would put in that kind of effort nagged at her sense of curiosity.

"Sarding abyss," Draya cursed under her breath. She squared her shoulders and marched to the mouth of the offending tunnel.

The wood from her waist up was decayed, but still rather solid. It creaked but didn't budge under the pressure of her palms. The planks below her knees, however, were barely holding their shape. Water wasn't currently settled there, but there was evidence it had been submerged for quite some time. The floor was slick with old moss that was more akin to slime than plant life. She looked down at her new deer hide breeches. They were made for this kind of work, but that didn't mean she wanted to ruin them so soon. She kicked the toe of her boot into what remained of one of the planks. It gave way like unspun cotton. It wouldn't take much to clear out the bottom third of the barrier to allow her entry. Draya looked over her shoulder to the exit, but she already knew leaving was no longer an option. Once a path presented itself, she could never turn back, soiled breeches or no.

Once she'd cleared out a space large enough to crawl through, she unceremoniously got down on her hands and knees and thrust the lantern ahead of her. The light illuminated nothing but a continuing hallway that looked no different from the one she'd taken to the trophy room. Before she could change her mind, Draya pulled her legs through the opening and got to her feet. As she took her first step forward, she felt the stone tile beneath her left foot sink into the ground with an audible click.

3

Acting on instinct, Draya dove forward, rolling headfirst into a crouch. She heard the rush of air behind her and looked back to see a large, serrated blade wedged into the far wall.

"Stupid!" If she hadn't gotten to the ground in time, she'd be as dead as the stuffed trophies she'd left upstairs. Even with the rotten wooden planks blockading the entrance, she should have anticipated further obstacles. *Instead, I recklessly barreled through like a rank amateur.* She stood, straightened her tunic, and rolled her neck in an effort to recenter herself. She was better than this, and she knew it.

She knelt down and let the lantern light wash over the tile she had stepped on. Now that she was paying attention, the pressure plate stood out like a sore thumb. Unlike the stone floor it was painted to match, the steel plate was square and perfectly smooth. The centuries had worn away at the seams, and the two surfaces were barely flush with one another.

Tamping down her self-deprecation, she turned her attention to the serrated blade. While the surface had tarnished, the crucible steel used in its forging had held up surprisingly well. She tugged on the haft, surprised to find the blade moved silently backward on what was either a well-oiled or well-spelled joint. Judging by the braziers she'd ignited in the trophy room, she suspected the latter. If she wanted to, she was sure she could easily reset the trap. Instead, she returned the blade to its end point before making her way further along the tunnel. One less thing to worry about when she made her exit.

The smooth walls of the tunnel gradually gave way to haphazardly laid brick the color of charcoal. The matte surface seemed to absorb the meager light of her lantern. After a few twists and turns, she began to notice spots of reflected light up ahead on either side. Draya slowed her pace and carefully swept her lantern back and forth, up and down, squinting in the dark. "Got you," she whispered.

A thin line of gossamer thread shone across her path in the lantern light. Unlike the first, which only had the pressure plate as a trigger, this trap was more complex. Nearly imperceptible threads spanned the passageway, each tightly secured to bricks on opposite sides. If it was like other traps of its kind – and she was certain it was – the trip wires should be placed at varying heights, forcing those moving forward to step over, under, or through in the right sequence. Bypassing one could easily mean triggering the next. For reasons beyond Draya's understanding, the anchor bricks on either side were more reflective than the others, pinpointing the location and height of each thread. Careful to avoid touching it, she followed the trip wire to the left. Upon examination, the material itself appeared to be the same. A light scrape with her knife, however, chipped off a flake of the reflective coating from the brick's surface. From its construction, she was positive the trap itself was nearly as old as the palace, but the application of the alchemical mixture was far more recent.

She cocked her head to one side. "Why didn't the Order just disarm the sarding thing?" She spoke her thoughts aloud, her words swallowed by the stretch of darkness before her. Marking the trap but leaving it in place didn't make sense. Draya knew she was good at her job, but any novice acquisitioner should have noticed the painted bricks. Someone wanted to be able make their way through easily while impeding anyone without any training.

What sort of treasure was valuable enough to be protected by traps when they have impenetrable vaults in Trifall? The sarcophilum sprung to mind but was quickly dismissed. That path had been clear, and to her client's benefit, the item had been completely missed by the Coronet for over a century. She smiled in anticipation. With any luck, she'd find out what they were hiding soon enough – she just needed to keep alert for anything more dangerous ahead.

Now that she knew what she was looking for, it was easy to spot the locations of the rest of the wires. She might have considered disarming the trap herself if it wasn't a two-person job. Likely, tripping a wire would simply activate an alarm somewhere in the highest levels of the palace. That didn't worry Draya much – anyone left to guard the palace would be stationed as high as the lake's surface, giving her adequate time to escape. There was still the possibility that the wrong move could trigger steeper consequences, like filling the room with poisonous gas, sealing up the passage on both ends, or releasing spikes from the ceiling. The other option, then, was to climb through without touching the threads. She suspected whoever marked the bricks expected as much.

Draya looked at her dangling lantern. There was no way she could contort herself with the cage in hand. She checked her belt to make sure her flint was still in its pouch, then carefully slid the contraption under the first of the threads. It spun as the momentum carried it forward, stopping just past the halfway mark. Draya let out a breath, glad she'd gotten the amount of force right. Murky light emanated from its settled position allowing her to still make out the faint differences in the bricks on either wall. She did the same with her rapier next, pushing it harder so that it would make the entire length of the trap. It settled easily on the other side. Looking over her shoulder, she sighed. The lump of her knapsack was not going to be ideal to work around, but it was too bulky to slide under the threads like her other items. She'd just have to hope for the best.

Draya took a steadying breath and then stepped over the first trip wire one foot at a time. The next was at chest level, and she ducked low, careful not to stand fully as the next would have cut across her neck. She high-stepped over two at knee and ankle height, tucking her neck to make it under another. There was just enough room for her to bring her foot down between them, and as she lifted her second leg the weight of her knapsack shifted, throwing her off balance. She teetered for a moment on the toes of one foot, her other leg held awkwardly high. Draya could only imagine what a ridiculous sight she made. Steadying herself, she brought her raised leg down and carefully tightened the straps of her pack so that it hugged her spine. It wasn't comfortable, but at least it wouldn't budge. She made it past the next three strands without incident, stepping over one, ducking under another, and then carefully navigating through a pair that ran parallel at calf and shoulder height.

Draya smiled. *Easy enough.* She stooped to pick up her sword and then spun. Her lantern still lay forgotten in the center of the web.

She still had the flint, but there was nothing to catch fire nor any chance she could avoid any future traps without some kind of light to guide her. It was a few threads away, not close enough to grab from where she was. She retreated through the pair of threads she'd just avoided, crouching low so that she could stretch her arm past the other two. Her fingertips just barely touched the metal casement, so she inched a little bit closer, wary of the thread just above the top of her head. As she stretched her fingers as far as they could go, she was finally able to use her nails to catch the edge and drag it towards her in a few stilted movements. She sucked in a sharp breath as she was finally able to snag it with her fingertips. She pulled it backwards quickly and then froze in horror.

She'd forgotten to account for the latch. Her fingers brushed the edge of the miniature door, popping it open. Draya watched what happened next in slow motion.

The tip of the lantern flame sprang upwards.

Sparks of cinder flashed on either side as the thread caught fire and broke.

The singed ends fluttered to the ground like dead moths.

She didn't have time to throw herself backwards. Her eyes squeezed shut as she braced herself, hoping she could survive whatever came next.

The air was still, and after a moment, the treasure hunter opened one eye. There was no poisonous gas. There was no loud crash of a slamming door. There were no spikes. The air was musty and damp, but that was no different than it had been. As she suspected, the trap was meant to sound an alarm rather than injure an intruder.

Or, even more likely, it had stopped working altogether before I was even born.

Draya laughed triumphantly and then carefully extricated herself from the remaining threads. Just in case that one was a dud, she didn't risk triggering any of the others. Ignoring the heavy feeling in her heart from yet another brush with death, she continued forward, the lantern held high.

Contrary to the previous tunnel that led her to the trophy room door, there was no incline to the floor. Beyond the first two traps, archways led to and from the central path. Draya followed her instincts, taking one and then another as if on a whim as she stayed vigilant for further hidden obstacles. Eventually, one of those branching tunnels transformed completely, changing from smoothly crafted walls to crude, hand-dug warrens. She stopped at the transition from one to the other, running her gloved hand against the raw stone. It was strange for a palace of this age to suddenly swap styles so drastically, and the seam was glaringly obvious. This connecting tunnel was a later addition, but for what purpose she couldn't discern.

From there, the route curled in and around itself as her sense of direction led her through an inscrutably convoluted labyrinth. Three times, despite her typically infallible talents, she turned a corner only to find a solid wall of rock forcing her to double back. She even stumbled on two skeletons huddled in the far corner of one of the dead ends. What looked like long, thin scratches trailed the stone at their backs, and the ribcage of one had caved in. She'd paused, searching for blood tokens, but the pair had been long dead, the cracked bones dry and yellowed with age.

Eventually, the narrow tunnels opened back up into the professionally carved hallways she'd started in. She wasn't sure how much time had passed circumnavigating the strange maze, but she was beginning to regret her earlier disregard for any alarm her mishap with the trap might have triggered. She considered cutting her losses. She had no desire to end up on the wrong side of an official inquest — or even worse, vanished into some secret Order prison. Draya took in a lungful of air and felt a muscle pull in her lower back. It had been a while since she'd had to do any acrobatics on a job. "I'm getting too old for this," she grumbled. She wasn't about to limp back through those passages with nothing to show for it, and she'd come too far to give up now.

She looked to the left. A cascade of heavy rocks filled the hallway. The obstruction looked like it had been there a long time, the ceiling of the hall caving in on itself. Instinctively, Draya knew that this hallway once made a straight shot back to the original tunnel she'd started from. There was no way to discern if the blockade was intentional, or just some unfortunate accident. She looked to the right and made her way around a bend in the hall. She expected more pathways to navigate, but she was proven wrong. The tunnel came to an abrupt end, the space filled with an ornate archway that framed a heavy ironwood door.

"Hello, beautiful," Draya said with a smile.

4

Draya had seen a fair share of doorways in her line of work. Bloodstained castle gates banded with cold iron; hatches to crawl spaces so small she was forced to slither in on her belly; shining metal behemoths built to safeguard those that could afford the luxury. She could say with authority that this particular door wasn't a modest construction – it was a work of art.

The impressive feat of architecture filled the far wall of a cavernous vestibule, flanked on both sides by another set of unlit braziers. An expansive frame of chiseled black marble spilled out around the perimeter, its languid swirls punctuated by a halo of spiking rays. The central panels of each door were left raw, the natural wefts emphasized with glossy golden wax, while the stiles were sanded smooth. Veins of golden filigree spun throughout the material and disappeared into the marble archway. That particular technique alone aged the door at least three hundred years, placing it well before the palace was built. How someone had transported it here from the Southlands was a feat.

Intrigued despite herself, Draya approached with caution, placing a gloved hand against the surface. Unlike the rotting barricade she'd busted her way through, this door was made to last the test of time. For some reason, great care had been taken to hide both its existence and whatever lay beyond. If the alterations to the tunnels were any indication, someone other than the original owner wanted to keep this doorway from being found.

The ironwood felt almost warm through her gloves, giving Draya pause. The door was enchanted, or the room beyond was made to fight the chill. She suspected the former, but it was impossible to tell from here. She moved her hand down to the latch and looked for a locking mechanism. With any luck, it hadn't rusted solid in the damp air and she would make quick work of the tumblers with her tools. Her finger trailed the woodgrain, and she realized she wouldn't need her picks after all. The lock, if there had ever been one, was gone. Instead, there was a large carved hole where she'd expect to find a bolt. Leaning closer, she recognized the tail ends of ink engravings along the edges. There'd been a sigiled lock there once, but at some point it had been removed. She wondered why, and more importantly, how long ago it had been moved.

Gingerly, she tested the latch. There was a heavy click, and then the door slowly opened of its own accord. Waiting for a trap to spring, Draya hid behind the threshold. When nothing came, she risked peering into the room.

The door settled against the interior wall with a muffled thump, followed by a sharp hiss as sparks ignited in the nearby wall sconces. Quickly, the candle flame jumped from wick to wick around the wall of the circular room, filling the huge space with a warm golden glow. She watched as the flame split into two paths, one coursing upward and through a hole in the vaulted ceiling. A gong echoed somewhere above her, then another and another, each further away.

Well, if the trip wire didn't trigger an alarm, they certainly know I'm here now. She made a mental note to dawdle.

A pair of bronze griffins stared blankly in her direction, their wings like flame in the reflecting light, but they didn't hold Draya's focus for long. Behind them, a series of pedestals topped with fine pottery created an intentional pathway through an eclectic array of antiques, jewelry, and gilded trunks stacked precariously high.

The Vault of the Undying. Her breath caught in her throat. She'd found the fabled palace treasury – the cumulative wealth of a Lich Emperor's unnaturally prolonged life. It was the stuff of bard songs and bedtime stories; a dream even the most wistful fortune seekers left behind as they learned the practicalities of the trade. There was no assurance the hoard had ever existed, and even then the idea that the Order would have left their spoils of war unclaimed was absurd. But here it was, frozen in time.

Draya took a moment to marvel, and then she got to work.

The stack of three trunks ahead of her was one of the shortest. Careful not to disturb anything, she examined the construction for any signs of mundane traps, contact poison, or runic spellwork. Spotting nothing suspicious, she tried the lock on the top chest and found the lid opened easily. A glistening sea of gold and silver greeted her, the coins representing a variety of denominations and kingdoms of origin. She lifted a particularly large bronze-gold disk embossed with a woman's smiling face.

"Empress Bonjukhar?" The name floated to the surface of her consciousness, her numismatics training triggered by the particularly rare coin. At a quick glance, she saw at least three others poking out of the pile. Immediately, Draya began calculating the worth of the room and let out an impressed whistle. Aside from the shoddily dug tunnels obscuring its entrance and the conspicuously missing lock on the door, there was no sign of looting here. The floor was covered in an undisturbed carpet of thick gray dust, and heavy cobwebs wove from one pile of spoils to another. If the convoluted maze was designed to keep the contents of the Vault safe, it had done its job well.

Draya took her time traversing the crowded pathway into the room. Her senses were on edge in anticipation of further traps or the tell-tale clack of animated dead. Instead, her gaze fell on the underside of a huge ironwood table carved in the same style as the Vault doors. It was out of place, tipped onto its side by what could only have been an incredible feat of strength. A few chests lay shattered beneath it, spilling coin and brightly colored gems across the bare stone of the floor.

Curious, she circled the large piece of furniture. The images carved into the tabletop were unrecognizable at first glance. The surface was cut into sharp peaks, concave ovals, and deeply etched rivulets. It would have been wholly impractical for eating on, let alone for writing. Turning her head to the side, the purpose of the design became obvious. It was a map, but not one the average traveler would recognize. It was at least two centuries old, depicting the land as it was before the floods changed everything. The thick band of raised peaks down one edge shared the curvature as the Mahdjor Steppes, and beyond were smooth lumps that must have represented the trees of

Loatra's forest. Most striking, however, was the detailed simulacrum of Aiylonia carved into two-thirds of the table. Here, the Sovereign Lakes were but dry ravines, and the thin river that would one day become the central Cimmrean Canal traveled the length of the kingdom. At the far end, what would be towards the north, was a large asymmetrical valley. At its center an oval bowl had been cut into the wood with a small star-shaped indenting its center.

Draya went to take a step closer but stopped when the toe of her boot struck something small and solid. She knelt down, expecting to find a broken piece of wood. While the object was carved, it was far from broken. Tiny spires and archways made of black obsidian curved from its star-shaped base. Standing, she fit the replica of the palace into its waiting slot. The shallow indentation around it was the desert that once stood in this spot, the pit in which the Radiant Sea had formed. When right side up, the miniature would have sat perfectly into the table, but as it was now, gravity worked against it. Rather than let it fall, Draya set the miniature palace back on the ground at her feet. Other carvings made from a variety of materials scattered the floor around her, the remains of replica armies, armaments, and architecture. The war map depicted the desolate wastes that had once been Aiylonia, before and during Occidrious's reign. Draya stepped away, a shiver traveling up her spine. She didn't want to know what could have thrown the table over without disrupting more than a handful of items in its wake.

She refocused her thoughts and continued along the winding path. As she rounded a towering leather bound trunk, the true extent of the room finally opened up before her. More riches of various kinds continued lining the rounded walls, but the center of the room was clear of debris. Instead, it contained something wholly unexpected. Recessed into the gray stone floor was a perfect ring of mottled black marble, and inside that a dilating door, the aperture of overlapping plates sealed firm. A vault within a vault wasn't particularly uncommon, but that wasn't the part that stood out to the seasoned treasure hunter. There was a translucent film over the surface of the depression, refracting the firelight of the surrounding sconces like the surface of a soap bubble. The prismatic shield thrummed with powerful magic, but as well-read as she was, Draya had never stumbled on anything like it, in life or in her studies. To prepare for this venture, she'd studied what little information the Guild library held on Occidrious and his powers. It hadn't been much, but it was hard to believe something so beautiful could be the result of anything necromantic in origin.

Before her rational mind could register the danger she was in, all of Draya's senses narrowed in on the oddity, her vision tunneling to a fine point. She found herself drawn in despite the growing realization that something ominous lay beneath the surface, compelled by forces outside of her control. In what felt like a blink, the tips of her toes teetered at the edge of the marble, hovering just above the translucent pool. She paused for a moment, logic screaming for her to pull back, to retreat, to run. The compulsion persisted. She knelt, leaning forward until her reflection stared back at her, and watched as the color of her hair, her skin, her eyes were sapped away, leaving only the pale silhouette of a stranger behind. She pulled off her glove and reached her hand out towards the mirrored surface.

A faraway part of Draya's mind registered the sound of boots striking hard and fast against stone. She ignored them. The air around her hummed with unseen energy, welcoming her into its warmth even as the fear rose in her throat like bile. The monochrome face staring back at her shifted, the features melting and changing, transforming into something – someone – else.

"Stop!"

She heard the shout, but it was too late. Her bare fingers brushed against the glistening film. It was as thick as honey, warm and thrumming with a living pulse. Her hand sunk in, and as it did, Draya's senses flooded back to her with a wave of nausea. She tried to pull her hand away, but her muscles had stiffened with rigor, locking her in place. Out of the corners of her eyes, she registered Loatrin sigils lighting up along the perimeter of the dilating door. She watched as a pinprick of light in the center of the web brightened, blasting her vision white as the gentle warmth turned to nerve-searing pain. The magical energy was all-encompassing, burning its way through her skin and into the marrow of her bones, traveling along her veins and into the clenching muscles of her heart. She was sure she was dying, but at the same time, she felt more alive than she ever had before. Pure elation washed over her, and with it something alien, something truly incomprehensible was there, too. Deep loneliness Draya didn't even know she held onto was lifted, replaced with what she could only describe as its opposite. There was no way to tell where the force of it stopped and she began. She felt complete. She felt whole. While her base instincts were screaming at her to fight, to flee, she found herself yearning for nothing more than to stay in that gentle embrace. She surrendered, and as she did, her rigid limbs went slack.

Suddenly, a heavy force crashed into her side, breaking the metaphysical connection and violently shoving her to the ground. Her tailbone slammed against the marble floor, the jolt of pain waking her from whatever stupor she'd fallen into. She looked up to find the profile of a strikingly handsome man hovering over her, pinning her body to the ground. He looked in his twenties, and his white-blond hair was neither long nor short enough to be fashionable, falling in short ringlets around his ears. He wore a simple baldric across his chest, and his linen tunic and pants were a uniform dove gray, meticulously dyed to match. As if sensing Draya looking up at him, he pulled his attention down to her. His brow was knit, his charcoal irises so dark they were nearly indistinguishable from his pupils.

In any other situation, Draya may have welcomed – or at least found a way to monopolize – the physical attention of the objectively attractive stranger. Instead, she raised an eyebrow incredulously. Before she could make a cutting remark, she found her own eyes drawn to the Vault door. "That can't be good," she managed instead.

The stranger turned his head. The field of magical energy had vanished, leaving only the glowing Loatrin sigils behind as the aperture of iron plates began to dilate open. Arcs of indigo lightning broke free of the center, striking the walls and the ceiling and sending down showers of sparking stone filaments.

The stranger's eyes found hers again. They weren't filled with panic or accusation, only sympathy. He reached down and clapped something around her wrist. Before she could protest, he lay his palm against the curve of her cheek, the act more familial than intimate. "It's in your hands now." His voice was soft but firm, brokering no argument.

More unnatural lightning shot out of the Vault, scorching the walls and shattering artifacts older than the kingdom itself. The stranger didn't look back as he lept off of Draya's prone form and threw himself forward. Before she could ask what he meant or even call out in warning, the widening aperture erupted in a column of indigo light. She threw her arm up to shield her eyes against the blast, but not before she saw the eldritch energy consume the man that had saved her life.

5

The crisp, alchemical smell of ozone filled the air and the brightness burned against Draya's closed eyelids. Within seconds, the unnatural storm went quiet, and when she allowed herself to open one eye, the stranger was gone. An eerie calm filled the chamber, the charred marks left by the destructive magic sending up rapidly dwindling streams of smoke. The only other evidence anything had happened at all was the state of the Vault door. The aperture remained partially dilated, but a much smaller pool of that same luminescent magic filled the opening that remained.

A new seal, Draya realized. It seemed so obvious now. She waited to see if she'd feel the same horrifying compulsion pulling her forward. To her relief, it did not. She blinked, then pushed herself to her feet. After the violent activity, the sudden peace was disturbing. Her back and shoulders ached from being thrown to the floor, but the pain seemed inconsequential compared to what she had witnessed.

The stranger's cryptic words rang through Draya's ears.

"Sarding abyss," she muttered to herself. The stranger was gone. She searched the room for any signs of life and found nothing. *Did he fall into the open doorway? Was he incinerated by the blast?* The idea that he quite possibly saved her life only to die himself discomfited her. She buried feeling by focusing on the present. *Whatever his fate, I'm alone now.*

Draya swayed slightly on her feet. Her head felt thick, her sinuses heavy with a throbbing pressure worse than any hangover she'd ever experienced. She was just getting her bearings back when she registered a low rumbling on the very edge of her hearing. As it grew in volume, its nature became clear.

Rushing water, she realized with sudden dread.

The explosion must have damaged the integrity of the palace architecture. Between the monolith's age and the crushing pressure of the surrounding lake, there was no telling the damage wrought. Enchanted glass meant nothing if the walls themselves gave way. The rumbling grew louder. She sighed as she mentally bid farewell to the hoard of treasure around her. She was unlikely to ever see such a score again.

Remorse – for the loss of the fortune or for the stranger, she wasn't sure – weighed down her limbs as Draya took off in the direction of the entrance. She was half worried the door would be blocked and was glad to be proved wrong. She grabbed her discarded lantern and paused, looking back over her shoulder.

Even just a few coins would be a fortune.

Just as she was about to turn back, the floor shifted beneath her feet. One of the stacks of chests toppled over with a crash. She had no choice but to move. She sprinted through the priceless door and into the shadowed hall.

Draya rode her intuition freely, letting her mind go blank as she navigated the twists and turns. She was maybe halfway through the labyrinth when a series of minor quakes shook the ground. The sound of falling stone followed, echoing around corners and off the walls. Her mouth went dry. Even before the sight of it came into view, she knew her way back out was gone. An avalanche of broken granite and slate filled the passage from ceiling to floor, trails of dust still trickling in the lantern light. She braced herself, waiting for her body to catch up with her mind, for feelings of dread and suffocation to settle in. A lot of work had gone into keeping trespassers out of the Vault. There was no reason for the Coronet to devise an alternate route to the surface.

A minute passed and the panic didn't surface. Instead, calm reassurance washed over her.

<This is not your end.>

The words surfaced in her mind, galvanizing her. As if guided by some invisible hand, she turned back the way she had come and squeezed her eyes shut.

Nothing happened.

Sarding abyss, Draya cursed. *You're alone in the bowels of a ruin, trapped in a secret maze carved by zealots, and you're hallucinating due to probable head trauma.* An incredulous chuckle escaped her lips. *In which case, what do I have to lose?*

She took a breath, centered herself, and tried again.

"This is not my end." The words came out in a whisper. She repeated them, this time with conviction. "This. Is not. My end."

On the final syllable, an image of the labyrinth's convoluted construction flared to life in her mind's eye. She saw the path that brought her here, and she saw it continue through the tumble of stones. On the other side, water rushed along the sloping path of the stone passage, leaking through thin fissures along the tunnel walls. That particular escape route was no longer viable.

She refocused on her current position, and a new path presented itself that she hadn't been able to see before. *How did I miss this?* Before she could dwell on the details, she took off in the prescribed direction. There was no telling how long she had until another avalanche blocked this escape route as well. She doubled back towards the Vault, this time her heightened sense of direction pulling her to the left.

She stopped short at another wall of crumbling rock.

Frustration welled as she sucked in a breath. Before she could let out an angry howl, her attention snapped to the side. She darted to a section of wall just beside the centuries old barrier. Something wasn't right. She ran her bare fingers along the smooth stone, desperately searching for a recessed lever, a hidden latch, anything that might reveal a way out.

There. Her nail snagged on an almost imperceptible seam. She followed the jagged line to the floor. A small indentation the size of a single finger was carved into the base of the wall. With a silent prayer to deities she'd never bothered to believe in before, Draya pressed her forefinger into the recession.

There was a moment of resistance, and then a satisfying click.

The seam Draya had found shifted. A curved section of stone pulled back, creating a crevice just large enough to squeeze through. She pushed her way in, and the hidden door closed itself shut behind her. A twisting spiral staircase, much like the one that had brought her to the trophy room, stood before her. The way upwards was illuminated by sconces covered in hand blown glass.

She tossed her lantern aside and took the steps two at a time, leaving the sunken tomb below. After an eternity, the stairs came to an end at a large wooden door. It wasn't a masterpiece like the one to the Vault, but the quality matched the aesthetic of the rest of the palace. Expecting it to be sealed shut, Draya threw her shoulder into the door. The well-oiled hinges gave way too easily, sending her sprawling face first onto the large stone tiles. Disparaged to find herself on the ground once again, Draya groaned. She pushed herself up onto her knees, wincing as the pain reignited in her side. As she moved to stand, something cold pressed against the tender flesh under her chin.

"Stay where you are."

Draya's eyes traveled up the length of the golden blade that threatened to cut her throat. Wickedly sharp twin tines curled towards her from the cross guard, giving the blade the appearance of a trident. There wasn't a soul in Aiylonia who wouldn't recognize the style of weapon. Draya groaned even louder. She knew running into an Aegis was a possibility when she took this job, but she'd sincerely hoped to avoid it. She continued her examination upward, taking in the segmented golden fingers of the gauntlet wrapped around the iconic hilt, and further past the intricate whorls carved into matching pauldrons. Finally, her gaze met the dispassionate stare of one of the Cresting Tide's most elite soldiers. A heavy circlet in matching gold perched on their brow, the broad band inlaid with swirling copper and silver accents. It looked almost incongruent against the shorn dark stubble on one side of their head and woven through a tangle of longer hair opposite. They loomed over her, their jaw firmly set.

Draya swallowed, careful to pull her throat back by a fraction. She raised her hands in surrender. "I'll comply, but staying still is probably counter to our best interests."

As if to prove her point, the flagstones bucked beneath them. The Aegis stumbled, throwing their shield arm up to balance themselves. Draya took the opportunity, ducking down and around their sword. She grabbed their gauntlet at the wrist, gritting her teeth as the sharp metal edges cut into her palm. Twisting backward, she forced their fingers open. The heavy blade clattered against the floor of the vestibule. The soldier's eyes flashed in disbelief, but they recovered quickly. Pivoting on their back leg, they threw the top edge of their shield forward. Draya danced backward into the open courtyard, narrowly avoiding the blow just as the ground stilled. The two combatants froze in concert, each taking a defensive stance as they assessed their opponent. With Draya's rapier sheathed and the Aegis's broadsword still lying in the vestibule, neither was equipped to continue armed combat. She quickly assessed the large courtyard around them. What must have once been an open air promenade several stories high had become a lonely island in the center of the Radiant Sea, one side buttressed against a huge square tower that rose up over the surface of the lake. Vestibules like the one she'd emerged from dotted the four cardinal directions of the platform, and two unconnected spires rose up from the lake on one side. There was no cover and no obvious watercraft to escape to.

Draya was considering her chances in an unarmed brawl against a soldier in full plate mail when an unnerving rumble rose from the direction of the spires. The vibrations traveled through the floor, the stone threatening to quake again at any moment. Draya hazarded a glance to the source of the noise. She watched as the walls of the ancient spire crumbled, the conical roof sliding away like a sheaf of wheat from the stalk.

It struck her that the corresponding splash didn't follow nearly as soon as it should have.

Even in the face of unprecedented destruction, the Aegis stood stoic. Only their fingers twitched without a weapon to grasp.

"Don't you see what danger we're in?" Draya shouted, hoping her voice could be heard over the scraping roar of stone against stone. She spread her arms out, emphasizing her unarmed state. "Aren't you curious what the abyss is happening right now?"

They were unfazed. "Where is Jierdan?"

"Who?" *I don't have time for this.*

"The Brightbourne Jierdan – the chosen one." While their expression remained unchanged, a hint of desperation colored the soldier's words, throwing Draya off guard. "You triggered the alarm, did you not?" they added, hazarding a careful step toward her.

Which one? Draya wondered if the earlier thread trap had done her in, or if it was only the one into the Vault. "I don't know what you're talking about."

The Aegis's eyes narrowed. Their sword was still in the vestibule, but they didn't need to be armed to be intimidating.

She forced herself to relax her stance in the hope they would do the same. "We don't have time to argue. Where's your boat?" Thunder crashed in the darkening skies overhead.

The soldier's gaze did not leave Draya. "In the name of the Cresting Tide, answer the question – Where is the Brightbourne?"

Draya's groan was lost in the howling wind. She wasn't going anywhere without a boat, and right now this insufferable metal mountain was her only chance. "Light hair? Boring fashion sense? Kind eyes?" Draya caught herself, unsure why she'd added the last detail.

The Aegis cocked their head to one side. "Yes?" They seemed thrown by her description.

Draya let out a humorless laugh. "Wish I knew." Their countenance darkened at her words. Hoping to avoid escalating things further, she adjusted her tone. "The Brightbourne, huh? Well, I guess he saved my life, or at least I think he did. Then he–" Realizing 'exploded' might not be taken well, she course corrected. "There was a flash of light, and he was gone." By miraculous coincidence, the raging winds calmed, and there was a respite from the disturbing rumbling below.

"Gone?" they prodded, their voice growing husky.

"He dove towards a big round door in the floor and vanished." She shrugged from her defensive crouch in an attempt to feign nonchalance.

The Aegis straightened, lowering their shield to their side. "What do you mean?"

"Exactly that. He was there one moment, gone the next." The storm had lulled, but she couldn't trust it would stay that way. She took a few furtive glances to each side, searching the rooftop courtyard for a way out. "Now if we aren't going to fight to the death, we need to get off this rock before it takes us down with him." When the soldier still didn't move towards her, Draya abandoned her defensive posture altogether and sheathed her sword. *If we don't move now, we're dead either way.* She took a few deliberate steps along a narrow path between the remains of two garden beds. Now only moss and scraggly grassweed grew in the hardened soil. She needed to get out from behind the decorative walls if she was going to get a look at the shoreline and figure out an exit.

"Wait! Did he say anything to you?" The Aegis crossed the distance between them in a few wide strides just as another small quake nearly knocked her off her feet. She heard the clang of metal behind her as the soldier slammed their shield into the stone to keep from falling.

Draya didn't bother to turn. Consciously, she knew she should be wary of the cleric, but something told her they weren't a threat. Besides, there were more pressing matters to deal with. She skirted a low wall and continued moving further from the central courtyard. As she rounded a corner, the flagstones ended abruptly at a parapet wall. A short wooden pier jutted out into the open air, and she realized the rumbling roar she was hearing wasn't from the wind. She looked over the side to see spouts of water pouring violently from various points along the wall, splashing like waterfalls into the waves.

Waves that were several stories lower than they should have been.

The Radiant Sea was draining around them.

6

Draya stared down in disbelief.

"I asked you – did he say anything?" The relentless Aegis came to a sudden stop next to Draya, following her gaze downwards. The soldier sucked in a breath. A small, well-appointed boat was bobbing along the surface, buffeted by waves. "That's our way back to shore," they said, their voice hollow.

"Not anymore." Draya looked at the naked pier. A line of discoloration marked how high the sea had been just moments before. Now the water level was receding faster than she would have thought possible. "I take it the palace doesn't experience a high and low tide?"

The Aegis gave her a confused look. "What do you mean?"

"Didn't think so." It was no surprise that they didn't appreciate her dry humor – it seemed unlikely the Coronet would include levity as part of their curriculum. A series of indigo flashes lit up the clouds, immediately accompanied by crashes of thunder. She wondered when the rain would start – or if it even would at all. It seemed odd that it hadn't already. She turned her back to the Aegis again and moved towards the central tower.

Their clear voice rang out, stopping her in her tracks.

"And the End will come at the Expense of the Light, her Trespass heralding the Undying's Blight."

She spun, the intoned words striking her like an insult. "What's that supposed to mean?"

Their shoulders slumped as the soldier shook their head. "It means I have failed in my duty to the Cresting Tide. I have allowed the prophecy to bear fruit."

Draya's eyes narrowed. "What do you mean?"

"What else?" they asked. "You are the Droughtbringer."

Draya rolled her eyes. "Right. And you're the Foul One in disguise."

They stiffened. "That...that is not remotely true, I can assure you." The Aegis pulled a telescoping lens from a pouch at their hip and used it to search the far shore. After a moment, they offered her the instrument. "Look southwest, towards the Cimmrean Canal."

She raised an eyebrow. "I don't know what that is supposed to–"

"Please."

The sincerity of the request took Draya by surprise. She put the lens to her eye, scanning the horizon. The levels of Aiylonia's central waterway were receding almost as quickly as the sea around them. If there had been any skiffs docked nearby, they'd already be beached. "That's impossible," she said in disbelief.

"Obviously not." The Aegis's voice was surprisingly calm.

Draya found her magnified gaze pulled skyward. The dense storm had gathered far above the palace, obscuring the light of the afternoon sun. The heavy clouds swirled clockwise like an inverted whirlpool, the billowing edges punctuated with jagged bolts of bluish-purple lightning. They were below the eye of the hurricane.

"The same kind of magic escaped the Vault door," she muttered as she watched, transfixed. Nearly imperceptible tendrils of smoke were pulled into the wake of the vortex. *Not smoke,* Draya realized. Jets of steam were funneling upwards, not only from the surrounding sea but from across the horizon.

The cleric stepped past her without comment. They shielded their eyes with one hand as they looked up at the violent storm. Without their judgmental eyes on her, Draya could see that they were younger than she'd expected, early twenties at most. Their skin was pallid enough to believe they'd spent most of those years hidden from the sun, or at least behind a helm. The latest addition to the line of Brightbourne had a formidable reputation, but it struck her as odd that only he and the Aegis had been left to safeguard something so obviously volatile.

She was considering why that might be when the Aegis dropped to their knees, a scarecrow cut from its post. Eyes downcast, they made the sign of the Helix, tracing a spiral shape over their heart. Another series of lightning bolts shattered the air, far too close for comfort. The wind was picking up again, whipping the loose hair on the right side of their head.

This is stupid. Draya spun, ready to leave the soldier behind. *There has to be another way to that boat.*

A sharp burn, like salt ground into an open wound, exploded through the bones of Draya's left wrist, stopping her in her tracks. She slapped her right hand over the source only to feel the surprising sting of cold metal.

The cuff.

In the haste of running for her life, she'd completely forgotten that the Brightbourne had slapped something onto her wrist. It was a simple band the width of her three fingers, the gold so pale it was almost white. The hammer work looked almost organic, the surface pockmarked like living coral or wind-beaten pumice. She lifted her hand away just in time to see the spiraling sigil of the Cresting Tide flared to life before quickly fading away.

When she looked back at the Aegis, their fore and middle fingers were pressed to each side of their golden circlet.

"What the sarding abyss did you do?" she barked. The burning sensation in her wrist lingered, pulsing quickly and unsettlingly out of tune with her heartbeat.

Resigned, the Aegis pulled their hands away from the circlet, and the same sigil glowed and then vanished into the metal of the frontispiece. The throbbing against her wrist went still.

"The connection," they replied softly. "It is confirmed."

No. Nononono. The horrible truth dawned on Draya. She scrambled, tugging at the cuff in an effort to tear it free, her fingers fumbling but finding no purchase. There was no clasp, no chain, nothing but a seamless band of pitted gold. Bile rose in her throat and she locked wide eyes the Aegis. As if weighed down by the same knowledge, they inclined their head in affirmation.

She rushed towards them, holding out her wrist. "Take it back," she demanded. The raging storm seemed far away in the wake of the revelation.

"I cannot," they said softly. She couldn't stand the wounded, withering look in their eyes.

"Don't say that. You can't mean that." Even as she said it, the truth of her situation sapped away her bravado. She recoiled, clutching the offending cuff to her chest.

She'd been bonded – tethered against her will to a member of the Order's most militant, most devout legion. The Aegii were raised on the doctrines of the Cresting Tide, adopted as children to be molded into perfectly disciplined soldiers.

"How?" she asked weakly.

"As I asked before," the Aegis said in an even voice. "Did the Brightbourne say anything to you? Anything at all?"

Draya's world spun. With effort, she found her voice. "It's up to you now, or something like that…No, that's not right," she remembered. "It's in your hands – that's what he said before throwing himself through that door."

They stood then made a show of adjusting their shoulder piece. "You are sure?"

"Yes, I'm sure." The image of the Brightbourne's face rose in her mind – the leonine slope of his nose, the calm in his eyes, the sad smile on his lips. She pushed the haunting visage aside.

The Aegis lowered their chin and, as if those words held some deeper meaning, made the sign of the Helix over their heart again.

A small quake rumbled underfoot, snapping Draya out of her existential haze. "That's it? That makes sense to you?"

"The words, yes." She felt the Aegis assessing her with their eyes. "The choice of recipient, I am not so sure."

Draya scoffed. "Is that an insult?"

"Not intentionally," they replied. "Quite literally, the cuff you now possess puts both of our fates into your hands."

"What the abyss does that mean?"

They didn't have time to answer. The ground bucked, sparks flew, and the Aegis threw themselves at Draya as the stone tiles of the vestibule's roof crashed to the ground. Before she could dodge, she was forced to her knees as she was enveloped in golden armor. She froze in place, rigid against the shield arm wrapped around her back. After a moment, the ground settled again and the Aegis released her. She sprang to her feet, ready to chastise them for their misplaced act of gallantry only for them to sprint into the badly damaged chamber. The reemerged a few seconds later, sheathing their great sword into a back sheath with practiced agility. They avoided her glare as their eyes darted around the courtyard. "We need to get out of this storm. It is not safe out here."

"Haven't I been saying that?" Draya barked back. They didn't deserve her ire, especially after what they'd just done, but anger was keeping her focus away from what she'd just learned. Anything to keep me from thinking about the cuff. Or the Vault. Or the dead Brightbourne. Or the ancient palace beneath us crumbling in on itself as a sarding cursed tornado spits purple death at us.

"This way," they said, ushering Draya towards the central tower. "We can take shelter until help arrives."

She planted her feet. "What help?" She gestured towards the far canal. The palace had long ago lost its curious appeal, and decades of the Coronet's guardianship had deterred all but the most tenacious visitor. "No one heads this far north anymore. And even if they did, they'd be mad to come out here in this. Anyone who could possibly deal with this catastrophe is fathoms away!"

"That may be so, but we have to have –"

"Don't you dare say faith, Aegis," Draya growled.

A deafening crash interrupted their argument. As many as three more bolts of menacing lightning had escaped the clouds above, the closest striking one of the courtyard's decorative pillars. The marble split in two, the larger half landing just outside the tower door. The sky was getting angrier, violent thunder growling from deep inside the swirling vortex.

We've run out of time.

"We do not have the luxury of time." The Aegis echoed her thoughts as they started back towards the tower.

"No shite." She sidestepped into their path, stopping them short. "What's the plan? Move a slab of stone the size of an ox? It's no safer inside that death trap anyway." Her eyes fell on the useless pier. "We're better off escaping to shore."

More thunderous cracks broke through the darkening sky. The floor beneath them rumbled in reply, further emphasizing the urgency of their situation.

The Aegis looked between her and the tower. "And how do you propose we do that?" they shouted over the noise.

"Working on it," she shouted back. She bolted back to the parapet, her eyes scanning the wall below. There was only open water beneath the pier, but she spotted exactly what she was looking for a short distance away. "Aegis!" she shouted.

"I do have a name," they said, already at her side.

She ignored them and pointed downward. "Look."

Below them, the receding waters had revealed a set of steps only a few arm's lengths from the bobbing skiff. Decorated with occasional archways of trellised metal, the staircase ascended the outer wall until it reached a small balcony only a story down.

"Blessed Helix," the Aegis muttered.

Draya braced herself for an argument. "It's our only option." An expanse of water lay between them and the safety of the shore. Wind whipped the surface into a frenzy, but the waves were still safe enough for a sturdy vessel to make its way across. There was no way to tell when that would change. "We don't have time to debate it. You can stay if you want, but bonding or no bonding I'm going."

"You may be right," they said thoughtfully. "The jump down could be dangerous though. Not only due to distance, but the narrow entry through that trellis and the palace wall."

They have a point, she conceded to herself. The arches crisscrossed over the balcony, leaving a fraction of the surface open to the floor below. One wrong twist or sudden quake could cause a limb or worse to get snagged in the crusted metal. It was a risk, but their continued cooperation was infuriating. "Scared?" she dared.

They didn't take the bait. "You can help row?" they asked instead.

"Better than you, I wager." She would have been insulted if they had any idea who she was. Only pampered outlanders didn't know how to row a boat in Aiylonia.

"And you are sure that retreating inside and taking the tunnels out is no longer an option?"

She kept her face neutral. If they knew about the tunnels under the Radiant Sea, she couldn't understand why they had been left practically defenseless. "I'd be surprised if most of the passages were still traversable," she confessed.

They considered this only briefly before nodding their assent. "Very well."

Draya let any clever retorts she'd been pondering die on her tongue.

Taking a moment to measure the distance, she climbed to the top of the parapet wall. Without sparing another thought, she turned her back to the water and dropped down the side, gripping the stone ledge with her fingers as she let her body dangle almost directly over the triangular gap. The distance halved, she pushed her feet lightly against the wall to adjust her angle and dropped the rest of the way. She landed in an easy crouch on the balcony floor. "Your turn," she called up.

The Aegis looked over the side of the parapet. Draya suddenly realized just how heavy and cumbersome their armor had to be. She was used to mild acrobatics in her line of work and dressed the part. The ability to maneuver in full plate and the dexterity needed to make a precision landing rarely went hand in hand.

Why do you care? she asked herself as worry tangled her insides. *Maybe an injury will break the bonding.* She knew that was false even as she thought it.

Unaware of her conflict, the Aegis lifted their armored leg onto the parapet. Their golden greaves alone looked like they weighed more than everything Draya was wearing combined. Even if they landed correctly, the chance of injury was high. She bit her lower lip and stepped to the side.

The Aegis brought their other leg up, only to teeter precariously on the top of the ledge.

7

In a flash, Draya's perspective shifted. She was standing firm on the balcony, but she was also back on the wall above her with the Aegis. Vertigo set in and her stomach dropped as her equilibrium struggled to adjust. As she reminded herself that the soldier's fate was theirs and theirs alone, an errant thought bubbled up in her consciousness.

There is no bonding if there is no Aegis.

Draya stamped the dark words down as soon as they surfaced, but it still had the effect of breaking the strange effect. Fully herself again, she watched as the soldier's heavy armor and weaponry acted against them, dreading that she'd jinxed their descent. After an excruciating few seconds that felt like an eternity, they managed to find their balance. Before they could lose their footing, they followed Draya's lead, letting their body hang from the edge before lightly pushing away from the wall and letting go. They landed with a perceptible thud, the weight of their clanking armor causing a few stones to tumble free of the ancient mortar.

The treasure hunter eyed them with begrudging appreciation. Despite the less than graceful landing, it was a feat to make the jump as well as they did. It took extensive training to move so effortlessly in full plate, and she'd seen older soldiers with more experience do worse. Before her look of respect could be seen, she turned and started down the narrow stone steps. They were slippery with algae and pockmarked with clusters of freshwater barnacles. She forced herself to look down and actively watch her footing. Falling into the cold water wouldn't normally be the worst thing that could happen to her, but she loathed the idea of trying to swim in an unpredictable storm with a knapsack full of plunder on her back.

The Aegis descended with even more caution. They hugged the inner wall as they took the steps one at a time, pausing at each of the increasingly common rumblings around the pair.

Moving with as much care as she could spare, Draya broke the silence between them. "What did you mean about our fate being in my hands?"

"Do you know what a bonding entails?" Their patient tone implied no assumption one way or the other.

She frowned, grateful they couldn't see her face. Draya hated admitting ignorance. "Pretend that I don't," she settled on as an answer.

"Very well. The ancient rite of bonding forges an unimpeachable link between an Aegis and the individual they are sworn to protect. The cuff around your wrist not only carries the tether itself but is meant to be a warning to those that might attempt harm against its bearer."

"I don't recall making any oaths," Draya protested. "In fact, it would be very out of character for me."

"Correct – we have not sworn oaths to one another. But oaths were sworn between myself and the Brightbourne. He gifted you the cuff, somehow transferring my oath – our bonding – to you."

"Well that doesn't seem fair," Draya said. "I don't even get a say in the matter?"

"Apparently neither of us do." There was a pause, then their tone turned introspective. "But why do it at all? And better yet, how?"

"Damned if I know," Draya muttered.

"Obviously, the Aegis to the Brightbourne can transfer their bonding to another Aegis," they mused without acknowledging her comment. "That is a necessity."

"Obviously." Draya rolled her eyes.

There was another pause, and Draya was fairly positive that if she turned around, the soldier's brow would be furrowed. They were conflicted about sharing this much with her. *Typical secrets of the Order*, she thought to herself. Thunder boomed overhead.

"There are…stories," they said when the sound faded back into the din. "It only happens in times of dire need – mortal wounds, imprisonments, anything that would disallow the Aegis to continue their stewardship. But never once have I heard of the Brightbourne — or anyone else with a bonding to an Aegis – doing the transfer themselves. Especially not to a…a…" they floundered.

"Heathen? Wench? Cur?" Draya supplied, drawing on the surplus of monikers flung at her at one time or another. Despite the calm demeanor of the Aegis, resentment smoldered in her gut like embers in a hearth.

"Uninitiated," the Aegis finished respectfully. "Can you elaborate on the events after…"

"After I was saddled with this shackle without my consent?" She shook her wrist over her head as she said it, but the cuff barely moved, the fit too perfect around her wrist. When the Aegis didn't respond to her goading she continued, recounting her escape. She made it sound like dumb luck and kept the details vague, leaving out the way she'd seen the exact route out in her head. She preferred to keep her intuition – or whatever that strange voice was — to herself for now.

"And when you left, the Vault door was secured," they finished.

Draya shook her head. "No, it wasn't. There was some sort of magic barrier, but it was over the opening. The plates just stopped dilating, leaving a hole the size of – well, the size of your shield."

The Aegis went quiet, but it didn't matter. They'd finally reached the point where the stairs met the sea. In the relatively short span of time it took them to get there, the surface had already lowered another two steps and it didn't look to be stopping any time soon. As the Aegis joined her on the second to last step, she slipped her knapsack off one shoulder and dug under the flap. After some fumbling, she pulled out a length of silk rope and began to unspool it around her forearm.

"Would that not have been useful earlier?" they asked with a hint of exasperation.

Draya shrugged as she looped one end into a slip knot. "We managed fine."

"Why do we need the rope now, then?"

"How else will we get the skiff?" She rolled her eyes and waved a dismissive hand. "Unless you'd rather sink to the bottom of the sea in that gilded casket of yours, swimming is out of the question. The water is draining fast, but I'm fairly certain you can't hold your breath long enough for the air to reach you down there." She circled the snare over her head and swung it towards the skiff. It fell just short of the bow, and she pulled the rope back and tried again. This time the loop hooked around the extended bowsprit. "Hah!" Draya smiled triumphantly as she pulled the snare tight and began hauling it towards them.

The smooth lines and fresh paint of the skiff stood out against the worn stonework of the palace wall. The hull was painted a light beige, stylized white waves decorating the sides. There were only two seats, and the aft was neatly packed with uniform crates held down with heavy platinum netting. The ostentatious nature of the design was entirely impractical, but so was everything the Cresting Tide built. Draya was about to make a disparaging remark when the vessel lurched to an abrupt stop. She braced her feet against the steps and tried again. The skiff didn't budge.

"The anchor chain," the Aegis said in sudden realization. "Perhaps it's snagged on something."

Draya pursed her lips and glared at the Aegis. The water level had lowered enough that there should be slack regardless. Her eyes caught on the series of metal archways leading back up to the balcony. The area above them was open to the sky, but that didn't mean there weren't more of the trellises below the surface. She groaned.

The soldier followed her gaze. Without saying anything, they wrapped a hand around one of the rusted bars and pulled. The entire arch bent against the pressure, but after a moment it broke with a satisfying snap. They let go of the metal and turned back to Draya. She could swear she saw a ghost of a satisfied smile on their face.

"Show off," she grumbled. Hands still gripping the rope, Draya looked pointedly between the stalled vessel and the Aegis. "Well? What are you waiting for?"

Their smile fell away as they dutifully took hold of the rope's tail end and nodded in her direction.

"On three," Draya coached. "One. Two. THREE!"

They tugged hard on the thin rope in unison. The tension reverberated slightly as something below broke free, and the pair reached up and pulled the rope again in a second concerted effort. She could feel the resistance of the anchor dragging against its metal snare. On the third pull, a sudden jolt along the line let them know another of the bars had snapped. The skiff was just out of reach.

"One more should do it," she breathed. The work was arduous, even if they'd only been at it for a few minutes.

"Will the rope hold?" the Aegis asked skeptically.

"Of course it will. Silk rope never breaks," Draya bluffed. She eyed the tether warily, hoping she was right.

"On three again?" they asked.

Draya nodded and repeated the countdown. The pair planted their feet again and made one last pull. The vessel jerked towards them, finally stopping only a short distance from the stairs.

The Aegis dropped their portion of the rope and reached one long arm out, grabbing the side of the hull with their gauntleted hand. They heaved the skiff the rest of the way towards the steps.

"Impressive," Draya admitted. She unhooked her rope from the bow, coiled it back up, and returned it to her pack.

The Aegis swung their legs over the side and landed deftly into the belly of the skiff. They crossed aft and diligently gathered up the links of the chain, pulling the anchor up and hooking it to the back of the ship without much difficulty. Draya watched as they methodically checked the entire vessel, testing every aspect from stem to stern. They took particular care testing the ropes that held the crates in place.

Draya eyed the skiff. Before she could second guess the distance, she took a wide leap towards the deck. She landed with less grace than she had on the balcony, and the skiff swayed violently against the waves. Some water splashed over the opposite side, but the crates didn't budge. The Aegis eyed her disapprovingly.

She wanted to scowl in return, but Draya executed an exaggerated courtesy instead. When she straightened up, the soldier was pulling a pair of oars out from beneath the seats. Disappointed yet again by their disinterest in her shenanigans, she accepted the one they held out to her. "What are you hauling?" Draya asked.

The Aegis didn't look up. "Just supplies."

"Supplies could mean anything," Draya prodded.

"Rations, camping gear, spare vestments. I'll stash what we can't carry on shore. It would be wasteful to abandon them to the elements," they said. "Are we ready to move?"

"I believe so."

She looked up. The sky had only gotten darker, and it was unsettling that no rain had fallen from the building clouds. She took her seat, hoping that at least this small amount of luck would hold out. The Aegis gave the vortex a dubious glance of their own. With a sigh, they lowered themselves into their own seat, leaning towards the center of the hull to keep it from listing to one side. With the din of the roaring winds as their backdrop, the pair began to row themselves toward the opposite shore.

"How often do you get resupplied? Do you have to travel back and forth yourself?" Draya tried to picture the Brightbourne and the lone Aegis paddling the canal without an escort. Not many would risk raiding a vessel belonging to the Cresting Tide, but there was always someone stupid or desperate enough to try.

"Monthly," they answered.

"You sail back and forth to Trifall every month? Do you trade off your watch with other clerics?" Draya looked back over her shoulder. The informants to the Hawkers Guild reported guards on site at all times.

"Not exactly," the Aegis responded.

Draya looked at them askance. "I'm confused – how do the supplies arrive?"

The Aegis kept their eyes focused on the waters ahead. "We have other means of transportation."

"Like what?" Her eyes lit up. "Portals? Do you use portals? Please tell me you can have a portal carry us away once we get to shore."

"Regrettably I cannot tell you that."

The finality in their voice made it clear the topic was not up for discussion. She pouted in silence, knowing they were likely oblivious to her show of disappointment. Occasionally, the Aegis gave a command and Draya corrected course, but otherwise, the journey was smooth. When they reached the shallows on the other side – which were much closer than they should have been – the Aegis jumped out over the side and pulled the skiff to a small docking port jutting from the shore. Once the craft was beached and tethered, the pair looked back towards the palace in the center of the dwindling sea.

"How long will it take, do you think? For it to be completely drained?" Draya asked.

The Aegis began unhooking the netting. "At this rate I suspect the palace will be fully exposed in less than two days."

Draya thought of all the rooms that hadn't seen the light of day in nearly two centuries. There was no doubt scavengers would descend on the palace to pick it clean in no time. Considering the instability of the structure, they'd be going in at their own peril. Draya was confused by the pang of concern that pinched her heart. *Less scavengers, less competition*, she reminded herself. The assurance felt empty.

To hurry their departure, she helped the Aegis pile one crate on top of the other and carry them towards a copse of tangled trees. The soldier stomped a spot in the silt with the toe of their boot, and a trap door sprung open in the ground. They pulled a fully equipped rucksack from the hiding place and dropped both crates inside before shutting the door and kicking dirt over top. The specially made pack slipped easily over their shoulders, leaving room for their sword and shield beneath.

As the pair started towards the Cimmrean Canal, Draya paused. "You're worried about something, aren't you?" She knew it was true, and to her surprise, she felt invested in the answer.

The soldier stopped and gave the Radiant Sea one last, long look. They were facing away, but she watched as they pulled out a piece of muslin and lifted it to their eye. They made a show of wiping their brow with it, but she knew better. She'd never partnered with anyone for more than a job here and there, and her romantic liaisons rarely lasted any longer than the time it took her to complete one. Regardless, she didn't need to know the intricacies of the relationship the Aegis shared with the Brightbourne to understand it was more than a simple assignment. The faint taste of salt echoed on her tongue as if a tear had fallen and settled on her lip. The bonding had made her a voyeur to a vulnerability best left private. It wasn't just an abandoned post they were mourning. Guilt rose like bile in her throat as she thought of the stranger – Jierdan – throwing himself at the dilating door. Unlike the borrowed anxiety weighing down her heart, she knew this feeling belonged to her and her alone.

Before she could fumble to find words of consolation, the Aegis turned on their heel and trudged toward the road with long strides. Their face was set with determination, and any evidence of their grief had vanished. The feeling of apprehension waxed and waned as they passed, confirming Draya's suspicion that the bonding allowed for some insight into their emotions. With horror, she wondered if it worked both ways.

"Aegis?" She started to broach the question but lost her nerve. Instead, she asked, "You didn't answer my question – what's wrong?"

"We need to move," they said simply. "Nightfall will be here soon enough."

8

For over a century, Aiylonians had relied on water vessels as their primary means of transportation. When the Great Deluge cut rivers into the dry, cracked earth and filled the valleys with fresh water, the grateful masses were eager to take advantage of their fortune. With the help of the Order of the Cresting Tide, streams were carved into canals, tributaries hollowed out into bays, and mountain springs diverted by aqueducts to the fields. Everything changed for the people of Aiylonia, and they were glad for it. The grand rituals of the Cresting Tide had saved them from the oppression of Occidrious and the feudal lords he called his Bastions of Vested Bone. They'd saved them from the constant threat of the bestial amalgams that ravaged the land. They'd saved them from the more mundane hardships of starvation and dehydration that had hung over them for generations. The Cresting Tide had provided salvation to their bodies and to their spirits, and its leadership would never let Aiylonia forget it.

Draya thought about this as she looked out along the Cimmrean Canal. Once, it had been a natural river that found its source somewhere in the Halloran Mountains to the north. To accommodate the increase in traffic, the sides were excavated wide enough for two water carriages side-by-side, buttressed at points along the way with levies and bulwarks of stone. It served as the country's main thoroughfare, spanning the many leagues from where they stood to Trifall in the south. The water levels were falling too fast to accommodate the Aegis's skiff for long, and they had no other vessel to speak of.

Without a second glance, the soldier started along the meager towpath that followed one side of the draining canal. It was narrow and more dirt than gravel, barely wide enough for a single horse-drawn cart. There was little call for land travel these days, especially this far north.

"You mean to tell me we are going to *walk* all the way to the Capital?" Draya looked down at her boots. They were great for skulking around a crypt and the occasional sword fight. They hadn't been made to withstand a hike.

"We do not seem to have any other choice." The Aegis took the lead, assuming a marching pace.

Draya considered her options. She could go her own way as she'd originally planned, splitting from the Aegis and avoiding whatever the Coronet might decide to do with her. She itched at the edges of the cuff. She didn't know the exact parameters of the bonding between the Aegis and herself but maintaining a specific proximity to one another was likely a factor. She'd read stories of bondings that acted like physical tethers, preventing one from going too far from the other; stories where one of the pair would be forcefully teleported to the other if they strayed too far; and of course, excruciating pain was a common option as well. Plenty of old magic rituals relied on corporal punishment to get the job done. Whatever the case, Draya didn't feel the need to test the limits just yet. For now, they were both heading south.

It's safer this way anyway, she reasoned. Traveling alone was never an ideal situation, and it was unlikely she was going to find a caravan to join up with any time soon. Taking a deep breath, she quickly caught up with the cleric. "So, what is it?" she asked.

"What is what?" the Aegis replied in a weary voice.

"Your name, Aegis. You said you had one before?"

"It seemed as if you did not care," the Aegis remarked. "At least you know to call me by my vocation – you have me at a disadvantage."

"True enough. Name is Draya," she provided, omitting her surname. "As to my vocation, I currently work as an archeologian for the Hawkers Guild."

"Ah. That explains your presence at the Palace," they replied.

"Oh does it?" Draya braced herself, fully expecting them to press her about the bounty.

"It has been a long time since anyone has tried, but it is not surprising that an organization of mercenary thieves masquerading as a legitimate business would show an interest in the Occidrian Palace."

Draya bristled at the insinuation, but as she didn't detect any malice behind their words, she chose not to be insulted just yet. "Aren't we all just masquerading, Aegis?" she replied in her most flirtatious voice. They ignored her sly grin and kept their eyes ahead. She kicked at a stone in the path. "Seriously. What is it? I assume it's 'Defender' or 'Guardian' or…"

"Sentinel," they answered, cutting her off. "Technically, Aegis Commander General Sentinel. Nel is my assigned abbreviation."

"Sentinel." Draya cocked her head to one side thoughtfully as she tested the name. "Not bad, all things considered. I've heard worse for members of your cohort. And Nel – the nickname even sounds like a real name."

They grunted dismissively. "Glad to have your approval."

"You seem a little young to be a general," she observed. She watched their jaw tighten out of the corner of her eye and smiled. *Something had to get to you eventually.*

"My age is inconsequential. A service was required, and it was my honor to accept."

Draya rolled her eyes before removing both of her gloves and tucking them into her belt. She appraised the condition of her nails, noting a chip in her left forefinger. "Why is that, anyway? The name thing?"

"What do you mean?"

"Well, Sentinel isn't exactly a normal name, is it? It's a title or a job description. Why are all you Aegii named different words for the same thing?"

"Do you really care to know?" Nel asked.

"Do you have something more interesting to chat about on our long, arduous trek through the wilderness?" Draya thought she saw the corner of their lip lift in amusement, but only for a moment.

"By edict of the Coronet, all children born into the Calling of Will shall be ordained Offspring of the Cresting Tide, each named in accordance with their function of service," they recited from memory. "Through this act, the Aegii will always remain humbly aware of their duties should danger come to pass."

She glanced over her shoulder. "Danger like a swirling vortex sucking away our kingdom's water supply?" The storm continued to rage behind them, an open wound in the darkening sky.

Nel nodded solemnly. "Yes – Dangers of this type. Brightbourne and their Aegii have been stationed at the Palace for generations in anticipation of such an event." They continued walking.

"Wait." Draya closed the distance and slipped in front of them so she could look them in the eyes. "Dangers *like* this, or this specific danger in particular? Did you know this could happen?" she asked in disbelief.

Pensively, they met her gaze. "The Order has always warned that a catastrophic event such as this could one day occur."

Draya rolled her eyes and continued to walk backward facing the Aegis. "The prophecy? Really? That's all just a bunch of propaganda meant to keep the Order's pockets full with protection money."

As if physically struck by her words, the Aegis stopped short. They clenched and unclenched their fists and took a deep breath. "The prophecy is the sacred word of the Oracles, passed down to us for nearly two hundred years. It is not propaganda, nor a tool of extortion." Their hazel eyes darkened as they bore into Draya. "To say so is blasphemy," they finished heavily.

It was the closest to angry Draya had seen them so far. She was so used to being flippant about religion in general that she forgot some people took the Coronet's teachings seriously. An unfamiliar feeling of regret welled up in her chest. "I'm sorry. It was not my intention to insult your faith," she said sincerely. For all her talk, Draya subscribed to a live-and-let-live attitude when it came to religious affiliation. As long as no one was forcing her to do anything, what did she care?

Except now this damn cuff is in fact forcing me to do something, she reminded herself grimly.

The apology had the expected effect. The tension in the Aegis's shoulders loosened and they continued their forward pace. "I appreciate that."

Draya resumed her position beside them, and they traveled in silence for a short while. A thought was nagging Draya, however, and eventually, it became too much for her to bear. "So? What is your plan?"

"My plan?" Nel asked in mild confusion. "My plan is to take you to

Trifall so that we may consult with the Order." Concern crossed their face. "Did you hurt your head during our retreat? Are you feeling faint?"

"No and no!" Draya let out a sigh of exasperation. "You said your name was to remind you of your role as a protector or whatever. How do you plan on protecting us from...from that?" Draya waved her arm vaguely behind them.

"The Coronet will know what to do."

"Ah. So you're just the muscle, not the idea person?" Her tone was more biting than she intended.

"Correct," they replied simply.

Draya was too aggravated to remark on the lack of offense they took from her intended insult. "Let me get this straight. They left you here, knowing full well what could happen due to some prophecy, yet you have to travel halfway across the country *on foot* to find out what to do about it?"

"If I have to."

Draya felt the grace she'd just given the Order evaporate. Her eyes narrowed. "That's rather short-sighted. You'd think an organization that relies on the prophecies of so-called Oracles would be better prepared – maybe leave someone with a little bit of information behind?"

The Aegis went quiet. Draya was about to gloat when they spoke again, this time far more softly. "They did prepare. They left Jierdan."

Guilt roared to life in Draya's chest. "Oh." She found herself at a loss for words.

Nel continued anyway. "We were stationed there, as our predecessors before us, to protect Aiylonia from the vengeful wrath of the Undying and his armies. We were the last failsafe – the one hope that the Oracles' words could perhaps be circumvented. But unlike our predecessors, we have failed. *I* have failed. The prophecy has come to pass, and the Droughtbringer has been allowed to bring about the beginning of the End."

"But that's a metaphor, right? Just like, 'the end of one thing, the start of another' – that sort of thing?" They didn't answer. "You don't mean like, the *end* end, do you? Like the End of the World?"

Nel's brow furrowed in confusion. "What else could I mean? The dam has been broken, the work of the First Brightbourne undone.

Once the waters recede, the way for the Desiccated One will be made clear."

"And if I'm this so-called Droughtbringer – you're saying I've started the apocalypse?" Draya felt unmoored. None of this made any sense.

"Yes." They considered that a moment. "More or less, anyway."

Draya took a moment to parse this information. "But I didn't *do* anything," she finally said.

Nel shrugged. "Perhaps nothing is what had to be done."

Draya felt a sense of resignation radiating off of the Aegis. It could have been acceptance of the prophecy, but Draya wondered if the loss of their companion had left them in a state of shock. Neither assumption was worth rooting around for. Instead, she focused on the situation at hand. She never took any stock in prophecies, but she couldn't argue that what had occurred in the treasury and the appearance of the vortex were merely coincidental. "Is there any way to reverse the damage?" she finally asked, dropping her flippant tone as the weight of her actions settled.

The Aegis considered this. "I hope so," they finally said. "That is why I am taking you to Trifall."

"Right, the Capital – you said that before. What makes you think I'll travel as far as Trifall with you, anyway?"

Nel gave her a quizzical look. "Because it's the right thing to do."

Draya raised her eyebrows. She wanted to make a retort, but the Aegis sounded so sincere. "You truly think that's enough, don't you?"

"Why wouldn't it be?"

Draya bit her tongue. "Never mind," she said simply.

"You will be coming with me." It wasn't a request.

Draya bit back a scoff. *We'll see about that.*

"Even if you choose to resist, we are bonded. We cannot part ways without considerable consequences."

So she was right after all. "What are the limits?" She thought back to the Palace. They had never been more than an arm's reach or two away from each other.

"I do not know precisely. The farthest I'd ever been from Jierdan was the length of the Great Temple's grounds. We never had any reason to test its limits."

Something about their answer struck Draya as strange. The Aegis knew quite a lot about some things and very little about others. One would think the details of such a powerful constraint would be essential knowledge for anyone who took on the responsibility of a ward willingly. If it were anyone else, she'd assume the Aegis was feigning ignorance, but she got the sense they didn't have an ounce of guile in their entire body. *Which means one of three things,* she reasoned. *The Order has kept the Aegis in the dark intentionally; they were greener than glade moss at their job; or the rank of Commander General held far less weight among the Aegii than it did in any other militant organization in existence.*

"How big are the grounds?" she asked aloud. She had things she had to do once they reached the city, and a gold-armored escort wouldn't exactly bolster her credibility.

"One hundred and sixty-two hectares," they answered easily.

About a third the size of Northtown, Draya calculated just as quickly. *I can make that work.*

9

If they'd been able to take the skiff downstream, they'd have been in Northtown hours ago. Instead, Draya had no idea how much longer it might take to find some semblance of civilization. The reliquary weighed heavy against her back despite its inconsequential size. She didn't favor the prospect of carrying her illicit cargo any longer than she had to, especially in the company of the Aegis. Seeing they'd already outright called her profession thievery, she doubted they would allow her to fulfill her obligation to her client without protest. At least she had faith that their honorable nature would prevent them from searching through her belongings. She hazarded a glance in their direction. Nel's hands were curled around the straps of their rucksack in an attempt to look casual, but her trained eyes could practically feel the tension in their fingers. Something was spooking the Aegis, and they weren't sharing why. Her hand settled nervously on the pommel of her rapier. It was a nervous habit, she knew, but it assuaged her nerves knowing it was close at hand.

 The pair continued along the towpath as the diffused light of the sun slowly dipped toward the horizon. The cloud cover had thinned, the unnatural purples giving way to lighter and lighter grays. Anyone who hadn't seen the vortex may not have noticed anything but an overcast day, but Draya couldn't help but recognize the uniform cords of steam overhead, curling wisps trailing behind like cigar smoke. There was no question – they carried the kingdom's water north and would likely continue doing so until the ritual she'd triggered was sated. She looked down at her feet, glad night would fall soon and obscure the ill fate she'd inadvertently brought upon Aiylonia.

Night came quickly after, sapping the world of color. When she could barely see a few strides ahead, Nel stopped their march with a raise of their hand. "We should make camp."

Draya let out a heavy breath as she surveyed their surroundings. "Here?" They were in the middle of nowhere, without even a substantial tree trunk for shelter. She'd been clinging to the meager hope that an inn would somehow appear. She imagined the proprietor welcoming them at the door with buttered rum, steaming stew, and the promise of soft beds.

Sarding abyss, she thought. *I'd settle for a haystack in a sheep shed at this point.*

"Did you expect to find formal lodging this far from a city?" Nel cocked their eyebrow up with honest curiosity.

Draya scowled. Her appreciation for Nel's insight into her thoughts had just about waned.

Without waiting for a response, the Aegis looked both ways along the far shore. "There," they said, pointing a few strides behind them. "We just passed it." Nel backtracked a few paces and then dropped down over the raised lip of the canal wall, disappearing over the side.

Without thinking, panic rose in Draya's chest. She rushed over to the ledge, fearing the worst. Nel looked up with a placid expression, the top of their side-shaved head only a hand's breath away. The distance was less than they'd jumped from the palace roof to the balcony on their way to the skiff. The water didn't even reach their waist.

"Do you require assistance to get down?" They extended a gauntleted hand towards her.

Draya ignored the offer and dropped down beside them. She bit back a yelp as icy water seeped through her breeches. She was surprised to find the dwindling canal was still high enough to crest the top of her thighs and fill up her boots.

Unaware or indifferent to her plight, Nel turned and began to trudge through the water.

"Where are we going?" Draya managed to ask through chattering teeth. She fell in step behind them.

"There's an old rest site this way. Just some rock formations, but they should provide some shelter," Nel explained.

She squinted into the darkness. "You can see that far?"

To her surprise, Nel let out a small chuckle.

"What's so funny?" she asked.

"I cannot see the rocks from here. I'm amused that you think I could though." They pointed to a short stone that lay ahead of them on the shore. "There – It's an old marker, from the early days when the canal was first built."

Draya could just make out a numeral etched into its surface. "There are markers to point out rock formations?" she asked incredulously.

"Not exactly. Some point to potential campsites, others to now-defunct resupply caches, that sort of thing. Most are no longer maintained or viable, but the Order demands their memorization regardless." When they reached the opposite wall, Nel laced their fingers together and nodded to Draya.

"What?" Draya asked.

"I'll give you a boost," they said.

Draya eyed their offering with suspicion. "How will you get up?"

"I can manage." The soldier's eyes were earnest as they continued to hold out their hands.

Draya glared on reflex. "So can I." She eyed the obstacle. Bending her knees, she jumped, wrapping her fingers around an errand root that had broken free of the canal wall. She pulled herself up and then used the same root as a step to launch herself over the ledge.

Nel followed without comment. Despite the weight of their armor, they jumped, their reach grasping the lip of the canal without the aid of the root. They pulled themselves up with both hands and then dusted off the front of their armor. "This way," they said, starting into what could barely be called a wood line. Draya wiped the look of astonishment from her face and continued after them.

The ground beneath them sloped upwards as they walked away from the canal's edge. Unchecked cypress roots became more common, their pronounced curves jutting into the arches of her feet with every step. She bit back the complaints she wanted to make – it wasn't as if they had another option at the moment. Once they'd passed through a grove of trees, the ground ahead dipped out of sight. A small valley spread out below them, buttressed by a ridge of jutting rock formations along the far side. The aforementioned outcropping was small in width but twice Draya's height, a solid wall of granite flanked by two wedge-shaped rocks that jutted from the ground. Nel signaled her to stop again and entered first, swinging the lantern into each corner. Rocking back on her heels, she judged that the center space was just large enough to fit three or four bed rolls, leaving more than enough space for just the two of them. Assured it was safe, the Aegis ushered her inside.

Draya took a step and immediately felt the soil drop out from beneath her foot. Pain spiked up her leg as her ankle twisted and her body pitched to the side. She threw her arm out, catching her balance against the boulder just as she felt a hand wrap around her other shoulder.

Nel looked down at her, their face in shadow. The lantern lay discarded within the stone circle. "Are you all right?"

She took a moment, mentally cursing her clumsiness before shifting her weight away from the Aegis and fully against the rock. Carefully, she extricated her foot from the strange hole it had fallen into. "Fine, I think," she answered. She flexed her foot and tested it against the solid ground. The tendon ached slightly, but nothing a night's rest off her feet wouldn't cure. "I stepped in some kind of –" The lantern light pooled across the ground at her feet, revealing what appeared to be one of a series of holes dotting a shallow channel. "Is that...?"

Nel had given her space but moved closer for a better look. "A borehole moat, yes."

Draya knelt down, her stumble forgotten. She touched her fingers to the curved depression that had once circled the outcropping. Until a century ago, it was common practice to dig rings like these around Aiylonian homesteads. Believed to protect against misfortune, they were regularly sealed along the bottom with tar so that captured rainwater would take longer to seep into the dry soil. Time had smoothed out the moat's edges and the floor was uneven mud, but still the old marks remained. "I guess that confirms the age of this rest site, doesn't it?"

"As I said, it is one of numerous locations established in the years following the Great Deluge." Nel reached down their free hand. This time, Draya accepted the offer and let them help her stand. A sense of anxiety filled her core, and as they stepped into the light she could see the emotion in the lines of Nel's face as they looked out into the night.

Draya looked away, making a show of investigating the space. "It hasn't been used for a while, has it?" Inside, a few half-buried river rocks were all that was left to denote an old fire pit, the center overgrown with scraggly grass.

When she looked over her shoulder, the sense of dread had lessened. It remained, but it was as if it was muffled, like a loud noise through a heavy door. Nel shook their head. "Not that I know of."

She took the opportunity to shift the mood. "Yet they still make you memorize its location as part of your training," she sniped. She shook her head as if the very notion was absurd.

"It does not seem inappropriate at the moment," they replied simply.

Draya couldn't argue. Circling the campsite, she found three viable entrances into the interior. Technically, dropping in from above was an option, but it seemed an unlikely choice. There was also a narrow space between the cliff face and the boulder to the right. If it came to it, she could squeeze through in a pinch. The only truly reasonable way into the camp was from the front, where the entrance was wide enough to fit Draya hand to hand if she spread out her arms. Overall, it seemed safe enough by her standards, or at least as safe as an ancient outdoor rest site could be in the wake of an apocalypse.

"I'll take watch." Nel placed their pack on the ground near where they had entered from.

"*First* watch, you mean?" Draya positioned herself in front of the narrow breach she'd discovered and unslung her pack from her shoulders. The attached bedroll was a little damp from crossing the canal, but otherwise, the quilted material seemed dry enough. She couldn't say the same for her ruined boots.

"I would not expect you to stand alert," they said.

Her eyes narrowed suspiciously. "What are you implying?" she asked.

"I just assumed you wouldn't, due to your particular inclinations. Do you wish to?" they asked.

"Inclinations?" Draya knew an insult when she heard one. "What do you mean by that?"

Rather than bite back, Nel went silent. She thought she saw their face flush in the shadows.

"I told you already, *Aegis*." She put emphasis on the title. "I'm an acquisitioner, not a thief."

"Is there a difference?" It appeared to be a genuine question.

Draya paused. As accustomed as she was to being called a thief and denying the accusation, no one had ever asked her that question explicitly. She preened at the opportunity to explain what separated her actions from that of a common criminal. "Substantially, yes. I am paid to recover specific lost artifacts and heirlooms. I don't just ransack property that doesn't belong to me and sell it off to the highest bidder."

They gave her a curious look. "But the Palace does not belong to you."

Draya shrugged. "No, but it's abandoned. No one lives there." She sat down on the bedroll and started unlacing her boots. She'd rather wear them for a quick exit, but they were more likely to dry near a fire than on her feet. *If they dry out at all.*

"Ah, but it is under the jurisdiction of the Order," Nel pointed out.

She scoffed, kicking off one boot and starting work on the other. "Why? Because they claimed it after the Deluge? That's not ownership, that's just opportunism."

Nel was about to protest, but then paused, considering Draya's argument. "No," they finally decided. "Perhaps that was the case when the Undying Emperor was first locked away, but now public consensus confirms the palace is property of the Cresting Tide."

Draya felt the blood drain from her face.

Nel took her lack of response as surrender. "Ah, good. You accept my reasoning." Nel smiled to themselves and pulled a cloak out of their pack. They laid it on the flattened earth and sat in the middle.

"What do you mean, 'locked away?'" Draya's words felt like ashes in her mouth. She was back in the treasure chamber for a moment, staring at the partially open door to the Vault. "Are you telling me Occidrious is alive?"

Nel let out an uncharacteristic curse under their breath before meeting Draya's eyes. "Yes, in a manner of speaking, Occidrious the Undying endures."

10

This time Draya didn't hide her shock. While there were always rumors Occidrious might return – his epithet was the Undying, after all – conventional wisdom held that he was long dead. The assertion that he was not only alive, but that Draya may have just been in his presence was like a slap to the face.

"This is why Jierdan usually does the talking." Nel's shoulders dropped.

Pressing the matter was cruel, but Draya didn't have the patience for their mourning at the moment. She yanked off her second boot. "What exactly does the prophecy say, Aegis?" she asked in a low voice.

Resigned, Nel unsheathed their sword and shield from their back and laid them both next to the cloak. "I suppose it's too late for secrecy now." They slipped off their gauntlets and then reached behind their neck to remove their gorget. "There are two versions of the prophecy – a popular one for the general populace, and one told only to those sworn to the Order."

"How is that possible?" She sucked in a breath through her teeth. "I suppose the public one is a lie, isn't it?"

"No!" Avoiding her gaze, Nel started work opening the straps holding the rest of their armor in place. "Not really anyway. Some of it was just…left out. To avoid panic." They removed their bracers and rerebraces first, exposing the deep blue sleeves of their linen gambeson. The two sets of armor were set down neatly next to the gauntlets.

Draya glared, then realized her look of disapproval was likely missed in the dim light. "So...what? All the stories of the First Brightbourne killing Occidrious were just, what, propaganda?"

"Not exactly," Nel protested. They fumbled with the line of heavy leather straps that secured the front and back plates of their chest piece together.

"You say that a lot," Draya pointed out. "I'd like to think I'm generally well-informed, so please enlighten me as to what exactly the truth is."

Nel continued clawing at the straps. "He *was* defeated. His body *was* destroyed by the First Brightbourne, just as the histories report. It's his life force – his spirit – that is trapped under the Palace."

Draya couldn't take watching them struggle any longer. She pushed herself off the ground and closed the distance between them. "Move your hands," she demanded.

They did as she asked and looked down at her, their eyes earnest. "You see – he's mostly dead, there's just a little something...left over."

"Left over?" This close, Nel's youth was even more apparent. *Twenty, at most*, she figured. A five-year difference didn't seem like much on paper, but to her twenty seemed a lifetime ago. She hadn't even earned full membership with the Hawkers Guild by then. Draya finished unbuckling the straps of the gilded chest piece, followed by those around his shoulders. Without thinking about it, she lifted the heavy set of armor away from their body, allowing Nel to slip out from under the pauldrons. She'd already pushed the metal mass against their chest and stepped away before she registered the ease at which she'd assisted them. She'd expertly removed their armor as if she'd done it a thousand times, which was strange since the kinds of people who wore plate mail were the kinds of people she tried to avoid.

Nel clutched their breastplate, an equally surprised look on their face. "I don't know the technicalities. I just know the waters work against his style of sorcery. Without them, nothing is inhibiting the rituals he'd left behind."

"What rituals?" Draya took a step back, her hands on her hips. "You know what? Don't tell me," she turned away in exasperation and crossed back to her bedroll before spinning back around. "Then why the lie of omission? Why not just tell the truth?"

The Aegis removed their greaves, then made a painfully meticulous show of arranging their suit of armor on the ground.

A nagging suspicion sprung up in Draya's mind. "Do you even know?"

They stilled but didn't answer, instead avoiding her gaze.

Sarding abyss I'm right. "You don't, do you? You – Aegis Commander General to the Brightbourne – have no idea why there is a secret version of the prophecy or what it could mean for the rest of us peasants. You've never even questioned it, have you?"

Their head snapped up. "I cannot speak for the decisions of the Coronet." Nel's momentary vulnerability vanished, replaced only by their devotion to the Cresting Tide. The Aegis placed their lantern in the center of the fire pit. Its meager light was a pitiful echo of the campfires that must have once burned there. When they spoke again, their voice was clipped and professional. "You should get some rest. We do not want to stay exposed here for long."

"There you go again. What has you so on edge? Is something else supposed to happen?" When they didn't answer, Draya put her hands on her hips and glared. "If we're in danger, I deserve the opportunity to prepare for it."

Nel ran a hand over the shorn side of their head. "You are right."

"Of course I am," she said, hiding her surprise at how easily she'd won this particular argument.

"I assume you are aware that without an ongoing source of magical energy, mundane undead deteriorate quickly in the presence of running water."

"I'd have died in my first dungeon crawl without that knowledge," she said with confidence.

"Then you are also aware that the canals keep – kept – such abominations from venturing into the kingdom."

"Are you implying Aiylonia is about to be overrun by undead?"

They shook their head. "Not exactly – At least not yet." Draya went still, unsure where this was going. "Any undead the Undying created have long ceased to be a threat, and he is unable to raise more while the Vau – While the Will of the Brightbourne keeps him imprisoned." They coughed into their hand to hide it, but Draya still felt them swallow back a wave of emotion.

"Then what's the worry?" She asked, hoping to move the conversation away from her feelings of guilt.

Nel's eyes met hers, their stoic expression intact once again. "The Undying created more than just undead. He specialized in the practice of necromantic amalgamation."

The horrid taxidermies of the trophy room sprung to life in her mind. "The amalgams. I thought the Coronet wiped them all out."

"Those trapped within Aiylonian borders, yes. It has been a few generations since the sighting of a wild amalgam in Order territory. But necromantic amalgamations do not suffer the same restrictions as undead. Water keeps them at bay, but they do not deteriorate when left to their own devices."

"They're immortal?"

Nel shook their head. "They can breed. Once the canals have drained enough, there will be nothing to stop their growing hordes from returning."

The revelation was a slap to the face. "So they've just been out there, making more and more little terrifying babies?" Before they could answer, she was struck with a far more sinister realization. "Why did you specify 'wild' amalgams, Aegis?" Draya didn't miss the spike of anxiety the soldier tried to hide. She stepped closer. "Please do not tell me that the Order keeps its own little stable of those undead beasts."

"Again, they are not technically undead."

"Sarding abyss."

The same unwavering glare returned to Nel's face. "The Coronet has its—"

"Reasons. Yes, yes, I'm sure they do." Draya wanted to press further but suddenly found herself too exhausted to try. It had already been a strenuous day, and once someone invoked the infallibility of divine authority, it was hard to muster the energy to argue. Blind faith was not something Draya would ever understand. *All the more reason to keep the Fellowship's sarcophilum a secret.*

Her stomach rumbled, a subtle reminder that she hadn't eaten since breakfast. She sat down on the center of her bedroll and dug into her knapsack. Sifting through the various items she'd plundered from the palace, she finally came across a short stack of metal containers. She could use a distraction. Popping apart the three stacked tins, she laid out her evening meal on her camp blanket. The first tin contained a hunk of hard cheese, the second thick slices of cured venison, and the last a small loaf of brown bread. She tore the loaf in half and stuffed the other ingredients inside to create a makeshift sandwich. As she took a bite, her eyes fell on Nel across the empty fire pit. There was a large strip of jerky in their hand. They took a bite, each grind of their jaw deliberate as they worked their way through the tough dried meat.

They looked up. "What?" they asked through their mouthful.

"Nothing." Draya turned back to her sandwich. Her stacked selection looked decadent compared to the Aegis's rations. An unfamiliar feeling of sympathy tugged at her heart and she forced the grimace off her face. "Would you...would you like some of this?" She regretted her words immediately. She was loath to share food even in the best circumstances.

Nel quickly shook their head and raised a hand in polite refusal. "No, but thank you."

Draya's eyes went wide in disbelief. "Really?"

They popped the remaining sliver of jerky into their mouth and then pulled a palm-sized disk out of their pouch. With significant effort, they cracked off a small pale chunk and placed it in their mouth, tonguing it into their cheek.

All the moisture evaporated from Draya's mouth. "That isn't hard tack, is it?"

Nel's right cheek bulged slightly, giving them a passing resemblance to a lopsided chipmunk. "Yes?" Their voice was muffled by the dense biscuit.

Basic hardtack was made from water, flour, and sometimes salt, if the chef was feeling fancy. It was dreadfully dry and lived up to its name. Out of curiosity, Draya had tried it once when she was a child with dreams of being a buccaneer. She had to soak it in tea for half an hour before she could even manage to bite into it. "And you're just...eating it? Plain?" She suddenly felt very possessive of her rations in the face of the alternative. "Won't it crack your teeth?"

They shrugged. "Not if you let your saliva soften it up a little. It's really not that bad." They bit down on the chunk they were sucking on with an audible crunch before chewing it up the rest of the way and swallowing.

"I think most Aiylonians would beg to differ," Draya drawled.

They snapped off another piece and stuffed the rest of the biscuit back into their pouch. "What's wrong with it? It's efficient, it's cheap, and it travels well. What you're eating wouldn't last a day on duty, and it's probably four times as expensive."

"Four times more expensive than nothing isn't much!" Draya replied in horror. "Is that how the Order keeps you Aegii complacent? Depriving you from anything that remotely resembles food?"

The soldier's nostrils flared. "We are taught to be grateful for what we are given, and not to be wasteful with the coffers of the Temple. Not all of us are driven by a selfish desire for profit."

Draya let out a bark of a laugh. "Right, and I'm sure the Coronet forgoes their private chefs and overflowing wine cellars. Do you think they stand in solidarity with your sacrifices?"

Nel shook their head, as if in disbelief at even having the conversation. "You do not know what you are talking about. It is neither of our place to question the wisdom of the Cresting Tide's highest authorities."

It was her turn to flare her nostrils. "I'll question anything I like!" Draya angled her body away from Nel and took a defiantly loud bite from her sandwich. She refrained from making obnoxious sounds of pleasure as she chewed through the mouthful of food.

Nel sat up straighter, their voice rising for the first time. "Perhaps if you took counsel with the words of the Order, the Seal would still be intact, and we wouldn't be fleeing from the Palace. Perhaps I'd still be at my post and Ji –" They cut themselves off, unwilling or unable to continue their train of thought.

It took all of her restraint to stay seated on her bedroll. "What? What do you want to say to me?" Draya's tone was equally heated.

The Aegis went quiet before continuing in a low voice. "It's nothing. It doesn't matter. Finish your decadent supper and get some rest. I'll wake you at midnight for your shift."

Draya considered protesting, but what little energy she had left evaporated. She ate the rest of her sandwich in silence and then curled up on her bedroll. Her wrist itched under the cuff, a nagging reminder of the freedom she'd lost only a few hours ago. She kept her back to the Aegis and faced the slim break between the rocks. If anything came for them, she'd be ready to flee – bonding be damned.

11

"It's gorgeous up here, isn't it?" The speaker's voice was hushed, almost reverent as she stared up at the blue-black sky. It was a clear night, and the stars spilled out overhead like so many chips of crystal.

"Mm," Draya agreed, although her eyes were on the gentle arc of the speaker's neck as she tilted her head back against the stone pillar behind them.

Draya knew where this dream was going, what to say and when to say it. She never let herself relive the memory in her waking hours, but some nights it sprung forth, unable to be quelled by her sleeping mind.

"Each star is like a spark of potential," the woman said. "A story just waiting to unfold."

"What are they waiting for?" Draya had fully turned towards her now, the delicate freckles that splashed across her nose far more interesting than the stars.

"I don't know, maybe the right person to show itself to."

Draya lifted her hand, brushing a stray curl behind her companion's ear. The color was washed out against the night sky, but under the sunlight it was the color of apricots threaded with gold. She leaned in. "I can be the right person to your star," Draya whispered.

The woman let out a laugh that rang like music before giving Draya an incredulous smile. "That doesn't even make sense."

Draya shrugged and leaned back against the pillar. "Look, if you want to be the right person, I can be the star. Doesn't much matter to me," she teased.

Her companion snorted. "You're insufferable."

"So you keep telling me." Warm fingers snaked through Draya's, and she felt her companion's thumb making small circles against the back of her hand. They both sat in silence for a moment. "If you did have a story to share, what would it be?" she asked.

"You want me to tell you a bedtime story?"

"Something like that – just make it something exciting."

"That I can do," she replied, her eyes back on the sky. In Draya's actual memory, the woman would start in on a less than sanitized version of the Swashbuckler's Bargain, where Todric winds up marrying both Marigold and the Anonymous Prince after the duel.

Not this time.

"Conquering the sweltering deserts of Aiylonia was but a means to an end," she began. "A tilling of the soil. A staking of the footprint. A planting of the seeds. No – Emperor Occidrious had ambitions far greater than merely drawing power from the horrors of the eldritch planes. He sought to usher in the arrival of the Desiccated One itself."

The sky above darkened with a preternatural storm, and the starlight vanished from the firmament. Draya watched, transfixed, as the scene manifested itself before her.

"A single mortal lifetime was not enough to accomplish his aims. The Bearer of the Tenebrous Crown had to master powers of necromancy, magic of bone and blood, rituals of sacrifice and amalgamation." The indigo clouds coalesced into vague forms overhead, moving like figures in a shadow play. "He constructed bestial hybrids to maim and kill as they gathered the essence needed to fuel his rituals. He transformed himself into the greatest of the ritualized undead, an immortal lich whose soul could persevere even if its corporeal form did not. He vested parts of himself into his Warlords and sent them to enforce his rule across the provinces. As long as these fail-safes persisted, Occidrious's power could not wane."

The violent clouds settled into a gentle calm, allowing the pale yellow light of the moon to wash the indigo purple shadows away.

"But cycles change and nothing is absolute. A rival was born in the darkness, one who was impervious to the Emperor's Calling of Coercion and who could execute a plan to overthrow his iron rule." A shifting figure, no more than a slip of twirling smoke, took shape beside the moon. They held a long rod in one hand, and the clouds below roiled like ocean waves. "Together with the priests of the Helix, the other-worldly Brightbourne imprisoned his generals, defeated the amalgams, and lay siege to the Radiant Palace with the Tides at her side." The figure danced across the sky, vanquishing the shadows of armies and snarling beasts. As they slowed to a stop, the raging storm returned with a vengeance. A pillar of clouds spiked with lightning loomed over the fragile form. "But even at his weakest, the Brightbourne could not devise a means to destroy Occidrious indefinitely. Just as he was on the verge of extinguishing her life, the Brightbourne threw them both into the fearsome torrent of energy trapped within the Palace Vault." The two forms coalesced and then exploded outward in a shower of gold and purple. Draya shielded her eyes with one hand, and when she looked again the starry sky had returned. "Both would be trapped, waiting."

Draya swallowed, a pit of fear forming low in her core. "Waiting for what?" she asked in a small voice. She knew this was a dream, but she couldn't help the panic from seeping into her words. When there was no answer, she turned her head.

The creature beside her was a grotesque perversion of the woman Draya once loved. Paper thin skin pulled tight against sharp cheekbones and the shriveled remains of her lips were cracked and split. Her eyes bore into Draya's, burning indigo blue from deep within sunken eye sockets dripping with ichor black as ink. Claws dug into Draya's hand, her fingers still entwined with the obscene facsimile of her companion. It smiled. "You."

12

An intoxicating aroma and the comforting crackle of a campfire lured Draya into consciousness. She felt raw and on edge, haunted by the afterimages of dreams she couldn't quite remember. She opened her eyes slowly, only to find the bare face of a boulder staring back at her. It took her a moment longer than it should have to get her bearings, and then the events of the day before came rushing back all too clearly. The palace. The labyrinth. The Vault. The cuff.

The Aegis.

She groaned.

The pale light of dawn was streaming into the meager rest site, and the air tasted dry on her tongue. Resigning herself to her fate, she turned over to find a charred catfish skewered over the flames of the fire. *That explains the smell,* she thought. Beyond the fire pit, Nel sat cross-legged on their cloak, already fully armed and armored. Their golden sword lay across their lap as they methodically oiled the blade with a white rag.

A yawn escaped Draya's throat as she sat up. "You didn't wake me," she said in a tone that sounded more accusatory than she intended.

The Aegis looked up from their work. "Good morning."

"Is it though?" Her lips felt oddly chapped. She reached for her waterskin and took a swig before remembering she should try to ration her drinking water. "You didn't answer my question."

"It sounded more like a statement to me." They reached forward and used the end of a stick to stir the embers of the fire. Draya was about to issue a retort when Nel continued. "By the time midnight came around, I was still very much awake. I'm used to sleeping very little and very lightly. You were in a deep sleep, so I thought it best to leave you be."

"That's ridiculous. I can wake at the drop of a pin," Draya argued. It was a point of pride to be a light sleeper in her line of work. It was dangerous not to be.

"Perhaps you usually do, but last night this was not the case. Heat lightning struck a tree not far from here, and you barely stirred."

She never slept through the night without waking up a few times, and it seemed strange that she would start now. "And the fish?" she asked, circumventing her unsettling behavior.

"When dawn arrived I went to fetch some fresh water at a stream nearby. Only damp rocks remained, but I found the catfish. The Tides always provide, even at the End of Things."

Draya couldn't help but roll her eyes at their unflinching piety. She eyed the catfish again. "Wait – was it alive or dead when you found it?" she asked.

Nel shrugged, setting their sword aside. They removed the makeshift spit from the campfire. "It should be done – I'll divide it up for us."

Her stomach turned. The fish could have been dead for days for all they knew. It could have died of any number of things besides the magical drought. She shook her head. "No, that's all right. I still have some cheese from last night." She didn't, but she turned to her bag anyway out of pretense.

"Are you sure? We still have quite a distance to travel before we get to Northtown."

"I'm sure," Draya said as she dug around in her pack for something – anything – to eat. "Ah ha!" She pulled out a wax paper pouch half-filled with dried blueberries. "See? I'll be fine."

"As you wish." The Aegis lifted the spit to their mouth. They bit into the meaty fillet on one side of the spine, and the blackened flesh gave way with a satisfying crunch. Draya hoped they'd already gutted and deboned the carcass while she'd been sleeping. Her stomach lurched again at the thought of its potentially decaying entrails.

It only took Nel a few minutes to finish off the fish. Once the campfire was doused with dirt and sand, the mismatched pair made their way back to the towpath along the canal. As they'd predicted, the water level had dropped even further. The once formidable canal was a dwindling stream.

"It won't be more than a trickle by nightfall, wet mud by tomorrow at this rate" Draya said.

Nel nodded solemnly.

She popped the last of the rationed berries into her mouth, savoring the subtle sweetness. "It's only this bad because these canals flow downstream from the Palace right? Once we get further south and away from the vortex or whatever, things will be normal."

The Aegis was quiet, their eyes on the road ahead.

"Aegis? It is localized, isn't it? It can't have spread as far as Trifall." Draya knew it was a pipe dream as soon as she asked the question.

Nel shook their head ever so slightly.

Draya grabbed them by the shoulder, stopping them in their tracks with the sudden motion. Their pauldrons were cold and lifeless to the touch. "How far does this sarding curse reach? Answer me, Aegis."

They took a breath, then spoke softly. *"The Droughtbringer's folly will ravage the land, decimate life and leave nothing but sand,"* Nel quoted with an air of reverence.

"What's that supposed to mean?" Draya felt her stomach turn for the third time that morning.

They met her eyes. "It's the opening words of Soriadne's Lament – the most comprehensive prophecy pertaining to the Creeping Drought." Draya had never heard of it, and her confusion must have been clear on her face. "It means, it would not be an Apocalypse if it was confined to the Radiant Sea." Nel cocked their head to one side thoughtfully. "Or I suppose, the Radiant Desert, as it was originally named."

Draya narrowed her eyes suspiciously. "There's that word again – apocalypse. Surely, that's just a metaphor. There is no way the mere spirit of a dead man – even some mythical lich – could have enough power to affect the whole kingdom in the short span of a few seconds."

Nel laid a hand over Draya's. Rather than provide comfort, they gently lifted it off their shoulder and guided it back to her side. "Normally I would agree with you. However, he didn't need enough time to cast a ritual over all of Aiylonia. He just needed the freedom to call upon his Bastions." Nel began walking again, their measured gait quickly outpacing Draya.

She paused to consider this, and then her eyes opened wide. She sprinted to catch up. "The Bastions? Are you telling me Bone Generals actually exist?"

Nel winced at the popular name of the feudal lords that once terrorized each of the country's fiefdoms. "Of course."

Draya's brow creased. She tried to recall the words of her history tutors. "How many were there? Five? Ten?"

They gave her an incredulous look. "There have always been seven."

"I'm better with things than people," Draya said more defensively than she'd meant to. She'd always had a knack for understanding the broad strokes of history and the objects that related to different time periods – maps, coins, architecture, even certain weapons. It was the fiddly details of names and politics that escaped her. She'd never had the patience to learn about dead men and their dead ideals. "So there are seven of his – his *creations* still alive somewhere?"

"They were imprisoned, yes. Beneath each of the Sovereign Lakes in each of the seven original provinces. Whether that remains to be true after your actions yesterday, I'm not so sure."

Draya couldn't believe what she was hearing. "The door was only open for a moment!"

Nel shrugged again. "A moment's mistake is often enough to have an irreversible impact."

The words stung, but she refused to accept that there was no turning back. She was a lot of things, but she was not some fated herald of the end of the world. "No. That's ridiculous. There must be safeguards in place. And if not, the Cresting Tide fixed everything once. They can do it again. There has to be a backup plan. You're just not high-ranking enough to know about it."

The muscles in Nel's neck tensed at the jab. "So now you believe the Coronet will save us? You didn't seem to think much of the Order last night."

"Yes, well..." Draya fumbled, "Just because I disagree with a doctrine here or there doesn't mean I think the whole Order is useless." She had, in fact, insinuated just as much in plenty of taverns over the years.

"Indeed, we are not." Exhaustion seeped into the Aegis's words.

"Regardless, I pray you are correct. I pray that my lack of knowledge is an oversight due to my relatively recent assignment as Commander General. I pray that there is a contingency plan, as you suggest. Whatever the case, all the more reason to get you to Trifall as quickly as possible."

Before she could process the comment about their promotion, thoughts of the capital flooded Draya's mind. In addition to her hand in the creation of the vortex and the death – if that's what it was – of the Brightbourne, she still had the sarcophilum tucked safely in her pack. She'd checked the hidden compartment before leaving camp and was relieved to find that no harm seemed to have come to the ancient artifact. She suspected it was a lot more durable than it looked. She could only hope that once they reached Northtown, slipping away from the Aegis would be an easy matter. She'd feel a lot more comfortable entering Trifall without a potentially incriminating artifact in her possession.

A low rumbling interrupted her thoughts, and she was embarrassed to realize it came from her stomach. Nel gave her a sideways glance, but she averted her eyes. The hunger pains she'd been dreading came on quickly. Part of her knew she should have eaten some of the fish, especially since the Aegis had shown no signs of distress. *I'll throw myself back into the Vault before I tell them that,* she thought to herself.

The cypress woods on either side of the canal opened up to reveal fields of rice paddies. The sheaths of golden panicles hung like strung beads amidst the thin green leaves, but something in the otherwise idyllic scene looked very wrong.

"Isn't it too early in the season to drain the fields?" Draya asked aloud.

Nel followed her gaze. "I cannot say that I am versed in horticulture, but yes — I believe it is."

They eventually came upon The Split. The Cimmrean Canal continued on, curving to the right and cutting through high walls of rock on either side. It was the fastest route to Northtown, but there wasn't any bank for a towpath alongside. To the left, a less artificially constructed waterway meandered through the countryside, providing access to the docks of small farmsteads and fishing hamlets. Nel started towards a bridge that connected one bank to the other. "We'll have to take the trade road," they said in explanation.

Draya didn't argue and followed them across. Navigating the rocky slopes of the canal proper would be miserable if not impossible. At least the smaller canal had its own towpath along each side to facilitate foot traffic.

As with everywhere else, the water of the river had receded much further than Draya would have expected. The naturally sloping shoreline was exposed, revealing piles of driftwood and dying plant life alongside the carcasses of catfish, shrimp, and half-buried mollusks baking in the sun. Large carrion birds circled the sky, diving down to the veritable feast that had presented itself overnight.

The first pair of fishers Draya saw barely looked up as they passed, their attention focused on righting a small raft. It had been tipped sideways between the exposed supports of an old dock and a once-submerged boulder. The lines of the simple mast were tangled, making the work awkward. She knew she should keep her head down and keep moving, but an unfamiliar feeling of empathy took root in her chest. She wanted to go to them, to help them – and not for acclaim or reward. Before she could act on the compulsion, the raft shifted free of the rock. The pair pushed it slowly into the shallow waters that remained in the center. It was only a third of what the river once was, but it seemed they were determined to do their work regardless.

More spindly docks and upturned watercraft followed as they made their way along the path. Locals looked with naked dismay at empty crab traps and sagging nets that had been deep under the surface of the water just the day before. Some looked up as they passed, casting their eyes downward at the sight of the Aegis in gilded armor. A feeling of ineptitude continued to nag Draya. She'd never desired to help so badly and yet have so little idea as to how she could.

The sun was high in the sky when they started to see the towering aqueducts that signaled they were nearing Northtown. The infrastructure of raised channels siphoned fresh spring water from the western hillside, allowing residents access to clean drinking water regardless of the conditions of the canals. The presence of such technological feats had become the hallmark that differentiated a thriving settlement from a minor hamlet or village. Now, Draya wondered if they served any purpose at all. She couldn't imagine that water still flowed freely through them. She hoped she was wrong.

Finally, the path skirted back to the main canal. The great pillared walls surrounding Northtown rose above them, sheltering a hodgepodge of old stone buildings beyond its gates. As they got closer, it was clear that the docks meant to greet travelers were abandoned, the water levels so low that a flat-bottomed skiff would be lucky to make the trip.

Draya's stomach growled again. "Tavern?" she asked. "We're in time for lunch."

Nel took in the sight with resignation. "May as well," they replied.

13

The Brick & Boar Tavern stood out against the neighboring buildings. Not only was it the largest establishment of its type, it was the only tavern that could date its location to the founding of Northtown. True to its name, the mottled stone walls of the original building were punctuated with sections of red clay brick. Draya had only visited a few times, but she was familiar with the building's history. It had previously been called the Stone & Steed before it was sold a decade or two ago. Ever frugal – if not cheap – the current proprietor spent as little as possible on repairs, replacing imported stone with locally made brick when the need arose. It was far less durable, with a price to match. Claims that the mantle of 'oldest tavern' had been usurped by the lesser-known Spotted Barrel Inn, with its crumbling but fully original walls and foundations, had been a subject of debate for years.

Over the door hung a worn wooden sign without any wording. It vaguely resembled a four-legged creature with stunted legs and a flattened snout, and bits of newer, paler wood had been hammered to the mouth to give the even more vague impression of tusks. If you squinted and used your imagination, what had once been a carefully carved horse almost looked like a malformed boar.

"The new owner never lets a coin go to waste, do they?" Not for the first time, Draya imagined what the horse might have looked like before it was butchered into the monstrosity before them.

"*Pious men use frugal means,*" Nel quoted from scripture.

Draya glared at them, but they were already pushing open the door and stepping inside. She somehow doubted piety factored into the proprietor's motivations.

It had been a few years, but the interior was just as Draya remembered it. She was immediately assaulted with the familiar smells of stale ale, sweat, and freshly baked bread. The common room was dimly lit, devoid of natural light save for a few high windows along the eaves. Wisps of pipe smoke curled against the rafters and made the air feel thick in her lungs. Once her eyes adjusted to the shift, Draya began to wonder if coming here was such a good idea. Long banquet tables stretched out on either side of the room, the benches filled with fishers, traders, and muscular warriors who could just as easily be traveling mercenaries as town guards enjoying a pint after their shift. It was like any average tavern in any other Aiylonian city, but something didn't feel right. It took Draya a moment to place it.

No one is laughing, she realized.

It wasn't that the room was silent – the hum of conversation filled the crowded room. Rather, there were none of the usual jovial chuckles or boisterous guffaws punctuating the din. The patrons were anxious, their nerves tight like bowstrings ready to snap.

And then Nel crossed the threshold.

A sea of heads looked up from their cups at the sight of their shining golden armor. It wasn't every day an average citizen saw an Aegis up close. Worried eyes filled with hope, or in a few cases, condemnation. What little light there was seemed to be drawn to the swirling designs of engraved metal, turning the Aegis into a practical beacon screaming for attention. There was no hiding who or what Nel was – which, Draya supposed, was the entire point of having such an ostentatious uniform. A feeling of unease settled in her gut. She much preferred choosing when and how she shed her anonymity.

Nel clearly didn't notice the shift in the atmosphere. After taking a cursory glance around the room, they strode forward, taking the central aisle towards the large counter that stretched along the back wall. Draya followed, her hand slipping protectively to the pommel of her rapier. Most of the curious heads quickly returned to their meals, but a handful of eyes stayed transfixed on the pair as they passed. She took particular notice of a pair of twins on the far end of the bar. The brother and sister had matching thin builds and an assortment of blades arranged about their persons, the former sporting an eye patch and the latter a severe braid that started high on the top of her head.

Their cruel stare could have burned a hole in Nel's armor if such a thing was possible. Draya dared to take her eyes off them briefly, scanning the crowd for any members of the Fellowship of the Sun. The adherents wore braided cords of white and purple across their chests or bound around their biceps, but she spotted no such markers.

She reached out and touched Nel's forearm, causing the Aegis to turn quickly, a confused look on their face.

"Let's take those open seats over there." Draya pointed to a table on the opposite side of the tavern as far as possible from the sinister pair.

"Are you sure? I thought an open bar stool was the best place to find yourself in an establishment like this." Nel nodded towards a pair of open seats separated by a large brute curled over his ale. "We'll just have to ask that individual to move for us."

Draya blinked, momentarily stunned by the idea of asking the large mountain of a man to do anything, let alone move for their convenience. Before she could voice her concerns, Nel had already crossed the distance ahead of her.

"Excuse me," Nel asked politely as they approached the empty place to the left of the mercenary. The man grunted and ignored them. Draya resisted the urge to distance herself from the Aegis. "My traveling companion and I require two seats – would you perhaps shift to the next stool?"

The man let out a low, menacing chuckle before lifting his head and slowly turning to Nel. To Draya's surprise, his furrowed brow softened as he looked them up and down. "Calm winds and clear skies," he said in a soft, gravelly voice.

"Full nets and high waters," Nel replied. Draya winced. The traditional call and response sounded incredibly inappropriate given the circumstances. "Aegis Commander Sentinel," Nel continued by way of introduction, conspicuously dropping their title of general.

"Cromdren Destrovus," the mercenary said. "Veteran of the Twelfth Armada. I must admit, it has been some time since I last lay my eyes on one of the Willed."

There was a pregnant pause. Draya could sense Nel was weighing that information carefully. "Indeed, we rarely leave our assigned stations," they finally said. "We are on our way to the High Temple in Trifall."

Cromdren considered this. "The March is upon us then, is it not?"

he asked. "I never expected to see the Sign with my own eyes."

Nel's complexion managed to pale even further than normal. "I...I cannot speak for the Coronet," they managed.

The mercenary grunted in acceptance and took a sip of his ale before lowering his voice to a hoarse whisper. "I understand. Regardless, I can speak for me and mine – the Twelfth will be ready for the Second Flood. We await our call to the Torrent."

"Yes." Nel swallowed hard. "I'm sure you will be...informed." Draya could feel the nauseating twist of anxiety rising in their gut.

"It would be an honor to vacate my seat to fellows of the Tides." Cromdren moved to stand, turning his attention to the acquisitioner for the first time. "Calm winds and clear skies," he said to her, inclining his head in greeting.

"Yes, umm...smooth sailing," Draya fumbled. Before the mercenary could question her blundered response, she continued. "Perhaps we'd be better off at a table? So that we can...sit amongst the flock?" she improvised. She had no idea if that was something the Order liked to do.

Nel met her eyes, "Yes, of course, you are right." Their tone didn't sound nearly as decisive as their words, but it was clear they agreed there were better places to sit.

Cromdren gave them a perplexed look but didn't argue. "Tides carry you safe, Aegis Commander," they said, settling back on their stool.

"And you in return," Nel replied.

They followed Draya to the empty seats she had recommended, doing their best not to look like a dog with their tail between their legs.

As they sat across from one another at the end of the long table, Draya leaned close. "What the abyss is the Torrent? And what sign?" she hissed.

Nel looked surprisingly sheepish. "There are...extremists among the Cresting Tide. The Twelfth Armada subscribes to some of the more...violent interpretations of the prophecies."

Draya raised her brow as they squirmed. She didn't need a bonding to sense their discomfort. "Interpretations?" she prodded. "Is that why you didn't use your full title?"

Nel flinched and let their gaze drop to their hands on the table. "I took note of the Spiral of Service affixed to his cuirass. If I'd given my full title, he would have known I am – was – Aegis to the Brightbourne. That seemed disadvantageous if we hoped to make it south without causing a panic."

"Right." She couldn't argue that. "And the Torrent is...?"

"The Final March. They believe the Creeping Drought is an invitation to...to..."

"To what?" Draya asked, impatient.

The words came out in a quiet rush. "To hunt down the Droughtbringer and any who oppose the Cresting Tide. It's a call to execute the Order's enemies."

Draya shuttered. "Lovely."

"Not particularly. We should steer clear of their ilk," Nel advised.

"Obviously." Draya rolled her eyes and then rubbed her temples. A new headache was coming on and the soldier's inability to grasp sarcasm wasn't helping. "What about this sign he mentioned? Some other part of the prophecy, I take it?" She glanced back at the bar. The twins were still staring at them, their eyes otherwise unreadable.

Before they could respond, a broad-shouldered woman appeared at their side from the rustling crowd. She wore an apron of undyed linen, and her tawny blond hair was pulled back into a high bun. Two pewter mugs were hoisted in her large hands, the brims spilling with foam from the hearty ale within.

"Welcome to the Brick & Boar!" The cheer in her words didn't match the coldness in her eyes. "It is always a pleasure to serve the Aegii of the Order. Please, take these, on the house." She set a mug in front of each of them.

Nel looked up and nodded politely, their anxiety masked with an untroubled facade. "Thank you. Do you still have hot meals available?" they asked without a beat. Draya felt the color drain from her face. If she had to guess, this was the tavern's barkeep, perhaps even an owner. Treating her like a server was inappropriate, if not insulting.

"Yes, yes – of course." Ignoring the unintended slight, the woman snapped her fingers. A serving girl looked over from across the aisle. She was a few hands shorter than Draya and looked at least half her age. "Two bowls of cod stew for our new friends! And the good brown bread in the back!" The girl nodded and hurried towards the kitchens without protest.

"We appreciate it," Draya said, pulling the barkeep's eyes from Nel for the first time. The woman nodded quickly and then looked back at the Aegis.

"I must say, I'm surprised to see you arrive so quickly. No offense meant, but news often travels so slowly to Trifall and back. We weren't sure when to expect you." The barkeep had a saccharine smile plastered across her thin lips.

"Expect me?" Nel cocked their head to one side. Their hands were politely laced together on the tabletop.

"We'd assumed our usual Almsman would return to assist in our plight. He'd only just been here last week to collect our quarterly tithes. But of course, it makes sense that the Coronet would send a specialist for this matter."

Nel's expression was terribly naive as they met the barkeep's gaze. "I apologize, I do not understand what you are talking about. We are passing through Northtown on our way to Trifall – we were not sent here by anyone."

The amicable expression dropped from the barkeep's face. "You mean to tell me you were not sent here to rectify the problem of our dwindling supplies?"

Draya and Nel exchanged glances. It all made sense to Draya now – the looks of hope, the glares, the silence around them. The people of Northtown all thought that the Aegis had come here in response to the Drought, or at least to lend material help in the interim. The serving girl returned with two bowls of steaming hot stew balanced on one arm, and a basket of bread hanging from the other. The barkeep held up a hand, stopping her from placing the meal down on the tabletop.

"I'm sorry, but no. You are mistaken." Nel looked between the two women in confusion.

"Well. That might be a problem then, lad." The barkeep's eyes narrowed.

"What do you mean?" Their brow furrowed.

"The Almsman's demands and quick retreat was worrisome in itself. But after the strange heat storm yesterday and the sudden issue with the water…well, it's clear the Order knows something they aren't sharing."

Draya surveyed the room again. Patrons had already cleared the area around them and all eyes were on Nel. Men and women started standing from their seats. Eye Patch and High Braid had already inched their way across the room until they were a scant few steps away. The woman pounded one fist into the palm of her other hand while the man reached for something beneath the long open vest he wore. Some of the more seasoned mercenaries, including Cromdren, stayed seated, pretending not to notice the exchange. Draya guessed they were waiting to see how things played out.

Her fingers tightened around her hilt. It wouldn't be easy to draw the blade from beneath the table, but she might not have a choice. Things were about to get ugly fast. She kicked Nel's armored boot with her own. "Exactly what she said," Draya hissed under her breath. "We've got a problem."

14

Recognizing the simmering tension at last, Nel moved to stand. "I apologize. I regret that I have no knowledge of what you speak, but I'm sure this can be worked out amicably. I have nothing to do with–"

Draya grabbed them by the shoulder and shoved them back into their seat. She ignored the painful shock as the metal ridges of their pauldrons cut into her palm. "People of Northtown, please, hold your ire!" She was surprised by the clarity of her voice given the circumstances.

"Who the abyss are you?" a thin man in a blacksmith's apron shouted.

Most of the patrons were townsfolk. She'd be surprised if they'd ever even been in a bar brawl, let alone a fight with a trained soldier.

"I am –" Draya paused. As recently as three days ago, she wouldn't have hesitated to drop her mother's name to give herself a bit of clout, especially if it could get her out of a bind. But namedropping her way out of an alleged trespassing charge or the accusations of a disgruntled client was one thing. She was relatively certain hitching the family name to the start of the apocalypse wouldn't be met with the same begrudging tolerance. "It doesn't matter who I am!" Draya raised her hands to show she was unarmed and stepped up onto the tabletop. "I know you must be scared. I know you are looking for answers, or at least someone to blame." She looked down at Nel. "But this lowly Aegis is not worth your frustrations. They do not know why the Drought has occurred, nor any insight into the Order's business with the fine people of Northtown. They have been stationed far, far to the north for..." Draya looked down at Nel, searching for some kind of excuse that was decidedly not guarding the Palace of the Undying. They looked up blankly, their brow creased with confusion.

She would have to wing it.

"...for the last five years!" she finished. "They are headed to the Capital in search of answers themself."

A low murmur spread over the crowd. At least half the patrons relaxed their stance, listening now instead of preparing to pounce.

"Where to the north? And why?" The barkeep eyed her shrewdly, the gears in her head turning.

An idea came to her from years past, when she'd studied cartography under the guidance of her tutor. "The Aegis had been stationed in the Halloran Mountains!" She didn't have to look down to feel Nel's eyes boring into her. She pressed on. "When the devoted disciple of the Helix realized something was amiss, they left their post to reunite with their kin in this time of need. It was only by chance that I met them on the road. We are but travelers, trying to get to Trifall on foot now that the canal is unavailable to us!"

More patrons relaxed their stance, their expressions turning from anger to pity. The barkeep looked Nel up and down. To their credit, the Aegis kept a neutral expression, neither confirming nor denying the explanation.

Finally, the barkeep threw their hands in the air. "Fine! So be it." She turned to the masses. "Back to your seats, all. If what this woman says is true, this Aegis is nothing to waste our breath or brawn on."

Nel's jaw tightened. Draya understood why. The meditation caves of Halloran were well known but rarely discussed. For some, it was a quiet retreat, but most of the clerics were assigned to the mountains not for lack of faith, but rather for lack of muster. Not all children born with the Calling of Will were cut out to be soldiers. When a well-meaning acolyte couldn't live up to the expectations of their order or were too injured to carry out their duties, they were allowed the mercy of completing their oaths in quiet solitude. Few if any Aegii returned from these ceremonial posts, and even the dead were often left unburied, their bodies offered up to the mountain's dire vultures.

Rather than address the hurt she most assuredly caused to Nel's pride, Draya dug a small pouch of emergency coins from her belt. "Here," she said, tossing it to the barkeep. "Buy the house a round –

ON US!" she shouted the last, convincing the final few still standing to turn the other way. It was most of the coin she had on her, but she'd replace it soon enough once she ditched the reliquary.

The barkeep shrugged. She poured the glistening slivers of metal into her hand and appraised the contents. "One round on the Aegis and their Herald. Let Bessie know what you want," she said to the room.

Draya breathed a sigh of relief. Conversations picked up again as the locals turned back to their companions and their cups. She was almost relaxed when she noticed Eye Patch and High Braid hadn't moved. They were frozen in place, muscles tensed. "What are you two looking at?" Draya finally demanded.

They looked pointedly at one another and turned, absently tossing a few coins on the bar top before they strode out the front door without another glance.

"That was too close," Draya muttered as she slipped back onto the bench.

The Aegis looked less than relieved. "Halloran? Was that entirely necessary?" Their nostrils flared, but they kept their voice low.

"*That's* the part you're concerned about?" Draya threw back the contents of her mug. Her stomach rumbled as her eyes fell on the bowls of stew the server had left languishing on the bar. "Trouble couldn't have waited until *after* lunch?" she moaned.

"I trialed at the top of my cohort," they continued in a low voice. "I was *field* promoted to Aegis Commander General and bound on the spot to the Brightbourne. The idea that I'd been exiled to the caves –"

Draya grabbed a hunk of stale bread from an abandoned plate nearby and shoved it into Nel's open mouth. "Hush! Don't you get it? If they think you're that important we're as good as hung. You just need to lay low, maybe get a change of clothes, and get back on the road as soon as possible." She conveniently left herself out of the plan. She had a contract to fulfill and a payment to collect, after all.

Nel spat out the bread and narrowed their eyes. Draya looked at the sodden chunk and immediately regretted using it as a gag. "I still do not understand why everyone is so angry. If only they had given me a chance to explain, I could have assured them of their safety under the auspices of the Coronet and –"

"Are you insane? I just saved your life, you do know that, right?" It took all of Draya's restraint to keep from shouting through the smile plastered on her face.

Before Nel could respond, the young barmaid appeared at their side. "Here," she whispered with a shy smile. She slipped them each a parchment-wrapped package tied off with string. "You more than covered this and the drinks with that pile of coins you gave Marah. Not as good as the stew, but it's something."

Resisting the urge to devour whatever it was then and there, Draya placed her hands over the offering. "Thank you – Bessie, right?" She kicked Nel's ankle under the table.

"What? Oh, yes, thank you." Nel took the package and awkwardly held it between their gauntleted hands.

The barmaid gave Draya a small nod in confirmation. "I'm sorry about all of that. Northtown – and the Brick & Boar – are usually very welcoming."

"Could have fooled me." Draya softened the words with a dry smile. The girl seemed sweet enough, and she'd done nothing to earn her ire in particular.

The woman threw a glance at Nel. "Can you blame them? After what the Order did last week...Well, I think we have a right to be concerned."

"What did the Order do?" Nel's tone was too curt, startling the young woman.

Bessie stammered a second, looking between the pair and finally settling back on Nel. "The Almsman? The additional tithes? You really don't know, do you?" Her wariness turned to a kind of pity as Bessie seemed to recall the unflattering backstory supplied by Draya.

"What happened?" Draya asked, pulling Bessie's attention away from Nel.

The barmaid's faint smile returned as she faced her. "Ah, well. Last week, the Almsman came for his quarterly tithe, but he didn't come alone. A higher ranking priest was with him, and they demanded twice what the town usually gives. When the Regent didn't have that available, they surveyed the public food stores and confiscated anything they deemed to be...what did they call it? Oh yes. Superfluous or overly extravagant."

Nel's brow furrowed. "There must be some misunderstanding."

Draya shot them a scathing look before turning back to Bessie. "The size of the tithes, I take it, are compulsory?"

The woman cocked her head to one side. "Of course. How else would we be protected?"

This is exactly what Draya had been telling the Aegis the day before. When Occidrious was vanquished, the Cresting Tide had anointed themselves the protectors of Aiylonia. It was their self-appointed duty to oversee each hamlet and city. In exchange, they often requested donations made to their local Almsmen and their chapels. Draya had even heard of Almsman who exaggerated the dangers to extract more than their agreed-upon share. She couldn't be sure, but she hypothesized that the more coin sent back to Trifall, the more esteem the Almsman garnered with their superiors. For whatever reason, it seemed the local temple had taken great pains to convince Northtown that it was in danger only a week prior.

Draya changed the subject. "I see, and now with the sudden drought, there is worry rations will come up short?"

"Yes, exactly," the barmaid replied. "Seeing an Aegis so soon – I'm sure they just hoped you were here to make amends, or at least offer an explanation."

Nel's frown deepened but they kept their mouth shut.

"That is an unfortunate coincidence, isn't it?" Draya kept her tone even.

The barmaid looked back at Nel. "Really though – do you think this is the work of the Droughtbringer? Is the End upon us? I didn't see the strange lightning for myself yesterday, but some of the older folk are saying it's an ill omen."

Nel swallowed, averting their eyes as they lifted their mug to take a long pull of ale.

Draya was about to ask about the storm when there was a clap from across the room. The barmaid looked up. "Be right there!" she shouted to the distant patron. "Anyway," she said to the pair, "I have to get back to work before Marah docks my rations. Safe travels to you both." Her small smile widened into a show-stopping grin as she turned away from them.

"She must be confused," Nel whispered once the woman was out of earshot. "There is no reason an Archpriest or Prelate would demand such a tithe, let alone in foodstuffs."

Draya rolled her eyes. "You haven't spent much time among the common folk, have you?"

"What do you mean?" The Aegis's spine straightened.

"I assume that storm is whatever sign the zealot at the bar mentioned?"

"It seems likely. Perhaps a consequence of breaking the Vault's Seal?" Nel offered.

"Perhaps?" She was used to riddles in her line of work, but it would have been nice to get tangled up with someone with a little more certainty. Draya threw back the last of her drink. "You should head over to the guard house on the other side of town." She stood and unwrapped what turned out to be a sandwich of roast beef and hard cheese. She tossed the parchment on the table and took a big bite.

Nel looked at her in confusion. "I should? What about you?" They unslung their pack from their back and stuffed their own package inside.

She swallowed. "I have some business to attend to."

The Aegis's eyes narrowed suspiciously. "We should stay together."

"Can't." Draya went to take another bite and then stopped to point a finger at them. "Don't bother following me. I'll spot you a mile away in that armor, and you'll just muck things up."

Nel's nostrils flared at the assertion. "What sort of business is this?" they asked warily.

"Guild business. I know how your kind feel about us mercenary thieves." Before they could protest, Draya winked and flashed them a disarming smile. "Really though. Stock up on supplies, maybe get a cloak to hide that get-up of yours, and meet me at the southern gate. I shouldn't be more than an hour, tops. That should get us to Templekeep by nightfall." She hoped it would be enough to keep the Aegis out of her affairs.

Nel's expression softened with defeat. "I guess I cannot stop you, can I?"

"No, you cannot." Draya drained her mug and slipped out the side door. Just to be safe, she took a few alleyways before circling back around to the more direct route to the designated meeting place. If Nel was trying to follow, they were nowhere to be seen. A small part of Draya wondered if she'd come to regret that decision.

15

Northtown wasn't deserted, but it certainly looked that way. The spiderwebs of canals – both shallow and deep – were nearly drained. Brightly painted gondolas teetered low against their dockings, their iron prows tipped to one side. Walkways were littered with abandoned oarlocks, and ladders that had been submerged only yesterday sat exposed to the dry air, their ancient rungs caked in rust the color of dried blood. A scant few corner stalls, kettle shops, and dry goods merchants were open for businesses on the main avenues, but few people seemed to linger at any location for very long. Draya didn't know Northtown particularly well, but she'd spent much of her life in cities just like it. The central thoroughfares should be bustling with activity. Instead, she found the doors and windows of the residential districts barred shut. It seemed the majority of the city's inhabitants had chosen to shelter in place, perhaps believing the drought would pass like a violent storm or plundering army. The resulting silence set Draya's nerves on edge.

Confident the Aegis hadn't followed, Draya eventually allowed herself to follow a more direct route to her destination. As late as half a century ago, the district of Endchapel had served as home to a variety of faiths. Things changed as the Order of the Cresting Tide asserted itself as the kingdom's dominant religion. The eclectic temples and altars were absorbed, closed, or demolished as the clerics of alternate religious teachings sold their property or were run out of the city. All that was left of the diversity that once flourished in the district were the vestiges of antiqued architecture and their vandalized stone reliefs.

Draya was passing one such stoic procession of defaced statues when she heard singing up ahead. It was an untrained but not unpleasant voice, but the words were lost to the echo of the narrow passages. As she rounded a corner, the street opened up into a small square overlooked by the shell of a nameless temple. The owner of the voice was seated on the crumbling steps, picking out notes on her lyre as she sang. A crowd of locals had gathered at her feet, the first people she had seen since entering Endchapel. She could finally make out the lyrics of the familiar hymn just in time to hear a verse she'd never noticed before:

> *With neatly plaited mantle, as dead as brick red clay,*
> *her eyes a ghostly haunt in darkest empty gray.*
> *She will herald the end of all that we know,*
> *bring death and destruction wherever she goes.*
> *Only through the Tides will the Faithful survive —*
> *Raise arms against the Droughtbringer when she arrives.*

Draya pulled her long braid over her shoulder and gave the deep red tendrils an accusatory look.

"The Droughtbringer!" a man in the audience shouted.

She froze.

"Do you truly believe some mythical redhead is behind this disaster?" he continued, heckling the singer on the steps. He wore a canvas apron hung with an assortment of jewelers' tools.

Draya let out a nervous laugh, drawing the man's attention. He waved a hand in her direction but then turned back to the crowd. "See? She doesn't believe in this divine bullshit either! Only through the Tides," he mocked. "Only through the Tides do we lose the rations that might have seen us through this disaster. Or will the Coronet magically restore the canals if we empty our purses?"

A murmur wove its way through the small crowd. Most debated the man's heresy, but a few took his side. Draya noticed the bard sweep up her tips and slip away. Draya decided to follow her lead.

Once she was a safe distance from the square, she pulled a purple sash from her belt pouch and tied it around the crown of her head. She stuffed the tail end of the braid underneath her knapsack for good measure. *At least they don't have the eye color right,* she thought.

Draya usually chose a more neutral, public place for her meets, but she understood that the Fellowship handled things differently. They said they'd find her once she crossed into Endchapel, not the other way around. Some of the district's abandoned buildings had been turned into tenement housing, but most were small trade businesses and workshops, their craftsmen laboring among the remnants of esoteric architecture. She relaxed her gait, taking long, deliberate steps to make herself as conspicuous as possible. It was her intention to be seen, and she wanted the Fellowship's scouts to know that. She made a show of peering into windows at wares she had no interest in purchasing, hoping she'd reap some insight from the reflections in the glass.

She paused as she caught sight of her visage and ignored the dark grey pupils staring back at her. *Trick of the light,* she decided. *Blue can look black sometimes.* She didn't look into her own reflection again after that.

Draya was starting to wonder if the sudden drought had spooked her buyers when she caught sight of someone watching her from a nearby rooftop. They ducked out of view rather quickly, but not so fast that she missed the telltale purple flourish. She spotted another scarf further down the avenue, and then another past that.

Breadcrumbs. She smiled to herself and picked up her pace, following the flashes of color down twisting lanes and alleys. Anyone else may have found themselves hopelessly lost, but not Draya. By the time she'd spotted her sixth human marker, they'd made two different circuits around the district. She was ready to be done with their games.

As if anticipating the end of her tolerance, Draya found herself looking down a dark alleyway between two dilapidated warehouses. She stopped short, debating the risk. It would be tight corners if things got ugly, but the passage appeared empty. She let her hand fall to the comforting pommel of her rapier before she proceeded forward.

Her view to the opposite street darkened as a trio of robed individuals entered from a passage to the side. Three figures stretched out, forming a solid line stretching from one wall to the other. Despite the heat, they wore identical layers of black fabric, scarves of deep purple, and half capes over one shoulder. She fought the urge to glance back to see if more of the Fellowship had blocked her escape from behind, trusting her gut instinct that her escape route was still clear. She stopped a few feet from the group and raised her open palms in surrender.

"You know, most of my buyers just meet me in the dark corner of a tavern," she said. "Less theatrical, but at least we can get drunk after."

"The Fellowship does not sully themselves with inebriation." The man in the center snarled through the scarf wound across the bottom of his face. "Now where is the Relic?"

"No preamble?" Draya sighed dramatically and pulled her knapsack to the front of her body, taking the opportunity to covertly loosen her rapier in its sheath. "You Fellowship are a very serious lot, you know that?"

"These are serious times," the cultist replied.

"Yes, yes, Of course you're right. What do you want this old thing for, anyway? It can't be all that important if it stayed hidden for so long." She did her best to sound disinterested in the answer.

"That's none of your business," the figure to the right interjected. His voice cracked slightly as he spoke, betraying both his nerves and his youth. He couldn't have been more than sixteen.

The cultist in the center spared his companion a glare before turning back to Draya. "The contract stipulated no questions. Hand over the relic."

"Careful now, careful." She raised her eyebrow curiously. "See, this is why the brandy helps. Keeps everything relaxed." The three members of the Fellowship stared back at her blankly. "Fine. No small talk." Draya let her fingertips linger over the clasp that kept her pack closed. "Speaking of contracts – payment first, then the bauble. I almost died getting this thing."

The familiar feeling of sharp, cold steel settled against the hollow of her throat. Draya stilled but kept her posture relaxed.

"How is this for payment?" A fourth man's voice hissed hotly in her ear. The newcomer was taller than her by nearly a head, and he was holding her fast against him. She hadn't heard him approach, and she was sure he hadn't been there just a moment before.

"Now, now. Let's be civil, folks. Hawkers don't exactly approve of their agents sustaining injury after the job is completed. I just want what's due and I'll be on my way." Draya assessed her surroundings as she spoke. There wasn't much in the alley that could make a decent weapon, which meant both she and her enemies were restricted to whatever they had on hand. She'd fought her way out of tighter corridors, but the blade at her throat was going to pose a challenge.

The two cultists on either side of the central man stepped forward. One pulled Draya's rapier from her scabbard, while the younger man tore into her knapsack. Draya watched a scattering of odds and ends tumble to the ground as he dug into its contents. Finally, he pulled the small bundle of decayed velvet free. He took an awed breath and eagerly unwrapped a corner to peer inside. Draya watched as his eyes grew wide with avarice.

"The parcel is intact?" asked her captor.

"Yes, it's perfect – exactly as the They said it would be. We have it, finally, we have it, Vizier Erasmus." Reverence dripped from his words like honey.

There was a pregnant pause. Draya watched the speaker shrivel.

"You see," the lead cultist said, directing his words to Draya. "Normally I'd reprimand an initiate for revealing my name." The cultist in question paled even further. "But luckily for him, your success means we no longer have need of you or your particular…talents. Farewell, little thief." His grip tightened.

"Wait!" Draya stalled. "If you kill me, I can't tell you about all the other things I discovered as I fled the Palace."

She watched as the other three looked between themselves with excitement. Their questions overlapped.

"Did you see the vortex?"

"Has the Wake already begun?"

"Are you the Droughtbringer?"

"Silence fools!" The Vizier barked. "Anything you have found, we will discover for ourselves soon enough. Your purpose is fulfilled. Thank you for your service to the Fellowship."

Draya's throat was dry as she felt the edge of the blade tense.

16

"Oi! What's going on down there?" A baritone voice echoed against the stone walls, startling Draya's captor.

Seeing her opportunity, she moved into action. Draya threw her elbow behind her, connecting hard with the man's solar plexus. His grip on her loosened and she ducked to the side to avoid the blade. He stumbled in the opposite direction, and she swung her knapsack like a bludgeon, knocking him against the wall. His blade tumbled out of his grip, and Draya absently noticed there was blood along the serrated edge. She didn't have time to check her throat. If she was cut, the adrenaline was keeping the pain at bay.

She swooped down and grabbed the vicious weapon, turning quickly to face the other three attackers. The closest was caught flat-footed, still gripping the relic in both hands. The older two had managed to draw daggers from their belts. They looked back and forth, trying to decide if they should engage their original target or the source of the shout. As they hesitated, Draya feinted low with the stolen blade, distracting the one with the artifact. He threw his legs backward to dodge, and she followed with an upward swing of her knapsack into his overextended torso. As the artifact launched skyward, she darted forward, slashing at the cultist with her rapier. The serrated edge connected with his shoulder, tearing through the thick fabric of his tunic and slicing into flesh. With a flick of her opposite wrist, she flipped open her pack just in time to catch the sarcophilum inside, then swept her leg low enough to take out the wounded man's knee. He fell, his head colliding into the brick wall with an audible crack before his body landed prone to the ground.

Draya looked up to take on the third remaining cultist, but he'd already turned his back to her, running in the opposite direction down the alley. With him no longer a threat, she turned, only to find the young cultist getting to his feet. She threw her knapsack back on and snatched her rapier from where it had fallen to the ground, spinning back on the man in one smooth movement. The tip of the long blade came up under his chin, causing him to freeze. "Yield," she ordered. His body relaxed and he accepted defeat, letting himself fall back against the cobblestone street.

Draya's gaze shot upward to the Vizier. Before he flipped his fallen hood back over his blond hair, she was surprised to see he was rather handsome – or at least he would have been if not for the sneer turning up the corners of his mouth.

She lifted his dagger towards him with a taunting smirk of her own. "Looks like it's just you and me. I told your cronies we should have just shared a drink and be done with it."

"You are only delaying the inevitable, thief. You will wish you'd accepted a quick death instead of the suffering that awaits you."

There was a crash as a flash of light illuminated the space for a moment. Draya watched the cultist frown as he looked over her shoulder. She didn't dare take her eyes off him.

"We aren't done," he snarled. Before she could move, he took an elongated step backward, vanishing into the dark shadows behind him.

Draya blinked, taken aback. *Shadowmancy is a myth.*

She didn't have time to reconcile that fact. Seeing himself abandoned, the cultist on the ground lifted his arms in surrender. Draya cocked her head to one side and pulled back the blade. Taking the hint, the cultist crawled away, getting to his feet and running once he was out of range of an attack.

There was another crack of lightning. "Finally, some alone time."

Draya spun towards the familiar voice. The menacing twins from the tavern were advancing on her, Eye Patch brandishing a length of heavy iron chain as High Braid clashed her knuckle dusters together. Crackling sparks of blue light arced wildly with each impact.

Great. She's a Shock Caller. She clicked her tongue against her teeth in annoyance. "Now what do you want?"

The brother with the chain narrowed his eyes. "We want what's due."

Draya took a deep breath, slipping the confiscated dagger into her belt. "I thought we resolved this."

"Not in the slightest," High Braid growled. The light illuminated her features from below, distorting her face into a grotesque mask.

"Then what in the sarding abyss do you want?" Draya kept the point of her rapier trained on the pair but otherwise relaxed into a wide stance, her offhand on her hip. The potency of a Shock Caller's power varied wildly – most barely gave a jolt any stronger than wool in winter. High Braid obviously had more power than that, but Draya could work with it. *She can't stun me if she can't touch me*, Draya reasoned.

"The Cresting Tide owes us, after all they took last week," Eye Patch said. "Come quietly. I'm sure that Aegis friend of yours will shell out some hefty coin to get you back in one piece."

Draya barked out a laugh. "That's your plan?" She glanced upwards and saw the sun had fallen significantly. It was getting late. "I don't have the time nor the energy to explain to you all the reasons that will not work out the way you want it to."

"Good," the sister said, punctuating her words with another clash of sparks. "I'm tired of talking."

Draya sighed. Aside from the knick at her throat she was unscathed, but that was pure luck. The Fellowship obviously didn't expect a guilded archeologian to have military-level combat training, giving her the advantage. But now the twins had seen what she could do, losing her the element of surprise. Their brows knit in confusion as she slipped her rapier back into its scabbard and raised her fists into a defensive position. "Well, come on then."

They smiled at one another and closed the distance. Draya took two steps back, and then quickly snatched a throwing knife from the back of her belt and threw the tiny blade straight above her head. The twins didn't have a chance to react as it severed the clothing line that spanned the alley a few stories up. The heavily laden rope swung down, wrapping the two assailants in a large damp bed sheet. They tumbled to the cobblestones, a mess of flailing limbs and clinging fabric.

Draya had bought herself mere seconds, but her eyes caught on the myriad odds and ends the reckless cultist had spilled from her pack. They were worth a year's worth of wages at auction. "Sarding abyss," she groaned. Resigned, she spun on her heel toward the alley entrance behind her, but her moment of indecision had cost her. Shards of stone exploded from the ground at her feet with a flash of blue light. She recoiled on instinct and tripped on one of the fallen items just as something whirled violently through the space where her head had been. High Braid had managed to skip a lightning bolt from where she was struggling, but Eye Patch was clear of the sodden fabric. He pulled back the long chain for another attempt at her skull. Draya grabbed what she'd fallen on – a hunk of carved obsidian – and threw it back at the brother. It soared past him without making contact, but it was enough of a distraction for Draya to roll back onto her feet. She took off in a full sprint.

If the Fellowship scouts that had led her into the ambush were still around, they didn't show themselves. She took a different route back to the more populated areas of Northtown, but when she looked over her shoulder, the pair weren't far behind. They surged forward in an attempt to make up the distance, far more familiar with their city than she ever could be. She needed a clear path, and without ready access to the waterways, her memory wasn't much help. Draya closed her eyes for a second and then followed her intuition down the alley to her right, and then the next two to the left. A grand marketplace opened up to her, and while the crowd wasn't nearly as large as it should have been under normal circumstances, the sweeping tents and stacks of crates provided adequate cover. She darted amongst them, slipping under swaths of canvas as she avoided the bodies of patrons and vendors alike.

Her available camouflage was short-lived. When she reached the other side, she could still hear shouts of protest, betraying the continued pursuit of the twins behind her. She glanced left and right, then decided to continue straight, hoping the avenue would lead her to the southern entrance.

By the time she spotted Nel, Draya was breathing hard. To her welcome surprise, the Aegis had found a navy blue traveler's cloak to drape over their armor with a deep hood to hide their heavy circlet. They even had an extra bag slung over their shoulder, presumably full of further supplies. There was a thin line of travelers heading through the Southern Gate, likely hoping they could find water elsewhere. She'd lost the twins in the maze of streets, but she knew it wouldn't be for long. She slowed her breath and walked tall.

Nel's head turned on a swivel as she approached, their brow creased in concern. "Are you all right? What happened?"

"Why do you think that anything ha – Oh." *The bonding*, Draya remembered.

"When my heart rate increased, I thought it was a consequence of you going too far from me - that you'd tried to flee," they explained as they searched her face. "When the fear didn't escalate and eventually lessened, I wasn't sure if I should await your arrival or come looking for you."

Draya didn't like the look of worry in their eyes. "Jealous and missing me already?" she chided. "Aren't you Aegii under some kind of celibacy oath?"

Nel bristled, their expression hardening. "I didn't –"

Draya waved a hand, regretting the crude insinuation as soon as they left her lips. "Doesn't matter. We have to move." She latched her arm around Nel's elbow and tried to guide them forward. They didn't budge, instead peering more closely at her throat.

"Is that…blood?" They reached out to tilt her chin for a better look, but she pushed their hand away, touching the small cut with her own fingers instead.

"It's nothing," she replied, glad to find the bit of blood was already half dry and the wound was no larger than a pinprick.

"What trouble have you caused?" they asked.

"What makes you think *I* caused it?" she hissed. When they showed no sign of moving, she cursed. "Sarding abyss. I'm sorry I made you worry. Leave now, questions later," Draya said with a glare.

The Aegis clenched their jaw, but otherwise accepted this, following her lead towards the open gate. As she glanced behind, she let go of any notions she still had of ditching Nel in Northtown. The brother and sister emerged from the maze of alleys. They'd stowed their weapons out of sight, but that didn't make them any less dangerous. The last thing she wanted right now was to be on her own.

The city guards were stationed at the wall mostly for appearances, but as she darted forward she placed a hand on the shoulder of the closest of the two. "Excuse me," she said, her voice and breath suddenly calm through sheer force of will. "But those two people? They seem to be stalking me. Ever since I arrived," she added beseechingly.

The guard in question was a young woman with short blond hair. She looked beyond Draya and then gave her a small smile. "Harold and Grunda? Hmm, yes. A few drinks and the pair can get a little out of line." She smiled at Draya and nodded. "I'm sure they're just riled up from this drought. Do not worry, I will take care of it." The guard stepped between Draya and the oncoming pursuers. "Carry on safely."

"Thank you!" Draya cried in the most sincere voice she could muster. She continued through the gates at a walking pace, Nel following with a taciturn expression. It was only after they'd cleared the small crowd and were back on the towpath that Draya dared to look over her shoulder. The guard was talking to the pair, but they didn't seem to be interested in pursuing Draya outside the town borders. After a minute or two, the twins turned and headed back into town.

"Were those the two from the bar?" Nel asked as they adjusted the second bag more comfortably over their shoulder.

"They were."

"They followed you?"

"It seems so."

"So your heart racing – that was from running?" They cocked their head to one side.

Draya gave a noncommittal shrug. *Running was involved, at least.*

"Do you know why?"

Draya knew the truth was stranger than fiction. "They thought they could use me as ransom. Get you to pay the balance of what tithes were taken in excess." She chuckled. "Hilarious, right?"

Confusion wrinkled their brow. "Why would that be hilarious?"

She almost chuckled. "I doubt Aegii have such an allowance. And even if you did have that kind of coin on hand, why would you use it on me? If anything I'm sure you'd be happy to have me taken off your hands."

Nel remained silent for a moment. "I would, you know."

"Ouch." Draya clutched her hand to her breast. "Just because it's true doesn't mean you have to say the quiet part out loud. Trust me, I'm not exactly happy about this little forced partnership either."

"No! That's not — you misunderstand." They shook their head. "I mean to say, I'd find a way to pay should you have been captured."

Draya stopped short. "What? Why?"

"Because it would be the right thing to do." The sincerity in their hazel eyes was clear.

Draya fell into a stunned silence. She didn't even know this Aegis. They should be dragging her by the collar back to Trifall for interrogation. They should be penalizing her for her disastrous presence in the palace. Instead, they earnestly claimed they would have come to her rescue personally.

Even stranger, Draya believed them.

17

The unlikely pair joined the parade of bedraggled travelers snaking their way from the canal to Templekeep's front gate. They quickly learned that the unnatural storm of the vortex hadn't been confined to the Radiant Sea. Reports of the sudden appearance of dark clouds and brief flashes of blue and purple lightning circulated the gathered crowd. It didn't take long to confirm Nel's suspicion that the strange phenomena occurred in concert with Draya's escape from the Treasury. By the time they finally reached the walls of the waypost, they had heard more than one explanation for the onset of the Drought.

Most blamed the prophesied Droughtbringer, but to Draya's relief, only a few accounts were as incriminating as the description she'd heard in Endchapel. Some took the idea of fiery hair literally, painting the image of a woman made of living flame. Others claimed she was a giantess over seven foot tall, a creature half woman and half fox, or – in one particularly absurd case – a fabled astral drake with fangs as long as a human thigh. When they'd left earshot of the frantic fisher spouting that particular version, she asked Nel whether it was rooted in prophecy. They just shook their head with a sigh, muttering something about satirical folktales. Draya would have found it all funny if the fear hidden behind the tired eyes of the storytellers wasn't so crushingly real.

A sturdy drawbridge straddled the once formidable moat surrounding Templekeep's outermost wall, now reduced to a thin trickle of muddy water. Guards stood at either side of the entryway, each wearing the same shade of robin's egg blue as the pennants waving from the parapets – the same blue worn by lay citizenry officially employed by the Coronet. Their faces were hidden behind full helms sporting amphibious fins on either side, the rest of them dressed in silver plate mail similar in style to Nel's golden armor.

"That explains the bottleneck," Draya remarked. The legionaries assessed each group that came through, slowing the line down significantly. "What do you think they're screening for?"

Nel narrowed their eyes. "I'm not entirely sure. Templekeep is usually open to any traveler in need. Most wayposts are."

Draya's mind immediately went to the relic. They didn't seem to be searching people's bags, but that didn't mean they wouldn't make an exception for her pack.

Even if they saw it, would these rank-and-file soldiers even recognize the Sarcophilum as a palace artifact? Would Nel? If they did, what would they do? Try to arrest me? Portal me straight to the Order's dungeons? Execute me on the spot? Draya had enough reservations about traveling to Trifall in the company of the Aegis; she didn't like giving the Coronet more reasons to distrust her. At least Nel didn't seem to assign malicious intent to her status as the Droughtbringer, but her possession of whatever she'd gotten her hands on might jeopardize that tenuous understanding. Draya liked to think they wouldn't just throw her to the wolves, but there was no trusting a religious zealot. She felt a droplet of newly formed sweat slide down her spine.

Nel wove through the crowd, sweeping their new cloak aside and using their distinct attire to their advantage. When their turn at the front of the line finally came, the soldiers stationed there seemed to freeze. One stepped forward, pulling off her helm to reveal a head of hair braided in a crown around her head.

"Calm winds and clear skies, Lieutenant Rian." Nel nodded to the soldier in greeting.

She returned the gesture. "Full nets and high waters, Aegis Commander General."

Draya choked back a sardonic laugh at the irony of the sentiment, earning a sidelong glance from Nel. She shrugged.

The soldier didn't notice the exchange. "We are glad to see you here, Sentinel," she said, using their given name. Her brow furrowed and she scanned the crowd behind them. "Where is the Brightbourne?"

Nel pursed their lips but otherwise maintained their neutral expression.

Confusion, surprise, then understanding washed over Rian's face in quick succession. "I see," she said soberly. "Then the drought…?"

Draya tried to look anywhere but the legionnaire, bracing herself against Nel's emotional response.

Instead, all they did was nod.

Rian took in a deep breath before responding. "That is…unfortunate."

"It is." The voice was flat, almost cold, in response.

The lay soldier tucked her helmet under her arm and looked towards her counterpart at the other side of the gate. "Aegis coming through!" she announced.

The other legionnaire gently guided the family of four to the side, allowing Nel onto the drawbridge. Draya trailed quickly behind, simultaneously bewildered by Nel's lack of emotion and glad to avoid any undue attention herself. Rian beckoned an identically dressed soldier to take her place before leading them across the bridge and through the threshold of the compound.

In Draya's experience, every waypost looked much the same as the last. Aside from the outer walls, inner walls, and central courtyard, there were a variety of buildings, gardens, barns, and stables laid out in a vaguely circular pattern. The original foundations dated back centuries, each early fort built to safeguard a natural spring and harbor anyone that sought refuge from the dangers of the untamed wilderness. Most wayposts functioned independently from any local government entities, but the Cresting Tide had taken possession of all of the compounds along the Cimmrean Canal sometime after the Deluge. Even without the recognizable legionnaires at the entrance, the renovations to the architecture made it clear that Templekeep remained under the Order's control. The inner walls had been gutted and turned into airy colonnades, and as Draya passed between the columns a feeling of unease washed over her. The structures may have changed, but the memory of the original foundational footprint remained.

"Like walking through a ghost," Draya whispered to herself.

As soon as she spoke, her vision blurred. She teetered sideways, her palm catching against one of the supports. Just as it had in the labyrinth, a map of her surroundings flared to life in her mind. Pathways spun out around her, disjointed and confused. One pattern seemed at war with the other, the layout of what it had become struggling against what it once was.

"Did you say something?"

Rian's voice shattered the overwhelming sensation, leaving only afterimages behind. She and Nel had turned their heads to her, Rian's expression curious.

Draya forced a mask of indifference across her face. "Oh, nothing. Just commenting that you must enjoy being assigned this waypost. It has so much..." She floundered. She could see no benefits to forced service in a single location, particularly one without access to a decent tavern. "...rustic appeal."

The guard answered her with a shrug. "I serve where the Coronet wills."

When she turned her head away Nel furrowed their brow. *What happened?* They silently mouthed the words.

Draya lamented again the infuriating insight the Aegis had into her state of mind. *Later,* she mouthed back, dismissing their worry with a wave.

Nel narrowed their eyes suspiciously before turning back around, seemingly accepting her response.

Rian led them toward the central courtyard with purpose. As they rounded the corner of the residential wing, she and Nel stopped short at the same time. What should have been a large space of open green was packed with lines of cots and a scatter of canvas tents. Aiylonians of all ages and genders milled about, some tending cook fires and playing dice games, but most aimless, their eyes downcast.

"People are already seeking shelter?" Nel's voice was steady, but this time Draya could feel the dismay beneath their words.

"Sadly, yes," the Lieutenant replied.

"Is everyone here for well water?" Draya's eyes settled on a young girl wandering among the tents. *Where are her parents?* she wondered to herself.

"Oh." Rian shook her head. "Some, yes. We have an exceptionally deep reservoir, but even that is being tested to its limits. But many have escaped here from Laketop."

Nel sucked in a breath as Draya's heart dropped into her stomach, the shared distress transforming into horror. Very little of Laketop was built on solid land, their structures instead perched on floating platforms, each tethered to the next. Some of the larger areas were supported by struts secured to the lake floor, but that was few and far between. If the lake had drained, there was no way to save the cobbled-together town from collapsing in on itself. Even if every person on the central green were a survivor, it would only equal a small fraction of the town's population.

Draya's gaze traveled back to the young girl. She'd stopped moving, instead standing near the edge of the camp, her eyes wide. Before she could reason herself out of getting involved, Draya moved towards the child, kneeling to meet her face-to-face. She couldn't have been any older than six.

"Are you lost?" She surprised herself with the question.

The child's quivering lip was enough of an answer.

Draya prided herself on a calloused conscience, but she was stirred into action despite it. After taking a cursory look around, she took the girl's hand and instinctively headed to the right. "Follow me."

There was no rhyme or reason to the layout of the temporary encampment. Haste and necessity had rightly outweighed careful planning, and what might have started as personal campsites had been overrun with errant cots and a mix of quilts and bedrolls. Three small areas had been cleared for cook fires, each circled by men and women doing their best to stay busy. A triage center was being established in the far right corner, and while Draya couldn't make out the specifics, there was someone giving some kind of sermon on the opposite side. She snaked her way through the crowds, the child tagging behind. Unlike the vivid images that had flooded her senses earlier, this was the subtle knack for direction Draya was familiar with. *Though,* she had to admit, *it was one thing to reason out a hiding place of a bounty – finding a potentially mobile stranger in a crowded refugee camp would be a whole different level of uncanny.* Like the devastation that had befallen Laketop, she pushed the implications of the revelation down deep.

"Eva!" A small woman ran towards them from the closest cook fire, a handkerchief tied over her hair.

"Momma!" The little girl pulled her hand from Draya's and sprang forward, leaping into her mother's arms.

"Thank you." The woman's wizened face lit up with a smile of appreciation as she wrapped her daughter in a tight embrace.

Draya nodded absently. She felt unmoored. She wasn't used to doing things that elicited such gratitude.

The mother and daughter turned back to a tiny campsite, joining a man Draya suspected was the father. He looked up with a smile that immediately soured.

"Are you all right?"

Startled, Draya turned to see Nel at her shoulder, their armor glittering in the direct sunlight. The lines of concern on their face had deepened.

She shook her head. "No – I mean, yes." She cast a look back at the small family. The father was whispering to the mother, gesturing past the row of tents behind them. She shook her head and turned, walking with purpose back to where they'd left Rian. *I shouldn't be drawing attention to myself.*

Nel matched her pace, and the refugees parted before them with nods of respect and contrition in equal parts. "Where did you go? What is wrong?"

The acquisitioner set her jaw. She was unsettled, but she didn't have the words to describe why. It wasn't that she'd helped the girl back to her parents – she wasn't a monster. It was how quickly she'd moved to the task herself. Even in the best circumstances, she avoided calling attention to herself, and under the circumstances that seemed even more vital to her survival.

Rian or Nel could have handled it. Why didn't I just tell them? Draya shook her head to clear the confusion, glad the Aegis didn't press her further.

She was almost to the outskirts of the Green when she heard a shout from behind.

"It's you! Heretic!"

Draya blinked and turned.

The source of the shout was an old man, the pale blue vestments of a retired priest draped over his hunched shoulders. He limped towards her, brandishing a ceremonial salt censor in his hands like a weapon.

"How dare you show your face here, Droughtbringer!"

Weary heads snapped to attention, and she recognized his voice as the proselytizer she'd heard giving the sermon.

Acting quickly, Nel stepped between Draya and the priest, their palms out in a gesture of peace. "Calm winds, Father. We mean no trouble."

His rheumy eyes widened, but he didn't take his gaze from Draya. "Child of Will – are you blind to what stands before you? You are in the company of The Desolate Dawn! The Harbinger of Eternal Dust!" He stepped forward. "Do not be deceived! The words of the Sovran Oracles are stitched upon my heart. Even as my faculties wane with age, I recognize the signs of the Undying's cursed Herald!"

Nel opened their mouth to speak, but the priest had already turned to address the gathering crowd, his voice surprisingly loud for a man of his age. "The source of Aiylonia's downfall is among us, here in a fortress of the Blessed! Our Lady Soriadne laid out the signs! Perceive the heretic's plaits of woven embers! The dark charcoal in her eyes! This heathen stranger even arrives with an unwitting Aegis under her sway – could her identity be more clear?" He threw his long arm out, his bony finger pointing menacingly at Draya. "Do not be deceived! She is the Droughtbringer made flesh!"

Whispers rippled among the refugees. Draya felt eyes on her from every direction.

"Father, please." Nel took a cautious step forward, gently moving the old priest's censor aside. They lowered their voice. "There is no need to cause a panic. Let us discuss this in private."

"Blessed Helix! Have you been so corrupted by our enemy? You know what must be done!"

Nel shook their head and then looked over their shoulder at Draya. They were at a loss.

The growing whispers quickly became a cacophony. As a few people started to move towards her, Draya's hand shot to the hilt of her sword. She didn't fail to notice that her circumstances were an exact reflection of Nel's back at the Brick & Boar. This time, she feared the mob was even more desperate. Nel caught her eye, beseeching her silently with a shake of their head.

Draya grit her teeth but didn't draw her rapier.

<*These people are not your enemies.*>

A voice she didn't recognize rose unbidden in her mind.

<*They are frightened – do not allow fear to cloud your actions in return.*>

Draya's nostrils flared in Nel's direction, but they had already turned their attention away from her and toward the priest.

"Who the abyss are you?" she hissed under her breath.

The voice didn't bother to reply.

Whether real or a sign that her mind was growing unstable, the strange voice was right. The truth of their words was reflected in the eyes of the crowd. The refugees were scared, not bloodthirsty.

Intention doesn't matter if they decide to swarm us, Draya groused silently. Her heart was a drum pounding in her chest as questions sounded from every direction.

"What do you know?"

"Who are you?"

"Why have you done this to us?"

Nel unslung their shield, creating a barrier between Draya and the crowd.

"Does it matter?" A large woman's voice broke through the noise. "You heard Father Enoch's holy words! What more do we need to know?"

The questions turned to jeers. Draya and Nel locked eyes. They were surrounded.

The old priest's eyes were wild with fevered rage as he turned to the crowd. "Children of the Tides! She must be brought to justice! Only then will the waters return!"

18

Draya assessed the beleaguered masses. Armored legionnaires were only now starting to respond to the uproar, and she spotted Rian exactly where she'd left her at the edge of the courtyard. The Lieutenant looked confused, but still attempted to wrangle her unit, herding the legionnaires to create a shield wall against the frantic crowd. It was clear to Draya that despite their uniforms, Templekeep's guards were unprepared for violence. The waypost may have once been a military garrison, but it had been at least a century since it had been used as anything more than a religious tributary, serving the local villages as a central meeting place, trading post, and spiritual sanctuary. Their response to the burgeoning riot was too little and far too late. Realizing the growing danger, Draya unsheathed her rapier, and – almost as an afterthought – the cultist's serrated dagger from her belt.

This time, the mysterious voice didn't protest.

Draya turned and Nel pivoted, allowing them to stand back-to-back against the oncoming assault. Despite their earlier assurances to protect her, doubt surfaced in Draya's mind. The crowd was after her, not the Aegis. Aside from their conviction to deliver Draya to Trifall, the Aegis had more reason to hate her than to defend her. Despite their strategic positioning, Draya had no one to trust but herself.

Same shit, different day. She rolled her shoulders and widened her stance.

A wordless yell came from the right. Draya spun just in time to see two of the refugees breaking through the meager shield wall, the one in front brandishing a heavy walking stick, the other holding both ends of a weighted fishnet taut between his fingers.

Before Draya could brace herself against the onslaught, a spiral of golden sparks erupted in the stretch of space between her and the would-be attackers. She threw her arm up to shield her eyes and tripped falling hard into Nel's back. They scrambled to turn and catch her before she fell entirely, but the edge of their shield got in the way, crashing into her ribs and knocking the wind out of her. Spots floated in front of her eyes when she finally managed to look up, blurring everything but the silhouette of a single figure in the center of the fading circle of light.

"Yllari!" Nel shouted.

The figure spun as the final sparks winked out. Their jaw dropped at the sight of the crowd. The mob had pulled back, many cringing from the sudden appearance of the portal, but they were still a threat.

"What in the void have you gotten yourself into, Nel?" He didn't wait for an answer as he joined the pair, a rather modest staff held menacingly in his hands. As the afterimages faded, Draya was able to make out the man's features. Dark skin, dark hair, high cheekbones – he was handsome, she had to give him that. He wore robes of rich blue and yellow fabrics, each layer perfectly tailored to show off his tapered frame.

Undaunted by the man's sudden appearance, Nel grabbed Draya's arm and dragged her toward the floundering line of legionnaires.

"Rian," they said over the guard's shoulder. "We need a safe harbor."

The lieutenant's head swiveled from side to side, obviously thrown by all that had happened in such a brief span of time.

"Rian!" Nel barked. The crowd was starting to recover from the initial shock, their eyes narrowing as they realized the explosion of light had dissipated.

"Right, yes." The Lieutenant shook her head, clearing away any distractions. "The armory. It's –"

"I know where it is. Cover us." Nel turned to the new arrival "Fireworks!" they shouted, once again yanking Draya by the arm as they moved to leave the courtyard. She pulled herself free and glared, but the Aegis wasn't paying attention. They were barreling through the thinner crowd towards the entrance they'd come through.

"They aren't fireworks!" the man shouted. Draya turned just in time to see a shower of sparks fall in a wide arc behind them, crackling and fizzing in a way that very much sounded like fireworks.

"Are you coming?" Nel shouted, pulling Draya's attention back.

"Do I have a choice?" she shouted back as she cut between rows of cots and stray refugees. They raced along the colonnade, quickly escaping the open air into enclosed stone archways. Shadows fell across the flagstones as they passed door after door, and Draya instinctively knew the hall would end sooner than later. She rounded a corner after Nel, almost running into their back as they came to an abrupt stop in front of a huge door reinforced with iron bands. The walkways out of the complex opened up on either side. Opposite from the courtyard behind them, the sun was starting to set, falling behind the rear outer wall.

Nel tried the door handle, finding it locked. They took a step back, preparing to ram their armored shoulder into the door. Draya darted forward, holding them back.

"I've got this," she said.

Nel met her eyes and then looked back the way they'd come. The crowd wasn't visible yet, but they could both hear the shouts as they started to mobilize. When they turned back to Draya, there was doubt in their eyes.

"Trust me." Draya found the suggestion ironic, considering she held so little trust in the Aegis. Without waiting for permission, she turned to the door, crouching so that she was at eye level with the locking mechanism. She reached up and pulled two skinny lock picks and a thin wrench out of her braided hair, causing a few wayward strands to tumble out with them. Eyes narrowed in concentration, she slipped the tools into the cylinder, feeling around for the appropriate pins. The sound of the mob grew louder.

"Hurry, hurry, hurry!" Yllari cried as he slid to a halt beside them.

Draya ignored the commotion and concentrated on the lock. After a few clicks, she felt the last pin set and used the tension wrench to disengage the bolt with a satisfying clunk. She quickly stood and threw the door open inward. Yllari pushed her through, followed by Nel. The Aegis slammed the door shut and leaned against it, shoving a much more formidable interior bolt across to further lock it in place. It was just in time. Banging immediately followed, hard and fast against the iron-bound wood.

"How is it holding?" the newcomer asked.

Nel's brow furrowed. "All right." They relaxed slightly as they realized the door could hold its own. "For now, anyway."

Draya surveyed the small room's interior. One wall was lined with racks of weapons in various states of disrepair, while another was blanketed with small bucklers. There were one or two tower shields, but they were obviously not a priority for the waypost. The back wall was all shelving and emergency supplies, with a slim line of windows tucked just under the eaves. Dust coated every surface, and cobwebs trailed from every corner.

"You can't hide in there forever, heretic!" The shout was only mildly muffled by the heavy wood of the door.

"Watch me!" Draya barked over her shoulder.

The mage sighed and tossed his staff aside before flopping into a rickety wooden chair in the corner. It creaked but somehow managed to hold together.

Draya's adrenaline was at full speed. She turned on the new target and leveled the serrated dagger at his throat. "Who the sarding abyss are you?" she demanded. He seemed far too relaxed for having just outrun a mob.

He raised his eyebrows and looked between her and Nel.

The relentless pounding on the door paused. "An ally," the Aegis said obliquely as they peered out of the small iron grate in the door.

Draya was about to snap at them when the mage spoke for her. "Well, that isn't exactly helpful." Staying seated, he raised his hands in surrender. "Yllari Okessian – Apprentice Solaris Mage and Self-Appointed Aide to the Seventeenth Brightbourne. And you are?"

"I'm asking the questions here," Draya barked as her shoulders tensed. He was wearing a lopsided grin she knew all too well. It was the same one she used to charm her way out of a problem.

"And please, don't let me stop you. I'd just prefer to know the name of the person threatening me with an ornamental ritual knife." He glanced up at Nel. "Where is the Brightbourne?" When the Aegis didn't turn to meet his eyes, Yllari's cavalier look of amusement started to fall. "Nel. Where is Jierdan?"

"It looks like all but a few of the civilians have turned back. Those remaining are huddled on the far side of the corridor. They are debating whether they should find a battering ram."

"Wonderful." Draya rolled her eyes.

"Nel." The mage's voice was grave.

"They left."

"What do you mean he left?" Yllari pressed. He seemed wholly unconcerned by Draya's knife.

"Not he, they. The rest of the mob." Nel turned their back to the door and played at tightening the straps on their bracers. "Jierdan – the Brightbourne – is gone."

"Gone?" The mage closed his eyes for a moment, bringing two fingers up to pinch the bridge of his nose. "I see. Let me guess," he leveled his gaze back on Draya. "You must be the Droughtbringer, then?"

"I – I mean," Draya stammered in the face of the direct question. Just two days ago she didn't even believe in the prophecy, and now she found herself right in the middle of it all.

"Then Jierdan is…"

"I didn't kill him, if that's what you mean," Draya said defensively.

The mage cocked his head to one side. "If you had managed that, I somehow doubt Nel would have left you breathing."

Draya's arm dropped, the fight in her drained as suddenly as the Canal outside. "He pushed me aside – fell into the Vault. I think he sealed it – closed it back up – but it must have been too late."

"I see." Yllari bowed his head and performed the sign of the helix over his heart. After a silent prayer, the mage looked her up and down appraisingly. "Interesting."

"What is?" Draya narrowed her eyes.

A sparkle returned to his eyes. "I just always expected the Droughtbringer to be older. And less fetching."

Her teeth ground together in agitation. "Really? With all this going on," she waved one hand vaguely as she sheathed the dagger back into her belt, "that's where your mind goes?"

"My mind isn't going anywhere," he replied calmly. "I'm just stating an objective truth." He looked up at Nel. "I'm not wrong, am I?"

The Aegis slid down the wall and steadied into a crouch. "I must admit that I agree with the archeologian's assessment of your misplaced priorities."

Yllari shrugged. "I suppose you're right." He turned back to Draya, "Archeologian? Is that what I should call you?"

"Draya," she conceited. "I'm an acquisitioner contracted through the Hawkers Guild."

The mage considered this. "Should I infer you were in pursuit of a bounty, then? Some pre-Deluge artifact?" He dismissed the question with a wave of his hand. "Scratch that. It's none of my business."

Draya's shoulders relaxed. "You don't seem concerned about me."

"You? Of course not." They clapped their hands together. "So, tell me, how does –"

Before he could finish the question, a familiar voice called in through the grated opening in the door. "Aegis Commander General! Are you all right?" Rian called. The clamor outside had changed, grumbling voices replaced by the creaks of heavy armor.

"We are safe for now, Lieutenant." Nel stood and peered through the grate. "How are things outside?"

There was a pause. "Volatile," Rian finally admitted. "We've been able to calm things down for now, but Father Enoch will not be persuaded. He has insisted the greater authorities become involved."

"Does he mean the Order?" Nel asked. "Tell him we are on our way to Trifall now."

"I will try, but I don't know how effective that will be. He doesn't trust either of you nor the Magus."

"And you do?" Draya shouted from further in the room.

There was a sigh. "I trust the Commander General," Rian replied. "But I can't speak for the rest of the legionnaires here."

"What does that mean for us?" Draya shouted impatiently.

"It's probably best you stay put," Rian answered sternly. In a softer voice, she continued. "I am sorry about this, Nel. First Jierdan, and now...I can only imagine –"

The Aegis cut her off. "We will be fine. We needed a place to spend the evening anyway."

"Right. Very good." Formality returned to the guard's voice. "I'll continue trying to settle everyone down and set up a watch on this corridor. There should be some old tarps in the trunk along the wall. Might be better than sleeping directly on the floor, eh?"

Nel nodded, then remembered she couldn't see them. "Thank you, Rian."

The guard grunted and moved away from the door. The hall seemed empty now, but there would be plenty of bodies between the armory and the main entrance. Making it out with an escort would be more than a little difficult.

Yllari coughed into his hand. "As I was saying, how does it work?"

Draya looked at him in confusion and crossed her arms over her chest. "Context?" she prompted. "How does what work?"

His eyes lit up with excitement as he sat up straighter in the chair. "Your Calling – I mean, do you just know where to go? Do you see some kind of map in your mind? I've always wondered."

Draya thought back to her escape from the tunnels and averted her eyes. "What makes you think I have a Calling?"

"What? Of course, you do." He looked towards Nel. "Have you explained *anything*?"

They shrugged. "I didn't think it was my place."

"You didn't...?" Yllari shook his head and stood up from the chair. "Oh, Draya dear." She stiffened as he approached her, but didn't flinch when he placed his hands on her shoulders. "Only someone with the Calling of Navigation could make it to the Palace Treasury, and only someone who could make it to the Treasury could release the Undying One's Curse of the Creeping Drought. You have the Calling of Navigation, and you are the first of your kind I've had the pleasure to meet."

19

Draya shrugged off Yllari's hold on her shoulders with a scoff. "Horse shite. Kids with the Calling of Navigation are snatched up by the Order – just like them." She threw a pointed look at the Aegis, but when she met their eyes, all she could feel was a chasm of grief. Their despair hit her like a wave, dampening the force of her temper.

"Yes, you're right," Yllari said, pulling Draya's attention back. "Children who display signs of the Calling of Will – like Nel here – are adopted by the Order and trained as Aegii. Those with Foresight are trained as Sovran Oracles. Those with Navigation are trained as –"

"Reckoners." Draya finished. "As in dead reckoning. Everyone knows that." She steeled herself. The crush of Nel's sadness had waned, but its chill remained. "But I can't be a Reckoner. I grew up in Amphidon, for Rook's sake. I have a sarding family. Before I met Nel two whole days ago, I'd never even been around a cleric for more than half an hour, and that's being generous." She turned back to Nel. "You've been suspiciously quiet, Aegis. Tell him he's wrong," she demanded.

"I cannot," they replied. "Soriadne's Lament clearly states –"

"To the abyss with the sarding prophecy!" Draya threw her hands in the air. Frustration from the last two days boiled to the surface. Nel's body bristled in time with hers, but she turned her back on them anyway. She clawed at her wrist, tugging at the cuff in vain. "Sarding Brightbourne bastard," she mumbled.

Yllari sucked in a breath. "Is that…?"

"Yes," Nel confirmed in a low voice.

There was a pause. "I see." The mage looked between the two of them as understanding blossomed in his eyes. "That explains a lot – while leaving twice as many questions. It must be very difficult." He paused. "For both of you," he added.

Draya frowned, her anger settling to a simmer in the face of his sympathy. She might have every right to be wary of the Coronet, but neither Nel nor Yllari was responsible for the predicament she found herself in. *If anything, they might be the best chance I've got for escaping it.* A thought struck her, and she turned back to Yllari. "You have magic – can you break the bonding? Portal me out of this thing?" she asked.

He stifled a laugh. "Intriguing idea, but no. Manipulating the old magic behind a bonding is outside my wheelhouse, perhaps the known schools of sorcery altogether. I wouldn't even know where to begin if I didn't want to risk one or both of us dying. Skulls, I didn't even know a Brightbourne could transfer a cuff to someone else, but Jierdan always was full of surprises."

"Is," Nel cut in. "We don't know that he's gone for good."

Draya and Yllari looked to the Aegis, neither knowing quite how to respond. To Draya, the Brightbourne's survival seemed far-fetched, but so did everything else that had happened over the last couple of days. The remaining barbs of her indignation melted away. *Who am I to deny them the hope?*

Yllari must have shared her sentiment. "It's true," he relented. "Soriadne's Lament only states that the Droughtbringer will undo the sacrifice of the First and release the wrath of the Undying on the world. Nothing explicitly foretells the death of the current Brightbourne as a consequence." He waved a dismissive hand and turned back to Draya. "Back to the topic at hand. I don't know why you weren't taken in by the Order as a child, but it doesn't really matter. You have the Calling of Navigation – I am indisputably sure of it."

Draya raised a finger in opposition. "But you just said there are things the prophecy doesn't cover. This has to be one of those."

He gave her a soft look that bordered on pity. "How did you find your way to the Palace Treasury?" he asked.

"I have a knack for direction." She crossed her arms over her chest.

"Even in a labyrinth deep underground?" he countered.

"Mazes are meant to be solved."

"Not this one." Yllari mimicked her stance. "The Cresting Tide made sure of it. Without a Reckoner it's impossible to get to the Vault."

She scoffed. "Nothing's impossible."

To her surprise, Yllari chuckled. "You have me there." He returned to the chair, draping himself over the seat again. "In that case, I assume the Treasury was ransacked? Nothing worth taking?"

Draya remembered the towers of wooden chests, the layers of dust. Someone had been there some time ago, and someone had looted the upper floors, but the Treasury had been overflowing with riches. She said the only thing she could think of. "The lock on the door had been removed at some point."

"That's it? Everything else was untouched?" Yllari's half smile was skeptical. "Seems a bit odd that a century would go by without anyone taking advantage of that, don't you think?"

Yes, it was odd. Out loud she said, "Not really. The Order's had the place on lockdown for all that time. I'm sure anyone with enough time and planning could figure the thing out given the chance – and many probably have." She tilted her chin in Nel's direction. "Someone in armor probably just got in the way of an easy score."

Yllari shook his head. "I'm telling you they couldn't have."

She returned his cynical glare. "And why's that?"

"I don't know the details, but the labyrinth isn't exactly...stable. Without your Calling guiding you from the entry to the exit, trying to move through would be a death wish."

A dark laugh escaped her lips. "Sounds like more religious propaganda to me."

"It is not." Nel's sober assertion broke their bantering. "The layout can shift, sealing away any trespassers that may have made the attempt. Anyone that wanders too far from the predetermined path will find the walls closing up behind them."

Yllari coughed into his hand. "Or through them, I believe. Which I guess sounds a lot better than dying of dehydration but is altogether more morbid from a visual perspective."

"Have either of you seen this for yourself?" Draya asked.

"I have not ventured inside the Palace, no," Yllari answered.

"Aegis?" Draya asked.

"The Order forbids Aegii from entering the lowest levels of the Occidrian Palace."

"Well, there you go." Draya spread her arms wide. "Obviously propaganda." She turned away and wandered toward one of the weapon racks along the far wall. She couldn't look them in the eyes and bask in her bravado. Deep down, she'd always known that there was something more to her talents. The prospect had ultimately never mattered beyond providing her with a steady stream of clients. It seemed absurd, but she couldn't help thinking about her unsettling experience escaping the lower levels of the Palace. *And of course, there's that voice...* Draya repressed a cringe thinking about it. She knew she should say something, but she couldn't. Not yet anyway. If she was going mad, she wanted to sit with it a while first. She absently ran her fingers through the blanket of dust along the frame of the wooden rack. "Let's say, hypothetically, that you and this prophecy are right. That I do have the Calling of Navigation. What does that even mean for me?"

She could hear the smile in Yllari's voice. "How much do you know about Callings in general?" he asked.

"Only the basics - some people are born with some kind of unnatural ability. It might be hereditary, or it might be random. No one is sure, and most of them are pretty much useless from what I've seen."

He nodded. "That's the gist of it – although we like to call them *supramundane* abilities. Most Callings in and of themselves are relatively benign, as you say. They simply augment a skill that can otherwise be trained. Someone with the Calling of the Stream would be incredibly handy right now, for instance. Their ability to intuit underground springs is far more efficient than that of any farmer with a dowsing rod."

She turned back to face the mage. "Right. But Navigation, Will, Foresight, whatever you have – those are special for some reason?"

"Illumination," he said.

"What?"

"Illumination. That's my Calling. And it's not of the same ilk as the other three."

She looked at him askance. "The Calling of Illumination lets you make portals?"

His brow furrowed. "What? No. The ability to create portals is a Mastery, not a Calling."

"What's a sarding Mastery?" Draya threw her hands in the air.

"Callings are innate, passive. Masteries are trained through – wait, that's getting too far off track." He ran a hand through his thick curls. "Outside the practicalities, I only know one reason the founders of the Order would have focused on these three particular Callings."

"Yllari," Nel warned.

He spun toward the Aegis. "What? She deserves to hear it. She'd already know the whole story if she'd been brought into the fold when she should have been. There is no logical reason she can't know now."

Nel shook their head before leaning it against the door, their gaze diverted upwards. "That should be at the discretion of the Archpriests."

Draya stepped between them. "What do I deserve to hear, wizard?"

He raised an eyebrow. "I'm a mage, technically. But Yllari is preferred." Seeing her glare, he moved on. "The early signs of a potential Brightbourne are very similar to one of those three specific Callings. When one Brightbourne dies," he glanced at Nel then back to her, "or otherwise finds themselves incapacitated, the mantle of Chosen One manifests in one of those children. Gathering everyone with those Callings is as much a means of convenience as it is a practicality."

"Let me get this straight – that means any Aegis, any Oracle, even sarding *me apparently* – could become the Brightbourne any minute?" Her stomach roiled at the thought.

"No," Nel interjected. "We're too old."

Draya scowled. "Excuse me?"

"I did not – that is not what I mean." They sighed. "No one beyond their tenth year has ever been revealed as the Brightbourne. Jierdan was only six. If he is gone and, Helix forbid, a new Chosen One is to manifest, it will be among those who have not yet taken their oaths."

Yllari cocked their head slightly to the side.

"You disagree." Draya ascertained as she took a step closer to the mage.

"Disagree is a strong word." The corner of his lip rose conspiratorially. "As you said, nothing is impossible. There are stories–"

"Apocrypha," Nel corrected.

"Yes, technically apocrypha." Yllari shrugged. "Why does it

matter?"

"What's the point of talking about it if it's not sanctioned by Coronet?" Nel asked wearily. Draya sensed this was an old argument.

"Soriadne wasn't the only Oracle to write about the Droughtbringer. May I remind you of Elandir's Hymn of Redemption? The Dirge of Sands? Even Tyriadne – Soriadne's own daughter – drafted an amendment to her mother's Lament."

"*Alleged* daughter," Nel corrected. "And drafted yes, but not until after she'd retired to Halloran. You can't trust that she –"

"And you can't discount a person's entire life's work because of where and how it ends. Jierdan always said –"

Nel bristled. "Are you questioning Jierdan's faith in the Coronet?"

"You know very well I'm doing no such thing," Yllari admonished. "All I'm saying is that everything can't be divided into black and white, truth and fiction. The edges are always blurred."

Draya let out a frustrated groan, pausing the debate. "I don't care about any of that! The only truth I care about right now is how we plan to get out of this mess." A thought struck her, and she took a step toward Yllari. "Wait – Your Calling or Mastery or whatever – why don't you just portal us straight to Trifall from here?"

Yllari shook his head. "That's not exactly how it works."

"What do you mean?"

"I mean, I can't simply create another portal out of nothing, especially with the sun already setting." When Draya looked at him blankly, he continued. "I'm a Solaris mage. Our powers are fueled by the sun. Well, mostly anyway. Stars provide power as well but not in the same way. I have a theory that the two are interchangeable, but I haven't been able to effectively experiment with the concept yet. If that were the case, then maybe —"

"So, this was a one-way trip?" Draya cut in.

"Of course not. I just expected we'd spend the night someplace warm and comfortable. Then I could have recharged my energy and made a new portal with the morning sun."

She had to begrudgingly admit it was a solid plan. If she hadn't made a scene of herself, it may have gone off without a hitch. Uneasiness seeped into her thoughts. "How did you know where we were?" she asked.

Nel and Yllari spoke at the same time.

"Do not concern yourself."

"Oh, that's simple."

They exchanged glances, Nel's dour expression against Yllari's lackadaisical smirk. The mage seemed to win out. He turned to Draya. "Nel – the Aegis Commander General – is equipped with a solar marker. It's a beacon for my magic, allowing me to always find them. Otherwise, I can only travel to places I've seen for myself."

Draya absorbed that information. She considered asking about the apocryphal story Yllari was referring to earlier, but instead, a large yawn escaped her lips.

"It's been a long day," Yllari surmised. He stood up from the chair and strode to the back of the room, throwing open the trunk Rian had mentioned. He wrinkled his nose in disgust, then gingerly pulled out one of the canvas tarps. He tossed it to the floor with a thud and an explosion of dust showered the front of Yllari's robes. He sneezed a few times before letting the lid of the trunk close. "Well, here is one tarp. There are more inside. Utilize at your own discretion."

Draya eyed the questionable pile of canvas before moving to the far corner of the room. "I think I can make do." She unslung her knapsack and opened her bedroll. The floor of the armory was no worse than the forest loam she'd slept on the night before.

"Right." Yllari seemed less equipped than she did. He turned his head back and forth as if hoping one area of the dirty floor might be better than another.

Nel took a last glance out of the door's grated window. Seemingly satisfied with what they saw, they unslung their sword and shield from their back and sat rigidly against the door. Draya marveled at their clear disregard for even the semblance of comfort.

Yllari sighed and picked up the edges of the tarp, carefully shaking out the remaining dust. He eyed it skeptically before shrugging off the long open vest that served as his topmost layer of clothing. A few folds of plush fabric later, it was tucked under his head.

Draya smirked at the mage. "You didn't come prepared at all, did you? No rations or supplies?"

Yllari's face dropped with the accusation. "I assumed we'd have rooms at an inn – a shared one in a hostel at the very least. I didn't expect to rough out the night in a glorified closet."

Draya snickered to herself. While she certainly hoped for better accommodations, she'd spent enough time on the road to be prepared for the worst. "You don't travel much, do you?" she asked lightly.

"As a matter of fact, I do." Yllari fluffed his makeshift pillow. "Quite frequently in fact. I'm just particular about my accommodations when I get there."

"I guess if I could bounce from one place to the next in an instant, I wouldn't spend much time on the water, either." Draya wondered how her knack for direction would play out if she had the mage's abilities.

"We should sleep while we can," Nel interrupted. Draya expected a chastising glare, but when she looked over their eyes were already closed, their face placid as they rested their broad sword across their lap.

She turned onto her side, facing away from both Yllari and Nel. Getting a read on the mage would be easy after a few more conversations. She even suspected she'd enjoy a drink with him if circumstances were different. The Aegis was another matter entirely. Two days and two aborted brawls later she still hadn't found her footing. Aside from the certainty that their noble intentions were genuine, which was surprising in and of itself, she was at a loss. One moment they came across as the naive victim of religious indoctrination, the next as the war-forged soldier their title would imply. She'd never met anyone who could so easily balance arrogance, suspicion, and a sheer lack of guile. A little sanctimonious commentary was probably the least she deserved for her role in current events. *Skulls. They were probably even an optimist before I came along.* Draya nestled her head into her pack and closed her eyes. Ruminating wasn't going to do her any good at the moment. She let herself drift off to sleep.

The next thing she heard was the screams.

20

Draya bolted upright, torn from a nightmare of sickly churning energies as bloodcurdling screams echoed off the walls outside. She was disoriented in the unfamiliar darkness, and her heart raced as the mundane shadows of the armory took shape around her.

"Nel?" she called out. She didn't know how much time had passed since she'd fallen asleep.

"I'm here." There was a quick spark and then lantern light reflected gold off their armor.

"What's happening?" Draya scrambled to stand, realizing she'd shed her boots at some point during the night. She frantically worked to get them back on, fumbling with the tedious lacing in the dark.

Nel didn't answer. Instead, they carried the lantern over to where the mage was sleeping and leaned down next to him. "Yllari, wake up."

Outside, a guttural howl broke through the frightened screams. A second later, a bestial chorus responded in kind. Draya tried to swallow, but her mouth had gone dry.

"Yllari!" Nel shook the man's shoulder with a gauntleted hand.

"What? Wait — Who?" Yllari looked around blearily. A man's scream, louder and closer this time, finally seemed to register. He locked eyes with Nel, and then immediately gathered his belongings and got to his feet.

"You slept through this?" Draya looked at Yllari, dumbfounded.

"I'm a deep dreamer," he replied simply.

The sound of boots on flagstone grew louder before something heavy slammed against the reinforced door. "Let me in! Please!" a man shouted through the grated window.

Nel set the lantern down and leaned into the door. One hand gripped the hilt of their sword as the other wrapped tentatively around the heavy bolt keeping the door shut. "What is happening out there? Is the waypost under attack?"

A man's face filled the window. Blood dripped from his heavy brow and his eyes shone wide with fear. "Monsters!" he managed. "They're slaughtering everyone!"

Before Nel could move, Draya darted forward, her hands falling on the wooden beam. She was about to lift it free when she froze in place, disgusted with herself. "What the sarding abyss are you doing?" she hissed at herself.

Nel eyed her with surprise but quickly adjusted to help lift the beam. She couldn't do anything but follow through. They were just clearing the mount when a deep scream broke from the man's throat, only to be cut off by the sickening crack of bone. They were too late. There was a soft thud as the man's body hit the door. Wet sounds of teeth tearing flesh followed.

Nel's face paled as they released the beam back into its mounting. The crunch of bones continued on the other side of the door. Draya stared wide-eyed at the empty space beyond the grate in the door.

"Waergs," Nel announced before she could ask.

Draya immediately thought back to the Palace trophy room and the wolf-lion hybrids posed threateningly inside. She hadn't remembered the beasts had a name until the word left Nel's lips. With their broad skulls and stocky builds, they had been less impressive than the elk-bear and the tusked ram, but their massive jaws were no less lethal.

"Blood and bones," Yllari cursed. "I thought we'd have more time."

"Apparently not," Nel steeled themself, then peered out the window.

"Is it still there?" Draya asked, pulling her hand back from the door.

Nel's head turned left and right. They were about to answer when the door buckled. Fangs snapped at the grate and the Aegis jumped backward. Its vicious claws scrambled desperately at the wood.

"I venture that answers the question," Yllari observed.

The maw of the creature dropped out of sight. The clacking of its nails grew quieter as it moved away from the door, presumably chasing more vulnerable prey.

Nel straightened themselves with a look of embarrassment. They unslung their shield from their back, settling into a defensive stance. "We should move."

"Are you sure? That sounds incredibly unwise," Yllari advised.

Draya looked between them for answers before admonishing herself. *Make your own call, Draya.* She stepped up to the grate and looked out the tiny window for herself. The waerg was gone, and the remains of the victim lay torn across the threshold. His open eyes stared upward, frozen in fear. Recognition struck her – he was the refugee who'd come at them with the fishing net.

She pulled her eyes away from the dead man's. The columns of the colonnade framed a navy sky sprinkled with stars. Torchlight dotted the walls beyond, illuminating the carnage the beasts had wrought. Blood-soaked bodies lay in heaps across the courtyard, limbs torn savagely from hips and shoulders. The vicious creatures filled the interior of the waypost, fighting over the viscera and snapping at each other for scraps. Further away, she could see silhouettes of much larger creatures, all twisted horns and tangled antlers. The sounds of breaking bones and strangled screams filled the air.

Draya pulled back, her stomach turning at the gruesome sight. "There are more than waergs out there," she finally said.

"Necromantic amalgamations come in many forms." Yllari placed a gentle hand on her shoulder and slipped past so he could see for himself. "It's hard to make out the details, but yes – there are at least two, possibly three, other species among them."

"Any peryton?" Nel asked.

"Any what?" Draya glared at the Aegis.

"Possibly. I see the shadows of some antlers."

"That is not good."

"No, it's not."

"Excuse me?" Draya's patience waned. "What are you both talking about? It's a butchery outside and you're debating taxonomy?"

The mage turned to her, his eyes without judgment. "Do you know what an amalgam is?" he asked softly.

Draya scoffed. "Are you trying to piss me off, or will you be continuing with the inane questions?" When he didn't reply, she relented. "Yes, I know what they are. I also know I'd blissfully believed they were extinct until the Aegis told me otherwise. How many breeds are there?"

"Too many," Yllari said.

"Wonderful. Thank you for leaving out the details, Aegis," Draya grumbled. "They're just creatures though, aren't they? Shouldn't the walls have kept them out?"

Nel's voice was solemn. "No, but the moat would have deterred them. Without the canals, there is nothing keeping them from preying on this or any other settlement."

Draya's spine tingled. "The Coronet sure did a great job making us believe that was old superstition."

"The Order is always thorough," they said.

Draya didn't like what the Aegis was implying. *More secrets, more lies.* Choosing the more immediate concern, she asked, "What is a peryton?"

Yllari looked back out the little window. "You don't want to find out."

The door suddenly bucked as a new pair of waergs threw their bodies against the wood.

"Can you get us out of here?" Draya turned on the mage.

He ran a hand through his hair, leaving it mussed. "Not until dawn – and then I need to be able to see sunlight to fuel the magic."

Resigned, Draya looked back at the door. From the color of the sky, sunup wasn't far away. The waergs outside barked and growled, this pair seemed even more intent on getting inside than the last. "I guess we need to leave then."

"We should wait until dawn," Yllari argued. "The beasts will start to thin once we have some sunlight."

"How can you be sure?" Her hand fell stubbornly to her hip. "The water is gone. The rules have changed."

The hinges creaked as the waergs continued to test the door's integrity.

"She has a point," Nel said.

Yllari frowned in thought. "If I can get even a few rays of natural light, I might have something to work with."

With the matter decided, Nel angled themselves to cover the doorway. "Draya – on my signal, throw the brace. Yllari, get the latch."

She moved into position without comment, loosening her sword in its sheath. As an afterthought, she brought the dagger to her teeth and bit down before placing her hands on the wooden bar. Yllari's shoulder pressed against hers, his staff dropped to the floor nearby. His tanned knuckles paled as they gripped the latch.

"On my mark." Nel readied their sword and hunched behind their shield. "NOW!"

Draya and Yllari moved quickly, throwing the bar up and pulling open the door in quick succession. They both darted back, Draya freeing her rapier as the mage moved behind. The gaping maw of one of the waergs greeted them, bits of grisled flesh dangling from its yellowed fangs. It pounced without pause, but Nel's shield caught the beast as they bent their knees to absorb the impact. Not willing to waste the opportunity, Draya lunged, sinking her long blade into the soft flesh between its lower ribs. For a brief moment, the waerg's murderous red eyes turned on her as it clashed again against Nel's shield.

A low growl rumbled from Draya's left. Quicker than she could turn, a bolt of crackling light shot down from the sky, striking the haunches of the second waerg. It let out a pained yelp as it staggered back. The noxious smell of grease and burning fur filled Draya's nostrils. She wanted nothing more than to cover her nose and mouth, but instead, she succeeded in recovering her blade, pulling it out from the waerg's ribs before thrusting the blade forward again into its exposed belly. It shuttered and lost its footing, stumbling backward into its companion. They snapped at each other, allowing Nel the opportunity to bring their great sword down through the first waerg's neck, severing the spine. Even before the corpse had time to collapse to the paving stones, Nel's sword was moving again, this time slashing open the throat of its charred packmate. Black blood sprayed from their wounds, but the amalgams lay still.

"Two down," Yllari called.

Draya looked out past the breezeway. Corpses, mostly human, lay discarded in scattered piles of mutilated gore. A few of the more intact victims cried out wordlessly, their minds yet to catch up with the fatality of their wounds. More of the waergs – at least a dozen that she could see – darted between pools of firelight. Some bounded like wolves, while others slithered close to the ground with their haunches hunched like hyenas. None were close enough to take notice of the trio, but that wouldn't last long.

"The lightning," Draya asked Yllari. "What was that?"

"Not lightning. Starlight." He stood just over her shoulder, his staff again in his hands.

"Whatever. Can you do it again?" She looked out over the growing battlefield. They needed all the firepower they could get if they wanted to escape.

"Possibly. Stellar magic is unreliable – too many variables. If we had sunlight, however—"

"We don't," Draya interrupted.

"We don't *yet*." Nel lifted their sword, the tip extending towards the horizon. The hills were starting to brighten in layered color. "We just need to hold out until the sun crests that hill."

"Easier said than done," Draya said.

More than just the waergs haunted the grounds of Templekeep. Between the detached outer buildings, Draya spotted the silhouette of a gargantuan creature against the compound's high outer walls. A pair of antlers twisted from its heavy brow and feathered wings extended from its shoulders. Her heart sank to her stomach. "What – what the sarding abyss *is* that?" She swallowed hard. The shape she recognized, but not its size.

"Something worse than I'd feared." Yllari took a step forward, following Draya's gaze. "If a peryton that size made it this far, things are deteriorating much more quickly than I'd calculated."

"That's a peryton?"

"Yes, unfortunately. We would do best to avoid it if we can."

Draya shook her head. "I've seen one before – not alive, but a stuffed one. It was nowhere near that big. No wings either."

Yllari nodded. "A juvenile male most likely. Between the size and the wings, that's a full-grown female."

"When did you have time to make calculations?" Nel asked.

"Don't mind that." Yllari dismissed the question. "This way – we should keep the ramparts between us and cut through those passages." He started to move towards the left, but Draya grabbed his arm. For all his foppish pretense, she could feel the sinewy muscle of his bicep under her fingers. Like her, he was more than he appeared at first glance.

"Not that way," she said. Yllari glanced down at her hand.

Suddenly self-conscious, she quickly let go. "Something is blocking the way," she explained.

"You can tell that much?" His eyebrows lifted.

She shrugged in response.

He extended his staff. "Lead the way, Reckoner."

She scowled at the title but didn't argue. Glancing in both directions, she gestured to the right. In silent agreement, the trio took off into the fray.

21

A cacophony of howls echoed along the hallways towards them, seemingly coming from every direction. Waergs could be anywhere – around the next bend or far across the complex. Normally Draya could trust that her sense of direction – her Calling – would warn her of an obstacle in her path, but there was too much movement, too many bodies, and, to make matters worse, she was contending with the ghostly afterimages of the fort's original architecture.

It's too much. The errant thought slipped out, escaping her well-honed walls of blind bravado. As the trio came to a blind corner, Draya instinctively stepped to her left, wordlessly allowing Nel to slip past her, and then froze, confused. The movement was instinctual, coming far more easily than it should have. *The Aegis is just good with team combat, that's all.* The assurance was hollow, but she didn't have time to grapple with her potential loss of agency. *We have more pressing matters to deal with.*

Nel cautiously peered around the old stone blocks with their shield held high.

"Anything?" Yllari prompted.

"No creatures."

When Nel moved forward, Draya understood their meaning. A man's body lay prone near one of the benches in the otherwise empty courtyard. The Aegis paused, and she could feel a mix of complicated emotions clawing at her heart. Before she could succumb to Nel's overpowering impulse to help, her eyes fell on the cascade of roping intestines that spilled from the man's midsection. His eyes were glassy and fixed on the open sky above.

Yllari made the sign of the helix beside her. "Tides preserve us."

"Keep moving," Draya said as she hurried past the Aegis and put distance between herself and the gruesome sight. She half expected one or both of them to argue, but they followed her instead as she led her companions down the next alley and around another corner.

This time she stopped short, barely stifling her sharp intake of breath. "Well, that explains the noise," she whispered out of the corner of her mouth.

Whereas the last courtyard held only a corpse, this one was occupied by a pack of five waergs. Three of the beasts were muzzle-deep in a field of broken skulls and exposed entrails. The remaining two stood off against a small group of terrified refugees, a meager wall of makeshift weapons holding the beasts at bay.

Without even a pause, Nel burst forward in two long strides. They swung their broadsword wide, the golden blade flashing in the torchlight as it came down on the shoulders of the largest waerg in a spray of black ichor. It yelped but remained on its feet, abandoning its prey to face the more urgent threat.

Draya's eyes fell on an archway in the far wall. It was the only viable escape route. Her feet were already taking her there when she felt an inexplicable urge to turn back. If her normal innate abilities were a gentle nudge toward possible destinations, this was the yank of a choke collar, dragging her back to Nel's side and the endangered refugees.

As the Aegis was engaging the first waerg, another snapped forward unimpeded. It ducked under the broken chair one of the men was using as a shield and snapped at his ankles, finding purchase. The amalgam's fangs sank deep. The refugee dropped the piece of furniture and screamed with a mixture of shock and pain. Spurred to action, Nel bashed their shield into the snout of the larger waerg, stunning it before plunging their sword into the tender flesh beneath its jaw. The Aegis didn't wait to watch it die on the paving stones. They leaped forward in defense of the wounded man, striking out against the smaller waerg. Unaffected by the chaos, Yllari knelt beside the still-twitching corpse of the dispatched waerg and lifted its jowls to examine its impressive teeth.

A low growl caught Draya's attention. From her spot near the far alley, she watched in horror as one of the scavenging waergs pulled away from its near-finished meal, its bloodthirsty eyes fixated on the unguarded back of the Aegis. Rationally, she knew she should flee. She wasn't a front-line fighter. She had no armor, no shield to defend against fangs and claws. She was no match for a ferocious pack of reanimated monsters. Still, Draya's heart leaped into her throat, an indescribable force fighting against her better instincts. Heedlessly ignoring every one of those valid concerns, she threw herself towards the Aegis.

Draya slid to a stop just as the rogue waerg sprang. Its massive jaws connected hard against Draya's crossed blades. She buckled under the weight, falling back against the Aegis behind her. If not for her knapsack, her shoulder blades would have been crushed against the sharply segmented back of their cuirass. She didn't have time to dwell on the potential damage caused to the fragile merchandise she was couriering. Braced spine to spine, she held firm as the creature snarled in her face. Its fetid breath was hot on her cheeks, enveloping her in a baffling stench of wet fur, decay, cedar, and myrrh. It paused, its snout sniffing the air, and then dropped back on all fours with its tail between its legs. It whimpered as its haunted eyes narrowed suspiciously at Draya.

Refusing to question the moment of respite, she elbowed Nel lightly in the side. The group of refugees had taken advantage of the distraction, pulling the injured man into their ranks and ducking back into the building behind them. "We can't stay here," she hissed once the men and women were safely indoors. Nel nodded in agreement. They slowly pulled away from their bestial opponent. Like the one opposite Draya, it had backed off, its lip raised in a snarl of bloody fangs. She scanned the small courtyard until she spotted the mage. "Yllari!" she bellowed.

"Just a moment!" He'd pulled a vial out of his pocket and tipped the open rim against a wound in the first waerg's neck. A few drops of thick black blood pooled inside the glass.

The unaccounted-for waergs had been eating their fill, but Draya watched as their heavy heads swung in the direction of his voice. "Yllari!" Draya shouted again, her voice rising.

The mage looked up in time to see the depths of a great maw bearing down on him. Eyes wide, he slipped the vial into a pouch and rose slowly to his feet.

With a deftness she didn't know she had, Draya darted to intercept the imminent attack. Nel followed in perfect concert, throwing up their shield to barricade all three of their companions from harm. The scavengers couldn't stop in time, instead crashing into the golden armament and tumbling backward. The trio swiveled with their backs to one another, defenses raised against the circling abominations. All four beasts eyed Draya warily. On a hunch she took a quick lunge and swept the cultist's dagger forward. The closest waerg whimpered and pulled back, just like the others.

She eyed the serrated blade suspiciously. Either they were afraid of her, or they were afraid of the dagger. She was willing to put money on the latter. *For Rook's sake, what did I make off with this time?* "What's the plan?" she shouted, pushing the question aside. It was impossible to know how long their strange hesitation to attack would last in the face of such a large meal.

"Avoid the fangs?" Yllari offered. "Maybe the claws too?"

"I am open to suggestions," Nel shouted back.

"There's an alley over there." Draya motioned to the far side of the courtyard with her chin, never breaking eye contact with the amalgams. She swiped at the waergs with the cultist's dagger, forcing them further back with a low whine.

"How do you propose we get there?" Nel asked.

Draya gripped the dagger tighter and lowered herself into a crouch. "On my mark, run."

"And leave you here alone?" Yllari's voice rose incredulously.

The response turned Draya's insides. Even banded together for a job, when push came to shove it was always every mercenary for themselves. "Let me worry about me."

"I – we will not abandon you," Nel stated.

Draya hissed impatiently. "You aren't. I'll be right behind you." She held the dagger aloft, her rapier pulled back defensively. She didn't wait for a response. "One," she counted. "Two. Three. Go!"

Nel hesitated, but Yllari looped his arm through theirs and pulled them in the direction of the arch. The Aegis lurched forward and Draya covered their retreat. She didn't know what was so special about the dagger that the waergs seemed unwilling to attack her, but she was grateful to abuse the advantage. Once Nel and Yllari had reached the narrow threshold, she made a break for the alley herself, sprinting towards them at full speed.

"This way!" She slipped between the pair and ran ahead. Yllari followed and Nel guarded the rear, their tower shield filling the width of the thin passage. Two of the waergs barreled towards them, colliding with each other as they both tried to squeeze through the archway side-by-side. They snapped their jaws, their haunches wedged together at the threshold. They fought one another for the lead, but the trio didn't wait to see who won.

"Where are we going?" Nel didn't turn, unwilling to take their eyes off their retreat.

The cramped alley walls opened up into a columned breezeway and then split in three directions. Draya continued straight without slowing her pace. "Not sure."

"Not sure?" Nel shouted back.

"Do you have a better plan?"

Assured none of the waergs were on their tail, Nel turned to face forward. "No, but —"

"Do you trust me or not?" she barked, her breathing rapid.

"Don't make me answer that." Their tone was ambiguous, leaving Draya confused by their meaning.

"Yes – yes, we trust you," Yllari cut in.

Once again, Draya found herself uncomfortable. She pulled them around yet another blind corner without any coaxing. She was used to muscling her way out of a mess on sheer false ego – she reveled in it, even. It would have been easy for Nel and Yllari to underestimate her abilities after what little they'd seen her accomplish. Earnest trust was a rarity in her line of work. *Please guide me true*, she pleaded with the mysterious voice. She made another left, and then a right. She was second-guessing her last turn when she spotted firelight shining through a rapidly approaching archway. "There!"

She slid to a stop and strained to hear any bestial sounds out of eyesight.

"Is anything out there?" Yllari asked as he craned his neck to look over her shoulder.

"Doesn't seem like it." Even the screams seemed quieter on this side of Templekeep. Draya was about to step into the open air when a loud bellow stopped her short.

The gargantuan body of the female Peryton reared up in front of them, her tangled web of antlers forming a sinister crown. She dropped back down on all fours, her ursine paws cracking the tile with her weight. Tattered black wings spread from her shoulders, casting the trio in sudden shadow. Draya shot her arm out to the side, stopping her companions in their tracks. Her heart pounded in her ears as the beast's heavy brow lowered, her bird-black eyes narrowing on the young woman. Brittle skin stretched taut against her long skull like a macabre mask. Draya brandished the dagger in front of her, retreating backward. It sniffed the air and tried to follow, but its antlers pressed against the walls on either side of the alley. The peryton snorted, its hot breath blowing wisps of her crimson hair back from her face. Those same bewildering scents of myrrh and cedar enveloped her, but the peryton only tipped its head curiously to one side.

Draya laughed, the raucous sound erupting from her chest. Safe from the beast's advance, her shoulders relaxed as she glared back at the amalgam.

"Draya." Nel hissed her name in warning.

"What?" She did a half-turn, casually dropping the arm clutching the dagger to her side. "It can't get to us."

There was a crunch of stone as the peryton crashed its brow against the walls on either side of the passage. Dust rained down around them. The beast pulled back her massive skull to make another attempt. Draya leaped backward, colliding with Yllari.

"Alternate route?" he asked as he steadied her by the shoulders.

Draya shook her head, shaken from the sudden attack. "None that will get us out of the complex."

Yllari looked to the sky, then back to Draya. "Can you get us to the Eastern Wall?"

"Why?" Her brow furrowed, confused. "It's a dead end – literally."

"Not if I can help it – dawn is coming."

Draya looked up for herself. The night sky overhead had faded ever so faintly to navy blue.

"Whatever you are going to do, we need to do it now," Nel said.

Draya hesitated. "But what if –"

"It's your turn to trust me now."

Draya swallowed. He had a point. "There's a way, but we still have to make it past that she-beast."

Nel looked behind them. "You are sure?"

"The rest of the paths just circle back," she confirmed.

Yllari took a deep breath and gave Draya's arm a squeeze. "All right. Stand aside."

Before she could question him, the mage took a long step forward and struck the base of his staff into the floor. Rays of starlight crackled down from the dark sky, striking the peryton's bony skull like hail. She reared back in surprise, clearing the way out. Draya whooped in excitement, expecting Yllari to do the same, but he was dead silent instead. Before she could react, Yllari's knees gave out beneath him. Nel was already at his side, their shield arm catching him under the armpit.

"Move!" they shouted, their voice a grunt as they took on the majority of the mage's weight. He limped next to the Aegis, his head hung low.

Draya didn't waste any time. She rushed forward, skirting past the flailing front paws of the creature. The enormous wings remained unfurled, exposing more torn flesh and bits of ivory bone beneath. Idly, she wondered if the beast could actually fly or if the wings were merely vestiges from some earlier incarnation. She didn't slow her pace to think any harder on the subject.

The yard they'd come into was open on both sides, one end toward the front of the keep and the other toward the rear. Far away, sunlight slowly crept over the horizon, turning the dark blue sky shades of purple. They made their way between the remaining stout buildings, intent on reaching the high wall surrounding Templekeep.

As they came to a stop right against the stone, Yllari pulled away from Nel's supportive arm and planted his feet on either side of his staff. "Here goes nothing." He placed both his palms over the top of his staff and whispered a series of unfamiliar syllables.

Draya watched in awe as a crack of golden light formed in the space between the mage and the wall. Behind them, the cries of the dying and the howls of the waergs continued.

22

The portal started small, a slowly spiraling spark between Yllari's staff and the stone wall. The ember grew larger, its ethereal flames licking the ragged edges of a tear in the very air itself. The fissure cracked and burned with the same colors of the rising dawn and Draya found herself holding her breath. She'd read extensively about arcane magic in her studies; knowledge that served her well when confronted with the strange technologies left to rot in Aiylonia's ruins. None of that had prepared her for how beautiful the power actually was.

A shrill cry for help broke her state of fascination. More screams followed, and Draya spun to find the source. A woman was leaning out the window of one of the barracks, a terrified child clinging to her neck. Only two stories below, light and shadows danced against the foundations. Shattered oil lamps littered the ground and fire snaked quickly through the dry brittle grass, trapping the pair within the tower.

"We've got company!" Nel planted their feet and extended their sword towards a trio of waergs headed their way. The remains of a half-eaten soldier lay sprawled and abandoned in their wake, shreds of her crimson viscera still bright against their yellowed fangs. The woman's metal armor proved useless, the leather straps torn open at the seams. Draya could see the exposed bones of her ribcage even at a distance. Despite her helmet, she knew without a doubt that she'd been alive when they'd eviscerated her.

Yllari remained intent on his work, one hand extended forward. The thin tear had grown to nearly half his height.

"How much longer?" she asked.

"Hard to say." His voice strained with the effort. "Dawn is an unstable time for my magic."

"Is any time good for your magic?" Draya bit back. She took a deep breath and readied her blades. Another scream sounded from the tower, and her heart lurched. Every muscle tensed, an instinct she didn't recognize insisting she run towards the sound.

"What's wrong?" Nel asked over their shoulder, intuiting the warring impulses she faced. Their eyes didn't leave the advancing waergs.

"Nothing!" She grimaced as the lie soured in her mouth.

"The truth," Nel demanded. The first of the waergs prowled forward, salivating despite its recent meal.

Sarding bonding. She tipped her chin towards the barracks. "A woman is trapped by the flames. There's a child with her."

The Aegis glanced in the tower's direction. Their eyes were off the waergs for only a second, but that was enough. The creatures took advantage of the opportunity, pouncing at Nel with splayed talons.

"Aegis!" Draya cried. She feared her warning came too late, but the soldier was already in motion.

Nel expertly wheeled back and lifted their shield into the path of the closest waerg. Wicked claws crashed against the gold plate with an ear-splitting screech, and the force of the blow knocked the soldier off balance. They staggered back, falling into a crouch to recover their footing. The other two waergs broke off in either direction, parting like a wave around Nel as each narrowed in on new prey. Draya threw herself in a practiced roll to avoid one, but Yllari was in no position to defend himself from the other. Draya watched helplessly as the third beast barreled into his side, knocking the mage to the ground. A violent burst of light erupted from the nascent portal, the tether tying him to the arcane energy snapping in two. There was a shower of sparks, and the rip in the air was gone.

Draya didn't have time to mourn their lost escape route. Ignoring the waerg bearing down on her, she sprang up and recklessly charged at the one holding Yllari to the ground. Her shoulder collided with the corded muscles of its side, the rotting smell of wet dog and fresh bile filling her nostrils. The waerg tumbled off of the mage with a yelp, righting itself with its head low and haunches high. She ignored its deep-throated growl and held the cultist's dagger aloft, hoping it would have the same effect as before. With Yllari taken down and Nel grappling with the largest of the three to her left, Draya was on her own.

She'd resigned herself to lunging forward with her rapier when a bolt of light struck the waerg in the side. The force of the blow lifted its frame into the air and threw it backward. She heard the crash of another magical bolt and turned to see Yllari stagger, his staff raised high over the corpse of the third waerg. The amalgam's ear and upper lip twitched in its death throes.

The mage smiled triumphantly at Draya, but then all color drained from his face. He crumpled, falling to his knees as dark blood soaked through the tattered fabric of his pant leg. His eyes rolled back, and she and Nel reached him at the same time, holding him aloft between them. Nel's blade dripped with dark blood, the corpse of the last waerg lying in a heap behind them.

An unearthly bellow filled the air as another chorus of screams erupted from the direction of the barracks. The inhuman howl held a strange kind of magic, practically paralyzing Draya in place. It took all her effort to force her gaze upwards. To her horror, the gargantuan peryton was rounding the high interior walls and making her way to the woman in distress.

Control of her movements resurfaced as the echo of the call faded, but Draya's tongue felt like sandpaper in her mouth. "Can you walk?" she asked Yllari, already anticipating the answer.

"I can try," he lied, wincing as he leaned the bulk of his weight against Nel for support. His complexion was ashen, his striking blue eyes pitted with dark bruises. He was using every ounce of his energy just to stay vertical.

Draya looked back toward the barracks tower. The peryton had advanced on the mother and daughter, sniffing the air only a floor below them. The two pulled back from the windowsill and huddled in the shadows. The smoldering fires at its feet were little more than a nuisance to the monster. Draya pulled her gaze away. *Maybe they'll be fine on their own,* she reasoned. "Let's make a run for it now – while the peryton is distracted." Draya avoided eye contact with the pair, but she could feel Nel's disapproving glare boring into her. "Or not," she amended.

Yllari groaned unexpectedly.

"I'll go," Nel announced.

"No. You need to carry the mage," Draya countered. "Anyway, I'm quicker."

Draya didn't give them the chance to argue. Against everything she believed in, every tenet of self-preservation she possessed, she sprinted to the tower, dodging and diving between pockets of predators enjoying their meals. Whether it was due to her speed or their ongoing disinterest in her, none moved to intercept. Before she knew it, Draya found herself in the substantial shadow of the peryton. A sense of recognition washed over her. Even without seeing their faces, she knew the child above was the same she'd helped before being rushed by the mob of refugees. Protective fury washed over her. *I'll be damned if this sarding beast cancels out my good deed.* She watched the flames lap at the door. She hadn't thought this through. *How exactly am I going to put out a fire while simultaneously fending off the peryton?*

"Hey ugly!" she shouted, waving the dagger in the air. "I'm the one you want!"

The peryton pulled its intent stare away from the upper window. Its pitch-black pupils narrowed in and Draya's stomach dropped, her newfound bravado evaporating. The walls of the alley had protected her, but here she was exposed. There were no alcoves to dive into, no corners to dart behind. Its elk-like skull leaned close to Draya's pallid face and breathed deep. Inexplicably, its breath smelled of salt and sand in addition to the myrrh and cedar she'd smelled earlier. The amalgam cocked her head to one side and then pulled back. In a smooth movement that belayed her size, the peryton reared and bellowed a deafening call into the night.

An almost oppressive silence followed the peryton's roar, leaving only the whimpered cries of the dying in the wake of the sound. The ravaging waergs froze in obeisance. She let out three more short, echoing barks before turning and slowly lumbering away from Draya without a backward glance. Cowed, the lesser beasts pulled their snouts from their gruesome meals and begrudgingly followed. Within moments, the only amalgams left behind were those the people of Templekeep had managed to kill. The rest had retraced their destructive path through the compound, leaving through the mangled front gate and into the wilderness beyond.

Draya looked down at the dagger again, turning it curiously in her hand. The grip sparkled with embedded gems in the firelight, silver and pink striations cutting through the deep purple amethysts. *Is the Fellowship of the Sun related to the amalgams? And if they are, how are they both related to the Sarcophilum they meant to kill me for?*

Her pondering was short-lived. While the threat of the waergs had passed, the fires still raged. Above, there was no sign of the woman or her child in an open window. Draya hoped it was out of preservation and not because they'd been overcome by the heavy black smoke billowing from the eaves. She sheathed her blades and assessed the doorway. From across the field, the flames had looked like a wall, but up close she could see they trailed back and forth with space in between. While some flames were as tall as she was, most barely came to her knee. She'd navigated worse traps in her tomb-raiding career. With a few calculated leaps, she cleared the expanse without so much as a singed boot lace. The door was charred, the iron latch no doubt scalding even through her glove. She pulled the collar of her shirt over her nose and mouth, planted her feet, and kicked forward with the flat of her right heel. The warped planks buckled. With a second blow to the same spot, the wood around the latch splintered and the door caved inward. Smoke-induced tears seared Draya's eyes, blurring her vision. She ducked low to avoid the worst of it and forced her eyelids open long enough to find the base of the staircase. She need not have bothered. Even as she saw the smoldering stairs ahead, she found her body was already moving toward an unadorned door to the side. She pried it open to find a winding servant's stair clear of smoke and flame. It was her best chance.

She quickly shut the door behind her and raced upwards, mentally tracking the number of floors she needed to pass before reaching the woman she'd seen. Three floors up, she threw open the door, revealing a central chamber and a series of open doorways. Her instincts led her towards the room to the right, and she ran toward it, throwing her shoulder against the thin board that served as a door. Inside, the woman and her child cowered under a side table.

"It's all right!" Her lungs filled with acrid air, and she brought her collar back over her nose. A crack of timber and a shower of embers exploded from the opposite side of the room. "I can get you out!" Draya added, her voice hoarse and broken.

The woman's red-rimmed eyes went wide as she threw her arm out to shield her daughter. "Stay back, Droughtbringer!" she cursed. "Are your beasts not enough?"

Draya stopped short in surprise. "My what?"

"I saw you command the monsters – you cannot deny it!" The older woman spat at the floor.

Draya cursed under her breath. *So, it wasn't just my imagination.* She'd hoped no one else had noticed the strange behavior of the amalgams. "I'm here to save you!" she croaked, already regretting her sudden dalliance with heroism.

The woman made the sign of the helix over her heart. "We will not follow you to the slaughter, Harbinger!"

Draya did her best to swallow her impatience. She'd almost turned away when her vision cleared enough that she could see the child's panicked eyes. Her mother's arm was wrapped around her in an iron grip, preventing her from fleeing to safety. Draya's annoyance escalated to outrage. "Don't you understand?" she barked. "The building is *burning*. You need to come with me, if not for yourself, then for your daughter!" As if to emphasize the point, there was a loud crack and a hiss as something on a lower floor shifted and fell.

The contempt on the mother's face seemed to waver, but she held her ground.

"We don't have time for this!" Draya pulled the collar of her shirt tight against her face and coughed a few times into her elbow. "At least let me take the child!"

The woman's eyes hardened. "She will go nowhere without me."

There was another loud crack as a support gave way somewhere, and the child let out a whimper. "Mama!" she pleaded, finally moving the woman to action.

"Fine, we will follow," she said, angrily. She ushered her daughter forward.

"Thank the Fates," Draya muttered. She reached out a hand only to have the woman dismiss it with disdain.

The child mimicked Draya, pulling her collar up over her nose.

"This best not be –" The force of a cough cut off the mother's chiding words. Draya was about to grab the girl and run when the woman's grip reasserted itself around the child's forearm. "Best not be a trick," she finished.

Draya rolled her eyes and turned back towards the way she'd come. The black smoke was thicker than it had been when she arrived. "This way," she beckoned. Her eyes fell to the left, and she realized why the pair had been trapped. The main staircase had fallen in on itself, the supports burned through at the base. She was glad to see the servants' stair looked yet untouched by the flames, but there was no telling what they'd find on the ground floor. Hoping for the best, she pushed through the camouflaged door and beckoned the mother and child to follow.

23

"You're welcome!" Draya shouted.

She'd led the mother and daughter to the ground floor without incident. Even the trailing flames had already been doused with sand, eliminating any need to help them leap to safety. Seeing the way clear, the woman broke free from Draya without a word, her daughter trailing behind.

Draya grunted. She tried to dust the soot off her hands but only succeeded in smearing her breeches black. She pulled her gloves off and shook them out. Aesthetically they were ruined, but to her surprise, they were still intact otherwise. *Still liked the old ones better*, she thought before stuffing them in her belt. Once she'd taken a deep breath, she looked around the open field. It was littered with the bloody corpses of humans and waergs alike, although there were ruefully more of the former than the latter. She watched the mother and daughter melt into a huddled mass of survivors near the central courtyard. Shining gold armor was impossible to miss, so she trudged toward the Aegis. They were on one knee, wrapping the arm of an injured man with a length of linen.

"You wouldn't believe this wo –" Her complaining was cut short when she realized the entire group had gone quiet. Men stepped forward, angling their bodies as if to protect the women and children among them. The injured man Nel was tending to stood up quickly, tripping over the bench he'd been sitting on as he retreated towards the crowd.

"I'm not...done." Nel let their comment die as they took in the angry stares. They rose quickly, assuming a defensive position of their own beside Draya. The crowd formed an intimidating wall, and Draya began to worry the mob was about to resume the chase they'd started the day before.

Yllari staggered up behind them, his breathing heavy as he leaned against his staff. He tried to look unbothered, but it was clear he was favoring one leg. "What did I miss?" he asked as he took in the strained atmosphere.

Before Draya or Nel could muster a response, Rian parted the crowd. Her short hair was spiked in all directions with a substance Draya didn't want to think about, and dark splashes marred her recently pristine silver armor. There was no way to tell how much of the blood belonged to her, the waergs, or those she was duty bound to protect.

"Aegis Commander General," she said, her voice grave.

"Lieutenant, are you all right?" Nel strode forward to meet her, their calm facade slipping with concern for their compatriot. "Do we have any idea how –"

"Aegis Commander General," Rian sternly repeated. "While I cannot order you to do so, I suggest that you take your party and go."

Nel stopped short, their shoulders tensing. "I think that you could use our assistance, considering the casualties."

Rian's expression didn't waver. "No need, Aegis Commander General." The disdain in her tone was impossible to ignore. Draya felt herself stiffen in time with Nel.

"I see." Nel's voice had gone icy cold. "If that is the case, Lieutenant, we will take our leave."

She gave a curt nod, all of the kind familiarity she'd greeted the Aegis with gone. Watching the mob, it was clear the Lieutenant's authority was the only thing standing between Draya and their wrath. She swallowed nervously.

Nel turned their back on the crowd and took Draya by the elbow, steering her in the direction of the Waypost's main entrance. She didn't resist – she was well aware that her immediate safety currently rested in Nel's rather strong hands. Yllari followed, each step halting and slow. It wasn't until they'd passed the decimated outer gates and reached the other side of the empty moat that Nel seemed to relax even the slightest bit.

"Did the peryton do this?" she asked as she took in the damage. The road was churned to mud, and the cypress trees that had lined the road were uprooted and trampled.

Yllari answered, his voice weakened. "The aftermath, yes. But the original path was likely cut by a ceropel."

Anticipating her follow-up question, Nel added, "It's a rhinoceros-rodent hybrid with an armored carapace. They aren't much bigger than a waerg and are rather benign as far as amalgams go, but they're good at digging tunnels and clearing paths." The Aegis stopped their pace and looked out to the far wood line.

Draya tried to imagine the creature but quickly gave up. Instead, she took the momentary pause as an opportunity to assess her supplies. "Sarding abyss," she hissed, shaking her empty canteen. "All of this and I didn't even remember to resupply." She contemplated turning back. The well wasn't far past the entrance from what she could tell, and she had the strange blade with her should any of the waergs still be around. She shook her head, thinking better of it. The cultist's dagger might protect her from the amalgams, but it wouldn't ward off a vengeful refugee.

"Too late now," Yllari said as if reading her thoughts. "South, then?" He took a few steps past Draya and then stopped abruptly, his body wracked by a hacking cough.

"Are you alright?" Nel moved to place a hand on Yllari's heaving back.

With a painful finality, his coughing stopped and he looked down at the packed earth beneath his feet. "No," he said quietly. "I don't believe I am." His body went limp, his staff falling beside him. Nel managed to catch him as he collapsed, using the momentum of the fall to lower him to the ground. A large clot of blood was visible in front of where he'd been standing.

"Yllari? Yllari, stay with me." Nel gently tipped back the mage's chin and used their thumb to wipe away the traces of pinkish spittle that coated his lips. His eyes were even more sunken, his skin sallow and pale. Draya found herself already in motion. With no thought to propriety, she began pulling away the layers of fabric that enrobed the man's body. Starting at his shoulders, she probed his arms, his chest, his midsection for injuries. She'd just about reached his hips when her eyes fell on the slowly darkening patch not far from his kneecap. She sucked in a breath, remembering the injury that had disrupted the portal. She abandoned her methodical search and focused her attention there. The folds of his long robe had hidden a large wound, and she had to gently peel the ragged edges away from the bloody gash.

Draya fought to keep her face neutral as a wave of nausea swept through her core. A large, semi-circular tear was cut into Yllari's calf, exposing dark muscle and what Draya suspected was his fibula bone. It was hard to be sure as thick dark blood seeped sluggishly from the torn flesh. Looking closer, it was clear that the shape matched the jawline of the waergs they had just been fighting.

The back of his head cradled in Nel's hands, Yllari spoke with a quiet voice. "How bad is it?"

Draya looked up and met Nel's gaze, glad that the mage's eyes were still closed. She gave them a grave look, shaking her head once. Grim understanding crossed the Aegis's face.

"That bad, huh?" The mage burst into another coughing fit, sending flecks of blood across the front of his silk tunic. He wiped his mouth with the back of his hand and craned his neck down to assess the wound himself. "I knew I should have worn taller boots."

Draya looked down and saw that the top of his boot ended just short of the bottom of the bloody wound. A little taller and the thick leather might well have deflected the waerg's bite. Yllari managed a wink as she turned her attention back to his face. "My fault for trying to be fashionable."

Rakish to a fault – impressive. "Chasing trends has obviously been your downfall," she replied dryly, casting him a wry half-smile. She hoped her words wouldn't prove to be prophetic.

Nel lowered Yllari's head the rest of the way to the ground. They dug into a large pouch hanging from their hip and pulled out a small amber vial and a roll of linen. Before they could ask, Draya shuffled herself towards Yllari's head, leaving enough room for the Aegis to take her place. At a loss, she slipped her fingers between Yllari's, giving them a squeeze she hoped felt comforting. Anxiety whirled in her gut, and she wasn't sure how much was hers and how much might be Nel's. She didn't remember the last time she felt this level of concern for much of anyone, let alone a relative stranger. It was disconcerting.

Nel uncorked the bottle, all of their focus on Yllari. "Brace yourself," they said. With his curt nod of permission, they splashed the bottle's contents over the wound. The mage sucked in a breath through his teeth and squeezed his eyes shut. The smell of high-proof alcohol danced against Draya's nostrils. Within moments, Nel had expertly bandaged Yllari's calf. "Can you stand?" they asked.

"We'll find out." With a gentle squeeze, Yllari pulled his hand from Draya's and pressed his palms against the ground. It took some effort, but he managed to stand with only a little assistance from Nel. He tested his weight on the injured leg, and Draya watched as he bit back a wave of pain. "It's fine," he said through barely clenched teeth.

"You know how I feel about lying." Nel bent down and lifted the mage's staff, inspecting the integrity of the base. "Can you use this for balance?"

Yllari took his staff and planted it against the muddy path. "It's gotten me home after a few drinks, so I can only assume it can take a little more abuse." He leaned tentatively against it. Finding it stable, he wrapped his arms around it and put all his weight on his healthy leg.

"It doesn't need to last for long though, right?" Draya looked between the two. "Can't you just whip up another portal and...?"

Yllari sighed wistfully. "I wish it were that simple." He took a slow step forward, using the staff like a walking stick. Nel watched him warily but then took the lead down the path.

"What do you mean?" Draya adjusted her pack and stood.

Yllari moved slowly behind the Aegis. "The spell was interrupted."

"I could tell that much. But the sun will be out for hours. You can try again before sundown."

"No, I can't." The lightness in Yllari's voice was gone, replaced with a weary huskiness.

"Why not?" she pressed.

"It's just the way it is." His steps came haltingly. The mage didn't offer any further information.

Draya turned her attention back to Nel. They had already outpaced her. Draya rushed to the Aegis's side. "So, we're walking?"

"Looks like it," they replied.

She cocked her head to one side. "How long is that going to take?"

"At least a week on foot."

Draya scoffed. "What?"

"A week. Assuming we don't run into any trouble, anyway."

She lowered her voice to keep her words from reaching Yllari's ears. "I thought this would only take a few days?"

"With a portal, yes." They noticed her odd expression and explained. "I knew Yllari would find us eventually," they explained.

Draya groaned. "That certainly turned out well, didn't it?" Nel ignored her cynicism. "How long until he can cast again?" she asked.

"Normally, he would be refreshed with a good night's sleep. Having one of his spells interrupted like that is costly. It uses up all the stored magic that would have fueled the portal, without any benefit." They kept their eyes forward, intent on watching for any unseen threats. "But something about that bite is...unnatural."

Draya almost asked how they knew that, but even as she opened her mouth to speak she understood the truth of it. The wound was severe and should have been bleeding far more than it was. Instead of clotting, the flesh was seeping an ink-black substance Draya didn't recognize. The closest she'd seen in her time adventuring had been the result of a monitor lizard bite, but that was just rapid infection. Whatever this was, it wasn't like anything she'd ever seen before. "Why do you think that is?" she asked instead.

"The nature of the waerg perhaps? I've only encountered amalgams a few times during my early training days, and the victims of their attacks hadn't survived." Nel's emotionless tone left a sour taste in Draya's mouth.

She changed the subject. "Will Yllari be able to stay on his feet long enough to make it to Trifall?"

The Aegis hazarded a furtive glance over their shoulder. "We have to hope so."

Draya followed their gaze. She didn't need more than her rudimentary first aid training to understand what a long shot that was going to be.

24

"Now what?"

Draya knelt at the edge of the barren canal. Her fingers were wrapped around a heavily braided rope that trailed over the steep drop-off, and on the other end, a large square of pine planks hung limp against the wall. Across the way, its companion platform had not been so lucky. The rope on that side had snapped, leaving the soft wood of the platform to crash into the muddy canal bed below. Just days ago, the platform rafts floated on the water's surface, tethered on either side to allow those traveling on foot to row across with the provided paddles. Unlike a bridge, the rafts could be pulled against either side, allowing water vessels to move through unimpeded. With no water to speak of, the raft was as useless as the abandoned oar beneath it.

Nel surveyed the scene, rubbing a palm against the back of their neck. The only option was to leave the meager road they were following, but neither side looked promising. The ground was rocky and punctuated by the scrubby skeletons of dying trees. It would be hard enough to traverse if they all were able-bodied, but it would be nearly impossible for Yllari in his current state. Draya sucked in a breath. The catastrophic consequences of the unnatural drought could not have been more clear.

"There!" Nel squinted towards the horizon, shielding their eyes from the blazing noonday sun.

Draya tried to follow the direction of their finger, but the glare off the bleached rock hindered her vision. "What is it?" she asked.

"You do not see it?"

"Obviously not."

An irritated puff of air escaped Nel's nostrils. "There is a footbridge — or something like a footbridge – up along that hill. It looks like the width of the canal is thinner there."

Draya still didn't see it. "If you say so."

"There is a figure there too, maybe more than one. We should head in that direction."

Draya examined the landscape. Intellectually, she was aware Trifall lay further south, but she nevertheless felt the compulsion to follow Nel's lead. The Aegis was right - whatever they saw, her senses told her it was the most efficient route to take to their destination. She glanced at Yllari out of the corner of her eye. He looked worse than even a few hours before. His dark skin had taken on an ashen pallor, and she could even make out purple-blueish veins spider-webbing along his temples.

"Don't worry about me," the mage said, catching her gaze. "I've done worse."

I doubt that. Draya contorted her face into what she hoped was a look of encouragement and kept her mouth shut.

Nel was already high stepping over the rocky terrain, picking their way through the brittle branches. With a furtive glance at the chasm to her side, she made her way over the rocks. She had an easier go of it than she'd assumed from further away, but it was still hard on her feet. Exposed roots became their own obstacle, but eventually, she made out what the Aegis had seen from the main towpath. The opposite shore was much closer here, and someone had lashed together a series of fresh-cut tree limbs to construct a makeshift bridge across the short expanse. On the other side stood a long covered wagon and an old mule that was scratching at the dirt, munching on whatever shrubbery it could find. The bridge was just wide enough for the wagon to cross.

"Who did you think made this?" she asked as she approached Nel.

"An unfortunate soul." Draya followed their gaze downward. The crumpled body of a middle-aged man lay in a heap at the bottom, his arms and legs at unnatural angles. His head was twisted too far to the side, the sockets that once held his eyes picked clean by scavengers. A travel trunk lay upended nearby, gold coins spilling out over the mud.

Draya shook her head. "He must have brought the cart and the mule over first and then came back for his coin."

"But why would he have risked a second trip?" Nel asked, turning to her.

She approached the bridge, tapping her foot against the edge. It was sturdy, but the wood still had significant give. "Weight," she answered. "Bringing the mule and the wagon across would have been treacherous enough, and gold is heavy. Once his means of transportation was safe, he came back for the trunk he'd left behind."

"Makes...enough...sense," Yllari said as he caught up to them. His words came between painfully ragged breaths.

"I wonder what happened to cause the fall," Nel said, shaking their head.

"He slipped." Draya knew it was true as she said it but didn't know why she was so confident. "Nothing more nefarious than that."

"Let us hope...we have a more...fortuitous fate." Yllari slumped against his staff. His previously pristine robes hung like rags, the colors muted with layers of dried mud and dark blood.

"Hmm." Nel made a noncommittal noise. They reached out the toe of their boot and tested the integrity of the hastily constructed bridge for themself. Satisfied, they looked between Draya and Yllari. "How shall we do this?"

Yllari's brow furrowed.

"What's wrong?" Draya asked.

"Aside from the obvious dread caused by a cobbled together bridge already proved to be lethal?" Yllari's voice was hoarse, but his breathing had steadied. He took a few slow steps forward. "Under normal circumstances, we'd be on the other side already. I wouldn't even need a portal – just a simple swift foot spell."

"If it were normal circumstances, we would already be in Trifall." Draya regretted the cutting words as soon as they left her mouth.

Unperturbed by her bluntness, Yllari managed a small smile. "Well played." He almost chuckled but then coughed into his hand instead. When he wiped his palm against his breeches, Draya was sure she saw dark streaks of what could only be fresh blood.

"I'm the heaviest," Nel announced, ignoring the exchange. "I should likely cross by myself."

"Only because of that sarding plate mail," Draya interjected. "You could leave it behind, you know."

Nel's breath hitched. "That would – I don't see how…" Draya took some perverse joy in the brief moment of panic her suggestion elicited from them. They quickly recovered and looked Draya up and down. "Do you think you can help Yllari cross?" they asked through gritted teeth.

"Nonsense." Yllari waved a dismissive hand. "I can make it myself." To prove his point, he threw his shoulders back and strode confidently toward the bridge. He only made it halfway before another cough forced him to a stop.

Draya slipped her arm through his, steadying him. "Yes, you appear to be an exemplar of health and mobility." She eyed the bridge. If it was wide enough for the tinker's cart, it had to be wide enough for them both to cross side-by-side. "Yllari and I will cross together. Who should go first? Should we draw straws?"

"I will go first," Nel answered. They gingerly took a few steps forward along the raw wood. One of the limbs let out a creak of protest, but otherwise, the lashings stayed true. Within a handful of minutes, they were safely on the other side.

"Our turn," Draya said. She wrapped an arm around the mage's waist, and he draped his arm over her shoulders. "Ready?"

"As ever," he answered through a grimace. Slowly, they limped along the rickety bridge. It was sturdier than it looked, but it was no surprise the traveler hadn't wanted to test its weight limits with the trunk. She'd been watching her every step for hazards, when she risked a look to the opposite shore. She almost stopped in her tracks. Now that she was closer, she recognized a pattern of dots burned into the footboard of the wagon.

It's a Hawker's mark.

"Is everything…alright?" Yllari asked.

She strengthened her hold around his waist and picked up her pace. "Yes, I just want to get this over with." Once they were safely across, Yllari leaned his back against an outcropping of rock to catch his breath.

Nel watched the weary mage with concern. "I know you are pushing yourself, but we should probably keep moving. We might be able to reach a resupply shelter before nightfall."

Yllari nodded and pushed himself away from the stone.

When Draya didn't answer, Nel turned to her. "Did you hear what I said?"

"Keep moving. Shelter before nightfall. Sure, yes." Draya's eyes were intent on the canal they'd just crossed. Long-standing Hawkers on Guild business sometimes branded their mode of transportation as a means of covertly identifying themselves. Its use mostly secured safe passage through Guild territories, but sometimes signaled a level of import to the cargo or the passenger. Either the man at the bottom was a member of the Hawkers Guild, or he'd stolen the wagon from one. "Just let me do one thing first," she added.

Nel raised an eyebrow. "What would that be?"

She peered over the steep drop into the empty canal. Hawkers didn't have much in the way of a shared code, operating more like loosely allied mercenaries. Feuds between guildmates were common, and as long as no one jeopardized the integrity of the organization or its holdings, it was up to each member to manage their own business.

There is no hard-set rule you have to do anything, Draya reminded herself. *You can just pretend you didn't notice the brand and keep on going.* To her chagrin, she couldn't heed her better judgment. "I'm going to get that treasure chest."

"You have to be joking." Nel managed an even more dour expression than usual.

She wasn't about to reveal a Guild secret. "I never joke when uncontested loot is involved." Draya was already pulling the length of rope out of her pack. As she dug deeper, her hand brushed the hidden pouch containing the Sarcophilum, triggering a sharp, guilty pain in her core. *What would the Aegis do if they knew?* Ruefully, she pushed the feeling aside and wrapped her fingers around a thick leather pouch. She pulled it out triumphantly, undoing the knot that held it closed.

"What's that?"

She turned to see Yllari looming over her shoulder, his weight firmly on his staff. She assumed he wasn't any older than she was, but his sunken cheeks added years to his appearance.

"Grappling hook." She gingerly removed the three-pronged attachment from the protective pouch and secured it to the rope.

His obvious skepticism was undermined by a heavy cough into his fist. When the fit had passed, Yllari continued. "You don't –" he paused, coughing again. "– plan on trying to hook the chest and pull it up with that, do you?"

She returned his look with an incredulous one of her own. "I'm not going to dignify that with a response." She searched the canal edge. The trunks of a few widely interspersed cypress trees clawed up from the quickly drying earth. The closest was too fragile, but one to the right of it looked sturdy enough. She wound the end of the rope around its trunk, then used the hook to secure it in place. She eyed the long length of tether in her hands. The silk was tightly braided but not very thick. She briefly wondered if it would be strong enough, but if it worked on the Aegis's skiff hopefully it could bear the weight of the gold. She looked up at her companions. Yllari was eyeing her curiously, but Nel was baldly glaring.

"You're robbing a corpse," they said.

Draya ignored their scowl and perched on the ledge, the back of her heels hanging over the side. "You do understand that is what I do for a living, right?" She looked over her shoulder into the canal. "Just pull me back up once I'm ready."

"What? I will take no part in your…your…"

"You will if you want to get me to Trifall." Draya interrupted. She didn't wait for a response, instead repelling down the canal wall. The heels of her boots bounced heavily against the uneven soil until she safely landed on the muddy riverbed. It was only about two stories deep, but the surface was dotted with polished stone, each rock worn smooth from the water that had recently filled the space. As she left the rope hanging and carefully picked her way across the divide, the cause of the man's death became clear. It wasn't the distance, but rather the landing that did him in. The side of his head lay at a painfully sharp angle, a large rock puncturing his temple. The mud around his head had turned a ruddy reddish-brown and she steeled herself against the sight of his eyeless face. Despite the mutilation, he'd probably been dead for less than a day.

This explains how the mule is still alive and not starved tethered to a tree, she reasoned.

Avoiding the worst of the remaining gore, she knelt next to the corpse. Her hands safely gloved, she tilted the merchant's chin to one side. A heavy silver chain snaked around his neck and disappeared into the stiff collar of his embroidered tunic. She could feel Nel's eyes judging her from atop the ridge, but that only made her more defiant. *Let them think it's mere avarice,* she thought.

With one hand, Draya lightly ran her fingers under the fabric, blatantly following the shape of the chain to his sternum. She deftly pulled back the collar with her other hand, exposing the skin just above his shoulder blade. *Bullseye.* She was just making out the tip of a tattooed wing when felt the body's spine buck under her hand. Her heart jumped into her throat, and she bit back a shout of surprise. When she looked up, the head of the corpse had turned towards her, its jaw gaping open before her eyes.

25

Draya sprung backward, her hand snapping to the hilt of her sword. She had the blade half drawn before the triangular head of a black river snake pushed through the dead Hawker's teeth, its flickering tongue tasting the air. The rest of its body slithered free and Draya gave it a wide berth as she caught her breath. When her breathing normalized, she turned and shielded her eyes against the afternoon sun. As she expected, a bright glint of gold betrayed Nel's position at the ledge.

"Are you all right?" the Aegis shouted down.

"Fine!" she shouted back. *At least they aren't going anywhere.*

She looked back down at the man who was assuredly her Guildmate. She'd torn his tunic in her panicked backpedal, and something caught the light from the underside of his collar. She crouched back down for a closer look, and saw it was a dark iron pin the size of her fingernail, set with a faceted amethyst with silver and pink striations.

Draya didn't need her archeologian training to determine the gem was a perfect match to those embedded in the Vizier's dagger. She pulled the pin free and stuffed it into her pouch. Something told her she might need it later.

All the more curious about the trunk's contents, Draya stood and circled the corpse. The wooden chest was battered, but still largely intact except for a bent hinge that left the lid barely ajar, accounting for the spilled coin. An iron lock still latched the majority of the lid shut, and a quick shake confirmed it was otherwise secure. Draya bit the inside of her cheek, her hand resting on one of the thin pouches at her hip. She could take the time to pick the lock here, or she could wait until she got it to the wagon. If the metal casements had been damaged in the fall, she might need just as much brawn to get the lid open as she would skill. Her curiosity could wait. She wrapped both arms around the chest and slowly lifted it with a grunt. It was heavy, but she'd handled worse.

"I'm sorry," she murmured to the Hawker as she backed away. She was used to carrying away the belongings of the long dead, but this felt different. As the empty eye sockets stared up at her, she pondered Nel's disgust at her feigned intent. With a snort, she started back to the rope. *Who cares what he thinks of me.*

"Are you done scavenging?" Nel shouted down.

"Are you done judging?" Draya shot back. They didn't respond. She knew asking them for help would make her job easier, but she didn't want to give Nel the satisfaction. Instead, she carefully tied the excess rope around the midsection of the trunk, lacing it through iron handles that hung from either end. Thankful for her gloves, she wrapped her fingers around the hanging rope and began to pull herself up. Climbing was more work than repelling, but Draya had more than enough practice getting herself out of pit traps and sunken tunnels. The bundle acted as a weight at the bottom, keeping the rope taut as she ascended.

Finally, her eyes peered over the ledge. Nel extended a hand, but she ignored it as she pulled herself up. Following the line back to the trunk of the tree, she pulled the grappling hook free and unwound the rope.

"Now what?" Yllari asked with an amused expression.

"Watch." Draya pulled the rope around the tree trunk and let out the slack. She began to heave the rope towards her using the cypress as a fulcrum. Every few pulls she looked over the side, monitoring the gradual progress of her quarry. It was only a third of the way up when her arms started to burn. She paused, wiping her arm across her forehead.

"Would you like assistance?" Nel asked.

"No." Draya heard and dismissed the genuine concern in their voice. She started pulling again, arm over arm when suddenly progress stopped. She tugged a few times, but the rope wouldn't budge. She looked over the side to find the corner of the trunk lodged against a stray root. "Sarding abyss," she cursed under her breath. *Not again.*

Nel was already moving towards her. "Stuck?" they asked.

Draya sighed. "Looks like it."

"I doubt the problem is a submerged trellis this time." Nel said in line with her thoughts. They looked over the edge and then took up the loose rope behind Draya. "On three, pull." They planted their feet.

Draya swallowed her pride and accepted the help.

"One. Two. THREE." On the final word, the pair pulled backward. For a moment, she thought they'd succeeded, but suddenly the resistance gave way, sending Draya tumbling into Nel. They fell backward in turn, and both tightened their grip on the rope, but it was too late. The silk rope finally met its match, tearing against the rough bark of the tree. The end Draya and Nel held went slack, and the frayed end on the other side lashed out like a whip as it retracted around the trunk and slithered over the side of the canal.

She threw herself to the edge of the canal drop, desperately trying to grab the twisting end of the lead. She landed hard on her stomach as the rope slipped out of her reach and she couldn't help but wince at the splintering crash that followed. Inching forward, she saw the remains of the chest shattered against the barren river rocks, sparkling gems and shining coins spilling everywhere.

"I suppose that's it then." Nel stood, straightening their breastplate. "Can we go now?"

"This is just a setback," Draya argued. "I can try again."

"How?" they asked. In the beat it took her to answer, they added. "You no longer even have a rope to get down there with."

Draya took in a sharp breath and looked down at the remains of her line. They were right. She was down to an arm's length of rope and one grappling hook, with no spoils to speak of. "Maybe there's rope in the wagon?" she offered. "We should check, it shouldn't take that long to –"

Nel cut her off. "Do you see the sun? We do not have the time to waste on selfish greed." They took a furtive glance at Yllari. He'd turned away from them, his forehead pressed against his staff. Nel lowered their voice. "We can't risk being caught out in the open. We need to find shelter – now."

Draya looked over at the mage. She itched to tell them the real reason she wanted the trunk and whatever the Hawker might have buried inside. Maybe it was just the gold, but having found the Fellowship pin, she wondered if there was more to it. *But I can't push any further without endangering us all.* It was clear Yllari couldn't hold his own against another pack of waergs, let alone something bigger. And that wasn't even taking into account any brigands they might encounter. She glanced down at the riches that lay just out of reach and sighed, only a fraction of her regret for the coin itself. She stood and grabbed her pack from where she'd left it. "So, what are we waiting for? Lead on to this shelter."

26

"Ow! Careful!"

"I'm sorry!" On her third attempt, Draya finished wrapping the new dressing around Yllari's leg. She didn't know if it was the barely used road, the wagon's old axles, or some unfortunate combination of the two, but the ride so far had been one jostling bump after another. She sat back and leaned her head against the smooth wood of the interior, glad for the tarp roof over their heads. The late afternoon sun was brutal with no clouds overhead to offer respite. Nel had insisted on taking the driver's box, claiming some kind of rapport with the mule, and Draya didn't argue the point. If they want to overheat in that scorching armor with very little water on hand, that was their choice.

"How does it look now?"

"Hmm?" Draya pulled her attention back to her patient.

"The wound. How does it look?" Yllari pushed himself up against the threadbare cushions that must have served as the merchant's bedding.

"It looks...the same," Draya lied. In truth, she didn't know what it looked like. The bleeding had stopped, but the ragged edges of flesh had blackened to an inky blue-black. The rest of his leg had taken on a corpse-like hue, skin laced with deep purple veining that seemed to be growing by the hour. She wondered if amputation would be necessary, but didn't want to mention it until she'd had a chance to talk it over with Nel.

"So, as disturbingly unnatural as ever?" The corner of Yllari's lip curled upward. If he could manage such a smile in his half-dead state, she suspected he rarely left a tavern without someone on his arm by the end of the night.

"Yes," she conceded. Draya pulled her knees up to her chest, wrapping her arms around them.

"Cheer up, little tomb robber. It's going to take more than a necromantic abomination from whose bite no one else has ever survived to take me out." His brave words were subverted by a hacking cough.

"No, it's not that." Draya looked up and blinked, realizing how callous she must have sounded. "No, I mean, yes. I mean, of course, that's troubling, I just –"

"Have something else on your mind?" Yllari turned his head to one side thoughtfully. "Please allow me to be your sounding board. I could use any and all means of distraction."

Draya wanted to tell him everything – the strange lure she'd felt to the palace treasury; the reliquary in her pack; the way the amalgams fled from the shadowmancer's stolen dagger. She wanted to shout she wasn't the Droughtbringer and that it was just a stupid story he and the Aegis had made up to feel better about their friend's death. Instead, she shook her head. "I just hope we get to this shelter before my tail bone is worn flat."

The injured mage closed his eyes and tipped the back of his head against the wagon wall. "You can ask me, you know."

"I don't know what you're talking about."

"Yes, you do. You want to know what I meant last night. About the apocrypha."

Draya swallowed. She'd pushed the reference out of her mind entirely. "I don't believe in prophecy," she said softly. "Let alone prophecy that's been deemed worthless."

"That doesn't sound very convincing, especially with your training. No matter what our taciturn companion says, as scholars, we both know what a group wants forgotten is just as important as what they want to be remembered."

She managed to smile a small smile. Few people respected archeology as a scholarly pursuit. Had she continued the more politically correct path laid out for her, she'd be an apprentice historian or even a minor librarian by now. Instead, she'd used her education to earn clout amongst the thieves and mercenaries of Aiylonia's black markets, then into a legally sanctioned position in the Hawkers Guild. Archeologians were seen as scavengers first, scholars second. *If at all,* she reminded herself. "What makes the apocrypha so controversial, then?" she asked just as the wagon floor bucked beneath them.

"Apologies," Nel shouted from the driver's box. "I do not think this road has been used for some time!"

"Big surprise," Yllari muttered. "How far are we from this sarding waypost anyway?" he called back.

"Wayshelter," Nel corrected.

"What the void is the difference?"

"Historically, the two serve very different functions. The waypost –"

"Size and purpose," Draya interrupted curtly. "Wayposts are like miniature towns within a fortress compound. Wayshelters are just that – four walls and a roof to spend the night in as you travel from one place to another."

"With staff and kitchens, of course," Yllari's statement was more like a hopeful question.

Draya snorted.

"Sometimes a previous tenant leaves some rations, and it is proper etiquette to replenish the firewood and leave things as clean as when you arrived," Nel followed up.

The back of Yllari's head flopped back against the tarp. "Blood and bones. I don't know what will do me in first – this wound or the accommodations."

Just a few days ago, Draya would have agreed. Instead, she deflected. "You were saying, about the prophecy…?" she prompted.

"Ah, right." He sat back up and met her eyes. "Every prophecy centered on the End shares two important acts – first, the Droughtbringer does the otherwise impossible and finds the Undying One's Treasury; second, that same person manages to break the Vault seal, thereby triggering the Creeping Drought." He choked on a cough. Draya handed him her canteen and he took a small sip. "The details change here and there, but the major ambiguity lies in the motivations and moral character of the Droughtbringer herself."

Draya swallowed the sour taste in her mouth. "I imagine the Coronet has a particular take on that subject?"

"You imagine correctly."

She spread out her palms impatiently. "Well? What do these

prophecies say? That she's some bumbling idiot?"

"That's the gist in children's parables," he conceded. "But there are a few different schools of thought within the clergy. Most of what we have from the Sovran Oracles paints the Droughtbringer as someone far more devious."

"Lovely." Draya was struck with the memory of the brute in Northtown. "What about the Torrent? The Twelfth Armada?"

Surprise colored Yllari's face. "The Torrent? How do you know...never mind, it's probably better you do." He pinched the bridge of his nose with two slender fingers. "The Twelfth is fundamentally a mercenary company, but ideologically they are religious zealots – and that's coming from someone who grew up in a Temple. They claim to descend from the armada that infamously broke ties with the Coronet during the Five Valley War."

The pieces started clicking into place. "I think I remember some of this now. The Five Valley War took place a little over a decade after the Deluge, yes? After the Order had taken most of the Canal but before they'd assumed control over the Splinter Lakes."

"Precisely, but keep in mind they weren't called that yet. It would take decades for those little springs to form the Lakes as we know them." Yllari paused. "Oh, and the Order prefers the term liberated."

Draya snorted. "Of course they do."

Despite the Coronet's assertions otherwise, the years following the Emperor's defeat were rife with conflict. Aiylonians no longer had to live under the yoke of the Undying and his armies, but not every province had a plan for what came next. The voids of power left plenty of room for minor despots to squabble over control, and once the Coronet had secured the advancement of Trifall, they claimed it was their righteous duty to steer the rest of Aiylonia into their vision of freedom.

"Remind me – what exactly caused the conflict?" Draya asked. "Division of spoils? Land rights?"

Yllari shook his head. "Worse. The Armada disagreed with the Coronet's decision to pardon soldiers from the opposing districts. They wanted to hold mass executions as a show of strength."

"Skulls, that's the legacy they want to uphold?" Draya's disgust was clear on her face. "What does all this have to do with the prophecy?"

"At this point? Everything. The Twelfth see the return of Occidrious as a chance to purge those they consider enemies of the Helix in what they call the Torrent — that includes hunting down the Droughtbringer and her accomplices."

Draya tilted her canteen to her lips, wishing for something stronger than a swallow of lukewarm water. "How many of the other factions want me dead?" She peered into the canteen – it was maybe a third full at this point.

"Not all of them. One thinks you're mostly dead to begin with."

She blinked. "Excuse me?"

He smirked. "If they've got it right, I have to say you hide being Occidrious's half-lich daughter very well."

"That's...what?" Draya felt her brain stop working for a moment. "Can a dead person even –"

"Undead technically."

She rolled her eyes and continued to speak. "– an undead person with the rather contradictory moniker "Undying" even have children? A lineage at all? How would that even be possible?" She vaguely waved toward Yllari's lower half. "Would they even have the right equipment for it?"

Unperturbed by the crude gesture, Yllari tried to lean forward, groaned, and settled back against the tarp. When he looked back up there was amusement peeking through the pain in his eyes. "Maybe you were born before he became a lich and later became one yourself? Don't ask me. But as you can tell, depictions run the gamut."

Idiot. Evil. Astral Drake. Daughter of a lich. What's next? How many more versions of the Droughtbringer are there to contend with? "I had no idea I was so full of sarding multitudes," Draya grumbled.

"That's what you get for being the harbinger of the apocalypse." Yllari shrugged, and Draya vacillated between being impressed and annoyed at his glib nonchalance. She settled on the former.

"What does the official prophecy say? About the Droughtbringer, I mean."

Yllari's eyes met hers. "Depends who you ask." He waved his hand, dismissing her look of confusion. "Aside from a few poetic descriptors – charcoal-stained eyes, hair like coils of woven embers, and so forth – Soriadne mainly focused on the catastrophe rather than the Droughtbringer herself. Other Oracles left tidbits that range from generally accepted to outright denied by the Coronet – which brings us back to the apocrypha."

Ah, right. That. "I assume whatever it says falls on the 'denied' end of the spectrum?"

Yllari nodded. "Do you remember what I said about why the Order takes in children with particular Callings?"

"You never told me there would be a test."

He chuckled. "Just answer the question."

She rolled her eyes. "For whatever reason, the signs that a child has the Calling of a Brightbourne mimic the signs shown by children with the Callings of Navigation, Will, and Foresight. As a result, the Coronet collects anyone that shows aptitude for one of those Callings and locks them away in the Temple for the rest of their life." She wrinkled her nose in disgust. "Like collecting antiques in the hopes that one turns out to be worth something."

Yllari's brow raised but he only shrugged in reply. "A cynical – if more or less apt – take."

"Yeah, that's me. If I die a horrible death from an amalgam, make sure 'cynical but apt' winds up somewhere on my grave marker – or at least in the eulogy." She smirked at her own gallows' humor. "So if I have the Calling of Navigation, then somehow those early signs were missed, and none of the Oracles managed to ferret me out either. I'm an outlier, but I certainly can't be the only one. But that doesn't answer my question: what does all this have to do with Nel's temper tantrum?"

Yllari put a finger to his lips, flashing a look toward the curtain between them and the driver's box. "This is the controversial part. According to the prophet Tyriadne – Soriadne's daughter as I said – the Droughtbringer doesn't just bungle her way to triggering this apocalyptic mess by accident – no offense."

"None taken."

"In fact, Tyriadne wrote that the 'flamed-haired maiden' wouldn't even be the servant of the Undying that a subset of extremists fear." He leaned in, emphasizing the gravity of his next words. "Tyriadne declared she'd be more than that. That she is a Brightbourne – or rather, the Brightbourne – An embodiment of the First herself."

Draya barked out a laugh. "No wonder she was committed to Halloran."

He half shrugged and settled his head back against the wagon's interior. "It's far-fetched, don't get me wrong. As Nel said, as far as we know only children under ten have ever been recognized as the replacement Brightbourne." He paused as Draya opened her mouth to speak. "And before you ask, no, I don't know how a new Brightbourne is identified – I'm not even sure what the early signs of the relevant Callings are. I threw a temper tantrum when I was six and candle flames flared twice their size. You and Nel? Your Callings are all up here." He tapped a finger against his temple.

"But don't you work in the Temple? I thought all the potentials or whatever were brought back there to train." Draya eyed him incredulously.

It was Yllari's turn to laugh. "You assume I'm allowed anywhere near the dormitories. Mages aren't exactly high on the food chain in the Capital."

Why would that be? Draya tucked the curiosity away for a later time. "Maybe they just don't want you setting fire to the drapes," Draya said with a smirk.

"No," Yllari agreed. "Not again, anyway," The corner of his mouth turned up in a lopsided smile as he closed his eyes.

They fell into an easy silence, the wheels of the wagon rumbling against the unpaved track beneath them. As Draya idly tried to arrange all she'd learned over the last two days into a cohesive whole, one nagging question remained unanswered:

Why wasn't I taken in by the Cresting Tide?

Aside from being the only redhead among her dark haired, brown-eyed cousins, Draya's childhood was comfortable yet unremarkable. With her family's name and fortune, all of her needs and most of her wants were met. She grew up in a warm home with plenty of warm meals and wardrobes of warm clothes. Even as a child she had a knack for stumbling onto lost trinkets and she never got lost on the winding streets of Amphidon, but neither trait seemed impressive enough to make her think she had a Calling.

What am I missing? Is there something else to it? A question popped into her head. "What exactly is the Brightbourne's Calling anyway?" she asked.

"Immaculate Truth."

Draya and Yllari looked up at the sound of Nel's voice as the wagon pulled to a stop.

Before Draya could form a retort deriding the notion of integrity, her attention was pulled to the road ahead. Without the sounds of hoof beats and wagon wheels filling her ears, she could hear the din of a raucous crowd around them. She pushed her way forward and stuck her head out over Nel's shoulder. Silhouettes of travelers – on foot, in large caravans, on horseback – filled the horizon. "Please don't tell me they're all here for the shelter," she groaned.

"If you wish, but I am afraid I have no other explanation to give you." Nel's tone was bleak.

27

The low murmur of voices grew into a ruckus as the line to the wayshelter came slowly into view. Road-weary travelers loitered on both sides of the towpath as they argued with one another, their bodies and belongings clogging the narrow route. Whether it was due to far too quickly dwindling resources or fear of the unknown, it was clear people were moving south. Despite all she'd come to know of the Creeping Drought, Draya had been holding out hope that things would improve the further away from the vortex they got.

So much for that.

Draya could only make out snippets of conversation, and from what she could gather there were far more people than there was room. She could see the cause for concern. On the hill opposite the canal was a small building, more akin to a shed than a cottage. Firewood was stacked against the wall on one side of the door, and on the other was a long hitching post with room for three mounts – four if they were runts. The roof on that side extended over the packed earth beneath, providing any animals some cover from sun and rain.

"Thoughts on throwing our hat in the ring?" Yllari asked. He'd managed to stand and was leaning against Draya's shoulder.

"I've never seen the path to a wayshelter this crowded." Nel shook their head in disbelief. "Especially one of this style – only four walls and a hearth."

"Wait – there aren't even actual bunks?" Yllari coughed into his sleeve before looking on in horror.

Draya's veins ran cold. "It has a well, doesn't it?"

"Of course." Nel sighed at the revelation. "It does. A deep one."

"That explains it," she confirmed.

"Finally," Yllari said. "We've barely got a drop of fresh water to share between us."

Nel silently pulled the reins, and the mule stopped her advance.

"Am I missing something?" the mage asked.

"That depends," Draya answered. "So far our track record with new people has been rather poor. In the three days the Aegis and I have been together, we've already incited two mobs between us." A thought struck her. "But if water is out of the question, perhaps we could barter for some first aid supplies. I'm not sure how many more strips of linen I can get out of that dirty shirt." Draya looked down at Yllari's leg.

"Wait, they've been dirty? How dirty?" Yllari's brow scrunched in despair.

Nel ignored him. "We could try going in," they offered, their voice tinged with uncertainty.

"Maybe if you removed all that armor? A stiff breeze or a rough jostling, and that cloak becomes a piss poor disguise." Draya looked them up and down to emphasize her point.

"Absolutely not." Nel bristled at the suggestion. "Besides, they are just as likely to recognize you as the Droughtbringer."

She let out a frustrated breath. "It seems highly unlikely we'll find an excitable old priest at every pit stop."

Nel gave her a withering look.

"So, one or both of us could easily be recognized," she conceded. She glanced at Yllari.

"Don't look at me. It's becoming quite clear that I'm incapable of going anywhere on my own power. I know I'm enviable arm candy, but it makes sneaking in a little difficult." The mage gave Draya a smile that seemed to challenge both the difficulty of the situation and the pain he was most assuredly feeling.

"Staying still like this makes us even more conspicuous," Nel finally said. They started moving again with a shake of the reins.

"We've decided…what, exactly?" Draya asked. Nel sat rigid as she tugged at the corners of their cloak, tucking it in place around the segments of armor.

"There has to be an inn somewhere, don't you think? I can't say I was looking forward to staying here anyway." Yllari lowered himself back to the floor of the coach, manually adjusting his wounded leg so that it extended straight out in front of him.

"There are no roadside inns along the waterway until we're just outside of Trifall," Nel said.

"Well, that was rather thoughtless, don't you think?" Yllari's tone was just short of a whine.

"I doubt anyone anticipated this situation," Nel replied.

"Why not? There's a prophecy and everything," Yllari replied.

He'd be infuriating if he wasn't right. Draya swallowed, a sinking feeling growing in her gut. *For such an important prophecy, it doesn't seem like much has been done in preparation.* She wondered who was to blame for that – the Coronet, or the people?

A backdrop of rolling hills ascended higher and higher behind the shelter. The trees here seemed a little livelier than the ones along the barren canal, likely due to the underground water source. Looking at the mob that had formed, Draya wondered how long the spring would last before it was drained dry as well. Separate from the drivers along the road, a disheveled line of desperate people snaked back and forth around the side of a modest cabin on their way to the well. Angry voices boomed from the end of a line. Looking closer, Draya made out three distinct groups of people standing off in front of the stone pavilion that served as the well's access point. Draya could practically smell the seeds of chaos fomenting.

Nel must have noticed the same discomfiting air. "We should step in," they said as the mule slowed. A few eyes rose to assess whether their coach carried further competition for resources.

"Madness," Draya declared. "We won't get halfway up the hill without drawing attention to ourselves."

"Maybe that's not such a bad thing," Nel countered. "Maybe what these people need is the kind of reassurance only the Order can provide. Maybe it would remind them that they are being watched over."

"Watched over by whom? Do you see any clerics here?" Draya spread her arm out in emphasis. "There certainly weren't any watching over Northtown when the Archpriest took off with the food stores. From what I've seen, the clerics are doing nothing to help these people. Despite all of their resources, all of their promises of protection, the only clerics we've seen were holed up in Templekeep, and now half of them are dead." She bit down on the word, wincing as soon as the tactless words left her mouth.

A wave of Nel's justifiable reproach crashed into Draya as they answered defiantly. "There has to be a reason for all of that. We just have to trust –"

"Trust what? Their judgment?" Anger erupted in Draya's chest. The volume of her voice was rising, but she didn't care. "Their supposed plans for an event that could fill a library with conflicting prophecies?"

"Obviously, no one could predict the depths of greed and carelessness that would lead you inside the vault," they growled. Draya felt her anger reflected back at her. That level of rancor was out of character for the Aegis, but she was too incensed to care.

"Maybe if your masters had put up walls rather than parlor tricks I never would have found my way inside! Maybe if people knew the *actual dangers* of entering the sarding palace I never would have tried!"

Yllari's eyes scanned the crowd. "Nel, Draya – calm down, this isn't –"

The Aegis ignored Yllari's protest. "As if that would have stopped you from pursuing any job with the chance for illicit wealth."

"At least I'm good at my job! You trained your whole life to protect your precious Brightbourne and look how that turned out!"

The cruel words were surgically precise, but they only served to amplify the rage burning between the bonded pair. The two glared at each other, neither willing to break the stalemate, neither capable of backing down. Draya felt a nauseating pain emanating from the metal cuff secured to her wrist.

Yllari pulled himself even further between the pair. "None of this is helping," he hissed between clenched teeth. "Perhaps we should agree that everything's careened to chaos, and we should keep moving before the mob decides to redirect their frustrations at the two raving lunatics milling about on the road!"

Draya waited. She had no intention of showing weakness. Nel finally sighed and rubbed a spot in the center of their forehead – the same spot that had glowed with a spiral helix during their first meeting at the Palace. It took Draya a moment before she realized the loud arguments had gone quiet around them, only to be replaced by the hush of whispers.

"Too late," Yllari groaned with a sigh.

"Sarding abyss," Draya cursed under her breath. *Why can't I ever keep my mouth shut?*

The word 'Brightbourne' was already traveling through the crowd like a cool breeze. She adjusted the hood of her cloak to better cover her tell-tale hair, but Yllari was right. It was too late. People from every faction moved to block the narrow path they'd counted on as an escape route, eyes focused on their wagon with sudden interest. The anger seething between Draya and Nel dissipated to make room for a shared sense of dread.

"We could try the Halloran excuse again?" Draya whispered out of the corner of her mouth.

"I'd rather we do not." Nel's fingers tightened around the reins as they took in the sea of unhappy faces. Unlike the patrons at the Brick & Boar, there were no hopeful eyes to speak of.

"Probably wouldn't be enough anyway," Draya conceded.

"Again?" Yllari waved a hand. "Never mind, I'll ask about your exploits later. For now..." With a deftness that belayed his injured leg, Yllari unhooked the clasp at Nel's neck and yanked their cloak away. Rays of sunlight reflected off their golden armor, so bright Draya had to shield her eyes.

"Sorry," Yllari whispered in her ear. "Calling of Illumination and all that."

Members of the crowd gasped at the sight of the shining Aegis, and more than a few made the sign of the helix over their hearts. To them, Nel must have looked like an embodiment of divine light. She'd seen Yllari's Calling used for the occasional parlor trick – amplifying the reflection of a candle flame for instance – but she'd never considered the breadth of its usefulness.

We just might make it out of here unscathed, she thought.

"You dare show your face here, Aegis?"

Draya pinched the bridge of her nose. *Well, that hope died quickly.*

28

Draya turned towards the sound of the deep, feminine voice. The masses had parted to allow one of the three ringleaders she'd noticed near the well approaching through their ranks. She was tall and slender, but bare muscular arms and the waxed canvas apron she wore marked her as a member of the Shipwright Guild.

Their identity revealed, Nel looped the reins around the hitch of the driver's box and dropped to the ground. They raised their empty hands in a gesture of peace. "We have no desire to engage in confrontation," they intoned as they took two long strides toward the crowd. The authority in their voice was more in line with their high rank than Draya had yet to witness. "We apologize if our wild conjectures caused any concern."

"Concern?" The woman scowled. "Is that what the Order is calling this catastrophe? A *concern*?"

"Please, of course, the situation is serious." Nel stood stock still, and despite their show of confidence, Draya could feel their apprehension rising in waves. Overcome with a perplexing sense of loyalty, Draya leaped from the wagon and took position next to the Aegis. They continued, "We are on our way south now to –"

"To convene with the Coronet in Trifall?" the woman finished for them. "You and every other cleric from here to the Radiant Sea. You should be ashamed of yourself."

Rumbled agreements rose from all directions as members of the crowd closed in behind them. Draya could practically feel the escape routes sealing shut. *Why did you have to move so far from the carriage?*

Draya thought impotently. When Nel hesitated, Yllari chimed in from the driver's box. "We understand your distress, but we only wish for a small ration of water to carry us on our way. We swear we seek the same explanation for the Creeping Drought as you do."

Another of the three ringleaders – a shorter woman with a fishing spear strapped to her back – stepped forward. "You have the *gall* to take claim of a well that rightfully belongs to the hamlet of Fishtown?" Her voice boomed over the crowd.

The first woman scoffed. "You mean Overbrim? Our people have more of a claim to this shelter than any of yours do."

"Excuse me, but you speak out of turn." A bearded man with a shorn head – the third ringleader – interjected. He wore the simple gray robes of a lay devotee and a large iron helix hung from a cord around his neck. "It is the congregation of Safe Harbor that fill the shelter's larder, and therefore our taxes that support it. *We* deserve first refusal over the well."

"Is that a jest, Jericho? Without Fishtown, your entire compound would have nothing but rice and turnips to eat," the spearfisher scoffed.

"Rice and turnips that fill your larders all winter," he replied calmly.

The shipwright laughed, her attention pulled from the Aegis. "Nor would you have skiffs to catch those fish without Overbrim. Anyone can grow a garden or spear some dinner. Without us, you'd all starve."

"As if skiffs will help us now, Behelim," the spearfisher scoffed.

"My skills will certainly be more useful on land than yours, Quella." The shipwright turned on the lay priest. "Yes, yours too Jericho – can you build walls to protect us with turnips?"

The man scowled but did not respond.

Draya laid a hand on Nel's arm, cocking her chin back towards the coach. *Slip away now, while they're distracted,* she thought as hard as she could, hoping against hope that the Aegis would understand. To her relief, Nel nodded.

"People of the north – please, there is no need for these arguments," Nel called out. "I will personally bring your complaints south with us so that formal adjudication can be performed by the Order."

Well, so much for direct telepathy. Draya managed to repress her groan.

The shipwright and the spearfisher glared daggers at the Aegis.

"What's in the coach?" a voice shouted from the crowd.

"Yes," Jericho echoed. "What supplies do you carry?"

"Just an injured man with a bruised ego," Yllari called out. "Nothing to see here!"

"They have a mule, though," a man behind the shipwright remarked.

"Worst case," the spearfisher said as she punched one fist into her opposite palm. "I bet we can make a killing once we melt down that suit of gold."

Draya's hand dropped to her belt on instinct, only to curl into a tight fist at her side. Her rapier should have been on her belt. Even traveling by ferry and sitting at tavern tables, she always kept it close. Without any benches inside, there was no comfortable way to sit on the floor of the wagon with a weapon jutting out from her hip. She'd laid it next to her and never bothered to return it to her belt. *This wouldn't be a problem if I'd been the one in the driver's box,* she thought bitterly.

She dared a glance at the coach, but the ringleaders were already advancing. Turning her back on them would be suicide. As she pulled the Fellowship dagger from her belt, Draya watched Nel lift their fists in a pugilist's stance.

"Where's your thrice-damned sword?" she shouted to the Aegis. The spearfisher closed the distance, forcing Draya to duck and pivot to avoid the wide swing of her meaty fist. *At least she hasn't unslung her spear.* Draya sidestepped another punch and feinted with the short blade, creating a bit of breathing room between them. *I wonder how long that minor blessing will last.*

"Driver's box," Nel shouted back, their eyes on the approaching shipwright.

Unlike Nel and Draya, the shipwright wasn't so ill-prepared. She pulled a bladed adze and a mallet from her tool belt, moving more slowly than her fellow ringleader. As if anticipating a comment, she shrugged and spun the weapons in her hands. "Nothing fancy, I admit. But iron is iron," she said.

"That's a stupid place for your sword and shield to be!" Draya ignored the shipwright's attempt at banter and stepped closer to Nel, her back to theirs once again.

"I suppose only carrying that cursed dagger was a choice?" they said over their shoulder.

"Of course!" Draya lied. "And what do you mean cursed? You think it's cursed?" She glanced at the serrated blade. "Why didn't you say anything?"

"We have had more pressing concerns,"

The spearfisher paused, her dark eyes assessing the bickering pair. The shipwright was biding her time, slowly bridging the distance. Out of the corner of her eye, Draya saw that the rest of the crowd was frozen in place, either too pious or too scared to engage the Aegis in a fight. Even the third ringleader – Jericho – had stepped back into a throng of similarly dressed laymen.

"For Rook's sake!" Yllari shouted from the wagon. "Now is not the time to argue about that sarding dagger!" Draya wrinkled her nose but didn't argue. The mage followed with a call to the Aegis. "Nel!"

Draya's head spun, expecting to see a new threat attacking them from behind. Instead, she watched as the Aegis lifted their empty hand into the air. There was a brief blink of light near their palm, and then nothing. They looked up in confusion.

Using the distraction as an opening, the shipwright lunged with the adze at Nel's midsection. The small axe struck the overlapping plates of gold with a clang. The Aegis was forced a step back, but the metal remained unscathed.

Too hard to be mundane gold, then. Old enchantment, maybe? Draya watched as the fisher reached behind her back, untying the leather strings that held her spear in place. *A curiosity for another day,* she decided.

To her left, the shipwright came in with her mallet, but this time the Aegis grabbed her wrist with their other hand. They stepped in, twisting her hand backward and forcing her fingers open. The woman yelped in pain and the weapon tumbled to the dirt. Draya couldn't help but recognize the maneuver as her own.

"Yllari?" Nel didn't take their eyes off their opponent.

"Hold on..." His voice was strained enough that Draya risked a look in his direction. The mage was doubled over the front of the driver's box, his sallow features contorted in pain. Nel's sword hung limply from his hand. "I can't," he managed to croak out. He dropped to his knees and the broadsword tumbled to the dirt below.

Draya felt her chest squeeze. Before she could sprint to Yllari's side, the spearfisher growled, swinging the long iron spear at her face. Too slow to bring the dagger up to parry, she flinched in anticipation as she tried to duck in time. Then a flash of gold shot across her vision. Nel deflected the spearhead with their heavy bracer, shoving the weapon to the side. Thrown off balance, the woman toppled forward from the momentum, embedding the tip into the ground.

Unflinching, the Aegis spun back just in time to duck around a backhanded swipe of the shipwright's adze. Anticipating her position, they punched her hard in the kidneys. She cried out in pain and crumpled to the ground. At the same time, Draya kicked out with her boot, hooking around the fisher's ankle. The woman twisted and fell forward, landing hard enough that the crack of her wrist bone was only drowned out by her scream.

With both of their opponents incapacitated, Nel dove at the coach. In one easy motion, they grabbed their shield with one arm and scooped up their fallen sword with the other. Without needing to be told, Draya swung up into the driver's box and pulled Yllari back into the cabin of the coach. Nel planted their feet, guarding their retreat. The circling crowd maintained their distance, but there was no telling when they might make their next move.

"What the abyss was that?" Draya lowered the mage into the pillows he'd occupied earlier. Something slick coated his forearm, and when she looked down she saw the same black ichor that wept from his leg now oozed through the fabric of his sleeve. With less care than she should have, she yanked the edge of his sleeve up to his elbow. To her horror, a line of seared flesh wrapped around his wrist and ran down each of his fingers.

"It was supposed…to be magic," he stuttered. "I've blinked…Nel's sword to them…countless times." His bloodshot eyes shot wide open, but his gaze was unfocused. "They're taking my power."

"Who?" Draya asked, more to keep him talking and conscious than out of actual curiosity. She was too far out of her depth to make sense of things. She tore off her sleeve and wrapped the thick cotton around the new wound. The oozing had already stopped, but she couldn't imagine the raw wound should remain exposed. "The waergs…the amalgams…I don't know. Somehow, my power…it's being sapped."

"Like we need one more sarding thing," Draya said under her breath.

He managed to nod his head ever so slightly before falling back against the wooden frame of the coach. Draya was about to shake him awake when she heard a wail outside. Muffled voices erupted around them. Before she could debate leaving Yllari's side, clanking metal sounded from the driver's box. Nel took up the reins, their shoulders uncharacteristically hunched.

"What happened? What's going on?" she prodded, icy dread crawling up her spine.

"There's no reason to fight any longer." Nel's voice was flat as they draped the heavy cloak over their shoulders again.

Draya strained her ears. The timbre of the crowd's grumbling had changed. She moved to the back of the wagon and looked out the rear opening. Almost half of the travelers that had been surrounding the well had dropped to their knees, their empty jugs and pails littered at their feet. A few more were staring into the hole in the ground, but the rest were looking out amongst the crowd.

I recognize that look – they're desperate. "Nel?" Draya called over her shoulder. She didn't need to ask – the carriage was still behind a blockade of bodies.

"The well…it's dry, isn't it?" Yllari managed to whisper.

"That can't be possible," Draya said in stunned disbelief. People began segmenting themselves even further, those still in the winding line glaring hungrily at those who'd gotten their share of the dwindling water supply before it had run out.

"Nothing is…impossible, remember?" Yllari choked out between coughs.

Nearby, a handful of men and women had surrounded the injured shipwright and fisher, assessing their wounds. None had their eyes on the carriage, but Draya knew that wouldn't last long. The tension in the air was palpable, and who better to take out their frustration then on the strangers that wounded their leaders.

"Nel?" Draya called again. "We can't stay here!"

There was only silence from the driver's box.

"Nel!" She shouted their name just as her body was struck with an awful feeling of hopelessness. The tips of her fingers tingled with pins and needles, and she found herself short of breath. Draya fought the paralyzing defeat she was siphoning through bonding with every bit of stubborn anger she possessed. "AEGIS!" she barked between ragged breaths.

Her body abruptly relaxed, and she barely caught herself as the carriage lurched forward, the mule trumpeting a confident bray. She fell next to Yllari and braced them both, expecting to meet resistance ahead. With cries of surprise and anger from either side, the crowd scattered around them. It wasn't until they'd passed up and over the next hillock that the Nel risked slowing their retreat.

"Are we clear?" Nel shouted.

Draya scrambled to the rear. "Looks like it!" As far as she could tell, there was no one on their tail. She returned to Yllari's side and assured herself that he had only fallen unconscious and was still breathing. Then she slipped into the seat beside the Aegis, rapier securely at her side. The sky was still bright with afternoon sun, its rays diffused by a layer of clouds overhead.

"Where do we go now?" she asked.

"I have an idea," Nel replied obliquely. Whatever panic they had transmitted to her was gone, replaced with their habitual stoicism. They steered the mule to the right and the whole wagon bucked as the wheels bounced over the raised edge of the towpath.

From what Draya could tell, there wasn't even a deer path to follow on the other side. They were traveling over open land, snaking their way around the foothills. "Are you sure you know where you're going?" The previous animosity between the pair had fizzled, neither of them having the energy to reignite the argument.

Nel's eyes remained on the horizon. "No, I'm not sure," they confided. "But I pray we get there before sundown."

29

"Helix bless us. We made it." Nel sighed with relief as the wagon crested the latest of what had been a long succession of hills. The steeple of a provincial temple sprouted from the valley below, the iron silhouette of the spiraling holy sigil framed by the orange and reds of the setting sun. Beyond that, a small hamlet revealed itself, barely more than a long main street and a smattering of cottages to either side. The mule picked its way down the rocky hill that banked up against the temple's old but well-tended cemetery.

Draya squinted. "Made it where?" As she voiced the question, the answer came to her unbidden, although she couldn't remember if she'd ever actually heard the name before.

"Invranid," Nel confirmed, ignorant of her silent realization. "It's small, but I know they keep a boarding house. We can secure ourselves safe harbor before nightfall."

"I'm not so sure about that," Draya said.

The abysmal state of the hamlet became clear as they rounded the temple property. If the waypost had been a slaughterhouse, Invranid was a ghost town. The central thoroughfare was littered with debris, the windows and doors boarded up or torn from their casements. A fire must have recently broken out along the buildings on the left side. Sections of the wattle and daub walls were scorched black, and the thatched roofs were sunken and half eaten away. Nel pulled the mule's reins to a stop, tossing them to Draya before swinging down from the driver's box. They took a knee and traced a series of faint marks in the hard-packed earth.

"Amalgams," the Aegis reported. They scanned the town with hooded eyes. "They made it here first."

"Already?" The word was more a moan than a question as Yllari tried to sit up and failed. He slumped back against the pillows.

Draya cast the mage a wary glance before returning her eyes to Nel. "How did they make it this far south so fast?"

Nel stood and shook their head. "They didn't come from the north. They came from the west."

"The west? I thought –" Draya stopped mid-sentence as her eyes registered the range of mountains along the horizon. "Ophidaen Ridge."

Nel nodded solemnly. "Amalgams aren't exclusive to the northern wastes. The Great Deluge pushed the amalgams out of central Aiylonia in all directions. Without the free flowing waters of the canals, there is nothing to keep them at bay."

She shook her head. The Ridge didn't officially demarcate Aiylonia's western border, but for many, it may as well have. Trade relied on the canals, and the canals ended where the slopes of the mountain range began. Going any further required overland travel, and while passing through the Ridge wasn't known to be particularly treacherous, it was a lot of effort for nominal gain.

According to the last official cartographer's report, a few collections of simple homesteads – none big enough to even be considered settlements – dotted the landscape. It was a good place to escape the notice of the Temple, and therefore an even better place to disappear. It made perfect sense that amalgams would have retreated west once the water levels rose. Now nothing would stop them from returning to their ancestral haunts.

When she looked back to Nel, they were making the sign of the helix, their head bowed in silent prayer. Something strange – almost comforting – stirred inside of her. Draya quickly averted her eyes, then hazarded a glance at Yllari. His body was more relaxed than that of the Aegis, but his eyes were closed in respectful accord. Draya shifted on her feet and turned her attention to the buildings surrounding the square. As she looked from door to door, some broken open, others tightly shut, a sense of foreboding rose up around her. A clank of armor signaled the end of the moment of piety behind her.

"Where is everyone?" Even at a whisper, Draya's voice cut through the eerie silence that blanketed the town.

"Let's find out," Nel answered from over her shoulder.

When no one answered their knocks on the chapel doors, the pair began their methodical investigation. Yllari, already weary from standing, took a seat on a low stone wall and watched their progress. After knocking on a few more intact doors and receiving no response, Draya finally convinced Nel to let her pick the lock of the milliner's shop only to find the interior adequately clean and nicely organized, the living quarters empty and the lock box gone. It felt as if the proprietor could return any moment, wondering why visitors had broken in. The buildings with missing doors were not much different. One by one, the pair steeled themselves as they crossed the open thresholds, each time expecting to find gruesome scenes of clotted blood and scraps of flesh. Instead, they'd found nothing more ghastly than the occasional dark stain against a wall or the floorboards. Even pieces of furniture – tables, chairs, trunks – were inconspicuously missing, leaving the ghosts of dusty outlines behind. If any of those homes had sported tapestries or rugs, they were nowhere to be seen.

Yllari leaned heavily against his staff. "Still nothing?" he called in through the ruined doorway of the meager boarding house.

Draya made her way out as he spoke, shaking her head.

Nel followed. "The door has been rendered thoroughly unsalvageable, and there is nothing substantial enough to blockade the entrance," the Aegis answered. "We could hole up on the second floor perhaps, but we'd be leaving the mule unprotected."

"We certainly can't do that to Tabitha." Yllari cast a look over his shoulder to the mule. They'd removed her harness and she was busily munching on the sparse crabgrass that seemed to serve as a town's central green.

"You named her?" Draya followed his gaze, pointedly avoiding his eyes. It was getting harder and harder to keep her face neutral as the dark threads of corruption licked up his throat.

"It didn't seem like either of you were going to," he replied with a shrug.

Draya shot an incredulous look in Nel's direction, but they were kneeling again, their attention preoccupied with another set of prints barely visible in the dirt. She looked to the horizon instead. One-half of the sun was still visible over the rolling hills. Daylight was fading fast.

"Assuming those things are coming back, we don't have any more time to waste." She looked back the way they'd come. "I still think we should try the chapel again."

Nel stood, their eyes roving over the hamlet. "The doors are secure."

Draya already had her lock picks in her hand. "They don't have to be."

"It is sacred ground," they said. "Breaching the boundary without invitation is forbidden."

"For a lay heathen like me, sure." Draya smirked. "But you're an Aegis! A Commander General, in fact. We just need a place to hide. If anyone would be pardoned –"

"She has a point, Nel," Yllari cut off her cynical prodding. "Worst case, blame me. I'm neither a heathen nor an Aegis – just a faithful parishioner in need of shelter." He smiled encouragingly.

Nel hesitated. Draya took that as agreement and strode toward the building before they could protest. The Aegis sighed, then took the reins of the mule and followed, Yllari limping close behind.

As quaint as the small temple was, the doors were heavy and bracketed with old iron. Now that she was paying attention, Draya saw that the metal was freckled with engravings she was certain weren't sanctioned by the Coronet. She didn't recognize the language, which could only mean the symbols were ritual rather than cultural. Whatever they were, the glyphs reeked of old magic. She wrinkled her nose but decided against mentioning it. Most likely, her companions knew more about strange writing than she did. *And if not, things are complicated enough.* Draya checked for traps, and finding none, knelt low enough that she was at eye level with the inlaid lock. She dutifully slipped on her leather gloves, and for the briefest of moments, she was overcome with the inexplicable urge to stop what she was doing and back away from the door. She blinked, and it was gone. *Nel must be hating this,* she reasoned before turning back to her work. Like the brackets, the fixture was old iron, but not so ancient to have become brittle. Brass designs highlighted the central keyhole, and she got to work, slipping the minuscule wrenches inside. She could feel Nel's apprehension hovering over her, the shadow of their readied shield looming at her feet.

"It's locked, Nel. I highly doubt you'll need to be armed against whatever terrified townspeople are holed up inside, if they haven't fled already." She felt around, slipping the picks into one tumbler after another. It wasn't a complex lock, but its age required a gentle touch. She didn't want to snag against a bit of rust and snap off the end of her tool. It would be more embarrassing than inconvenient if the Aegis had to break the door down.

After less than a minute, she heard a solid click from inside the latch. "There!" She stood and threw open the door in one smooth motion, proud of her record timing.

"Draya!" Nel pushed her aside, slipping their shield into the gaping doorway. She stumbled backward, catching herself before falling into Yllari.

"Sarding abyss!" she snapped. "What was that for?"

Their shoulders were tensed as they peered apprehensively into the murky darkness of the unlit sanctuary. Yllari tried to warn Draya off with a gentle hand on her shoulder. She bristled, but then the force of Nel's emotions crashed into her.

Fear, she realized. *Fear for...me?* Anyone else might have been humbled by their concern, but Draya scowled. She slipped out from under the mage's well-intentioned hand and stepped back into the threshold. Inside was dark, the meager light of dusk filtering through the thick glass of the windows. The air was heavy with decades of burned incense and an undercurrent of something familiar she couldn't quite place.

"I told you," she said. "Empty."

"You could not be sure of that," Nel said, their voice low. "You just flung open the door. You did not even give us a warning. What if –"

"What if nothing." Draya tried to brush their shield arm aside, but Nel held firm. "I don't need to be coddled."

Nel flinched. Yllari was inconspicuously quiet.

"As you wish," Nel finally said, lowering their arm.

They don't mean anything by it, she told herself as she slipped past. *Misplaced chivalry is etched into their bones.* In defiance of an ever so slight pang of guilt, she almost heedlessly trounced forward before thinking better of it. She scanned the immediate area for anything dangerous, be it intentionally placed or as a result of disuse. She held out an arm, this time barring Nel from moving forward. "Careful." She unhooked her lantern and lit the wick inside, fully aware of the hypocrisy. A flare of orange light illuminated the flagstones at their feet. She swiped her gloved forefinger through a dark substance smeared just inches from the door. "Blood," she confirmed, rubbing the dried flakes between her thumb and forefinger. "It's at least a day old, maybe more."

"So not nothing," Nel muttered.

Her nostrils flared, but she didn't give them the dignity of a response. On some level, she was impressed with their sudden show of petulance. She lifted the lantern only to find that the dried blood didn't pool at her feet but rather continued straight up the nave towards the altar at the far wall. The edges thinned, brush strokes visible in the lantern light, but that wasn't all. The metallic smell in the air suddenly made sense.

"Blessed Helix," Nel whispered in disbelief. Yllari sucked in an unsteady breath.

Draya stood, dusting her gloved hands off on her trousers as the taste of bile rose in her throat. "Well, we found the missing furniture at least."

30

The lantern light illuminated more than just a simple smear of blood along the aisle. Mismatched rugs and swaths of fabric draped the pews, stained and spewing trails of dried and drying viscera. Unidentifiable globs of dull pink flesh ran in channels along either side of the central aisle before them. Draya had spent hours rifling through human remains in charnel grounds and catacombs. She'd studied corpses of strangers and associates alike to better understand the traps and poisons that killed them. Nothing could have prepared her for this gruesome display. As she peered deeper into the darkness, she could make out more and more pieces of furniture, all of which she assumed had been removed from the homes they'd entered earlier. These, too, were slathered with gore. Ruined chairs, tables, and the remains of missing doors were piled to the right of the altar in a precarious wall, blocking the transept doors that led into the far rooms. Her senses told her it was a viable escape route, but her lizard brain was on fire. Every animal instinct inside of her screamed to retreat, to get as far away from the nightmarish tableau as she could. This wasn't just the remains of a massacre or even a hard-fought siege – it was a deliberate act of intimidation.

"Draya," Nel said her name with quiet urgency.

She looked down to find her feet had moved of their own accord. To her horror, she'd taken three steps forward through the matted blood without realizing it. This time, Draya stepped aside for the Aegis, glad not to face what lay ahead on her own. She looked over her shoulder at Yllari.

"Don't even say it." He swallowed down a look of disgust and squared his shoulders. His stance was unwavering, even as he used his staff as a crutch. "I'm not standing out here alone as the pair of you descend into whatever madness this is. I'm coming."

Draya bit back a retort. Under normal circumstances, she would have insisted he stay put. It wasn't purely for his own protection; an injured teammate was a liability that could get her killed. *But nowhere is safe once night falls,* she reminded herself. She flashed him a practiced grin. "To be fair, it wouldn't exactly be standing. Leaning maybe, sitting eventually, but definitely not standing."

Yllari squeezed his eyes shut and Draya worried she'd gone too far. Then the mage raised his fingers to his forehead and let out an exaggerated sigh. "You're more infuriating than Nel sometimes, you know that?"

"Watch it," she answered, glad for the brief moment of levity. "I don't take insults lightly."

"We should shut the door behind us," Nel said, ignoring the exchange. "Perhaps lock it back up as well."

Draya wrinkled her nose. "Are you sure? Without the key, I'd have to pick it all over again. Won't make for a quick exit if things go sideways."

"A price we have to pay, I wager. At least if we'd like to avoid any amalgams following us once the sun sets."

"I didn't peg you for a gambler," Draya quipped.

Nel stared at her blankly.

Yllari coughed into his hand. "She's referencing your use of the word wager, Nel."

Seeing the Aegis was still confused, Draya turned to the door. "Never mind. Fair point." She felt the tacky pull of the half-dried blood on her boots with each step she took.

"No, I'm closer. I've got it." Yllari teetered back a few paces and propped his staff up against the wall. "Just let me guide Tabitha inside." He wrapped his long fingers around the latch and then stopped, his eyes transfixed on something in the distance.

"What is it?"

A chorus of sinister howls answered her question.

"Sounds like a full pack; at least five waergs, as many as ten," Nel calculated.

"Oh good. Just what we need." Draya unsheathed her weapons.

"I would disagree. It would have been better if we'd had more time." Nel said, taking her words at face value. They turned their body sideways, readying their shield to defend against the door while their sword threatened the macabre scene further inside.

"That's not what I –" Draya shook her head in bewilderment, calling out to the mage instead. "Yllari – how far away are they?"

The mage stood frozen in place. The wolfish sounds crescendoed, followed by a high-pitched braying. "They're not far – I can see their silhouettes on the horizon," he replied, transfixed. He sighed with relief. "She broke free."

"What?" Draya asked impatiently.

"Tabitha. It's a good thing I never learned how to tie a proper knot – one tug and she was gone."

Draya didn't let the good news distract her. "Take that as a lesson then!" she shouted instead. "Slam that sarding door and get back here already!"

Yllari did as she said, closing the door shut the rest of the way and throwing the locking bolt back in place. He was about to lean against it in relief when the scraping sound of wood on stone pulled his eyes to the opposite wall. Draya followed his gaze. The barricade had been moved to reveal an open door containing the vague shape of a short figure.

"Well? What are you lot just standing there for?" It was a woman's voice, low and gruff. "Get your arses back here before you've got more than a few mutts to contend with!"

Whether due to their bonding or sheer common sense, Draya and Nel didn't need to share a glance to spin toward Yllari in unison. In a few long strides, the Aegis braced the door with their shoulder while Draya sheathed her weapons and quickly slipped an arm around the mage's waist.

"Staff!" Yllari called out as Draya propelled them forward.

Nel grabbed the weapon from its resting spot and tossed it flawlessly into Draya's waiting fingers. She half-carried Yllari to the barricade, pushing him through the narrow gap despite his protests. She thrust the staff into his hands. "Go!" she shouted. His lips pressed into a thin line, but after a beat he obeyed. As soon as he'd limped through to the waiting doorway, a deep-throated bellow sounded from somewhere outside. The amalgams were getting closer, and there were more than waergs out there. This time, she managed to lock eyes with the Aegis. "Get moving!" she demanded.

"Not yet," they shouted back. "I will buy us more time."

"Not from there you won't," the stranger said. She'd already escorted Yllari through the open door and had an arm outstretched to Draya. "They'll smell you through that door if they haven't already." She turned her attention back to Draya. "Broken or picked?" she asked.

It took her a second to make sense of the question. "Picked," she stammered.

The stranger shouted back to the Aegis. "Then lock the thrice-damned door back up and listen to your elder!"

Nel didn't question her this time. After checking the bolt, they rushed to the barricade, waving Draya through before squeezing between a dresser and a stack of wooden chairs. As they barreled over the threshold, the woman knocked one of the chairs over to hide the way they'd come before roughly slamming the door shut.

"Don't stop now," she chided. "The scent of dead blood only works if they don't get a glimpse of you." She rushed them across the vestibule and through a set of heavy doors, shutting them firm once all three were clear.

Counter to the sanctuary, the inner chamber was bright with flickering yellow firelight. Stout tallow candles of mismatched sizes covered every open surface, their melted wax spilling over in layers. Even the central worktable was bifurcated long-wise with candelabras and candlesticks. Above, the rafters were strung with dismantled pieces of brass lanterns and gold censers in need of repair. To the right was a tradesman's cabinet lined with tiny drawers, and to the left were a pair of benches pressed together into a makeshift bed.

Draya felt a slight pull towards the back of the room and craned her neck to look. A dull blue braided rug lay conspicuously on the floor in front of the hearth. *Secret door,* she assumed. *Good to know.*

Yllari fell heavily against the edge of the table beside her. His breathing was shallow and quick from the brief bout of strenuous activity. Nel tossed their armaments aside to take the mage's shoulders in both hands. Draya watched as they looked him up and down with the marked concern of a bear to its cub.

"I'm no worse for wear," Yllari reassured them. Nel pursed their lips, but stepped back, satisfied. The Aegis retrieved their shield and sword, returning both to their back. As if sensing her eyes on them, they glanced in Draya's direction, daring her to comment on the exchange.

She rolled her eyes in a show of indifference, but the unbridled emotional display did strike her as uncharacteristic. Aegii were lionized for their restraint; for self-discipline honed through rigorous training of their Calling. Either the truth fell short of the myth, or Nel wasn't the paragon their rank would infer.

She heard the crank of heavy gears and watched as the older woman lowered a formidable iron beam across the double doors, bolting it in place with the spin of a wheel. "These doors stopped the Great Deluge from breaching these rooms. It's going to take more than a few waergs to take it down now."

"There are more than waergs outside. We've already seen a female peryton – anything could have crossed the Ophidaen Ridge," Nel pointed out.

She gave the Aegis a withering look. "The beasts would have to cleave the chapel from stem to stern to get in here. If they can do that in so little time that we can't scuttle away, we might as well drink ourselves stupid and wait for the end."

"What is this place?" Draya interrupted as she turned to admire the cabinet. Each tiny drawer was identical to the last, differentiated only by a minuscule number handwritten beneath the handles.

"A workshop. Please don't touch that." The woman stepped forward, gently guiding Draya away from the cabinet.

"Of course," Draya replied. Now in the candlelight, Draya saw that the woman was on the far side of middle-aged, her face creased with laugh lines. She wore layers of gray homespun, and a silver helix rested gently against her clavicle. "I had no intention of –"

"I may be older than you, but I haven't lost my wits yet, child. Don't fault me for being wary of a lass that can pick a rune-scribed lock." Her strict eyes softened. "Edifier Nyombe Tayit," the woman announced to no one in particular.

"Draya." She resisted the instinctual urge to thoroughly case the room. "This is Ne– Aegis Sentinel, and that is Yllari." The armor made it impossible to obscure Nel's allegiances, but she'd let them decide whether to drop their title.

"I wish I could say it's a pleasure, but frankly I'll reserve my judgment for now." She looked about to say something else when Nel spoke up.

"When was a Conservator assigned to Invranid?" They sounded both confused and a little surprised.

Nyombe visibly stiffened. She opened her mouth to make a curt reply, but her shoulders quickly dropped. "One wasn't," she admitted with a sigh. "I'd planned out a whole explanation, but honestly the technicalities seem rather trivial. What's one unsanctioned Conservancy in the face of Occidrious's impending return?" She shrugged and then moved further into the room. Pulling two mugs and a small clay bowl from a cabinet near the hearth, she deftly filled each from a decanter of dark liquid. She returned with all three held expertly in one hand and placed them on the table. "There only be three mugs on this side of the nave, and one be mine. You all can decide who gets the soup bowl."

Nel and Draya eyed the proffered liquid suspiciously. Yllari shrugged and grabbed one of the mugs by the handle. He looked to his companions. "How much worse can things get?" He lifted the mug to drink, but Nel moved faster, shooting their palm out to block Yllari's lips from hitting the rim.

The woman pushed one hand into her hip. "If I'd been trying to poison you, why in the Twelve Names of the Tidal Eterna would I have saved your arses?"

Nel looked like they wanted to reply, but Yllari elbowed them in the side. Instead, the Aegis picked up the soup bowl, peered inside, and took a tentative sip. Their brow furrowed indiscernibly. "Interesting," they muttered, waving Yllari on.

As if more suspicious of Nel's response than the drink itself, he took a sniff and then threw back a large swig. His eyes went wide in surprise and he raised the mug to the woman in thanks. In one smooth motion, he drained half of the liquid. "What *is* this?" Remnants of the dark beverage stained his upper lip a deep reddish brown. He held out the second mug to Draya. "You need to taste this."

"Far be it for me to turn down a drink." She accepted the mug and peered inside. It was a thick slurry, too viscous to be wine. She looked between her two companions for confirmation, but Nel had already put down their bowl – untouched except for their single sip. Yllari nodded encouragingly.

"May wings take you home," she said, lifting the glass in a toast. She tipped the rim to her lips and let a few drops into her mouth. The velvety liqueur coated her tongue like cream, and notes of bitternut and tart fruit mingled together to form a complex but balanced concoction. She took a full swallow and smiled. "Not my usual libation, but this is rather special." Draya looked back at the bottle. There was no label on the stoppered glass. "You made it yourself?"

The woman chuckled, deepening the creases at the corners of her eyes. "Sadly no, but it is unique to Invranid – as far as I know anyway. An old family recipe of the Shepherd family. They call it Buckling Dark, an old joke about a century past its prime."

Yllari choked on his latest sip and held the mug away from his body. "Buckling...as in..."

"A baby billy goat, aye," she confirmed.

His complexion managed to pale even further. "Please tell me it's not fermented from...from the removed parts?"

The implication dawned on Draya, but unlike the mage, the prospect didn't bother her. She gave her mug a curious look. *I've drunk worse.*

"Of course, it's not — and you're thinking of a wether, not a buckling." The Edifier clicked her tongue. "But that's the joke, aye?"

"Then what is it?" Draya asked.

"The joke?"

"No, no. What's in the drink?" she clarified.

"Ah, yes. This and that." The woman filled a mug she'd unhooked from her wide belt. "Mostly walnut cream liqueur and a dash of fermented bramble berries. Story goes that Oren Shepherd's great-great-grandfather lost his flock for a day or three, and when the herd was found they were fat, happy, and a little tipsy – and a few months later his flock doubled. Accounting the virility of his bucks to the wild walnut grove and overripe berries he'd found there, he invented this recipe." She admired her shot before throwing it back and wiping her mouth with the back of her sleeve.

Yllari visibly relaxed. As he resumed drinking, Draya just cradled her mug between her palms. She hadn't eaten or drank enough in the last few days to trust her usually formidable constitution. Getting drunk with waergs at the door seemed like a bad idea even to her, and the prospect of a morning hangover even worse.

A pregnant silence filled the air between the four vastly different individuals. The tension grew too much for Draya. "So, you were saying about this...Conservancy?" She'd heard the word before but couldn't quite remember the context.

The Edifier tilted her head back. "It occurs to me now, that the three of you seem a strange group to have been sent by the Order." She looked Nel up and down. "If you weren't wearing that armor so well I'd wonder if you'd stolen it from the real Aegis General."

"I assure you, Edifier, I am exactly who I appear to be," Nel confirmed.

"Good." She looked to Draya and Yllari. "So, which of you is the Brightbourne, then?"

All three answered at once. "Neither," Draya and Nel said in unison as Yllari hooked a thumb in Draya's direction. Nel shot the mage an exasperated glare.

Draya spread out her arms in conciliation. "None of us. He was..." she tried to find the words. "He was incapacitated."

"By the Droughtbringer?" The woman's eyes cut into her accusingly.

Icy anxiety flooded Draya's core. "Something like that." She resisted the urge to stuff her red braid down the back of her tunic and deflected. "I have to ask – where is everyone? Why are you still here alone?"

"Why am I here? Definitely not with the Order then." She laughed sadly as she returned her attention to the hearth. The fire had dwindled, and she stirred the coals with a poker, making them pop. "The Aegis knows why."

31

Draya and Yllari turned to Nel in open confusion, but they merely stepped past them, all of their attention on the Edifier. "It remains here then?"

Nyombe gave Nel a resigned smile. "I hope I'd be relieved of my duties if it didn't."

Nel lowered their voice but failed to mask their eagerness. "You are familiar with the contents then?"

"Please, child. You may be my senior by rank, but not by years. What I don't remember verbatim, I know where to find."

"Excuse me," Draya finally said, looking between them. "What are you sarding talking about?"

The Edifier's eyebrows raised. "Some mouth on you, aye?"

A loud clatter caused both Draya and Nel to spin toward the noise, but she was more nimble. Draya rushed to Yllari's side as he lay slumped against the cabinet. The remaining liqueur was spilling from his fallen mug.

"He's still conscious," she announced with relief before directing her attention back to the mage. "What happened?"

Inky dark tendrils twined up his neck and splayed out across his cheekbones. "I...I don't know. There was a flare of pain – then my leg gave out from under me."

Draya's hands moved quickly to the site of his injury. She pulled the folds of his robes aside. The dressings were stained with a mix of sluggish blood and black ichor.

"Stupid boy," the Edifier chided gently. She knelt next to Draya and rolled up her sleeves. "Why didn't you say something? Liquor thins the blood. I saw you were limping, but I didn't know you were still bleeding."

Draya considered whether she should allow Nyombe a better look at the wound. She felt no apprehension radiating from the Aegis. "Yllari...?" She looked to him for approval.

He weakly waved away her concerns with long fingers. "I'll take any insight we can get."

With a nod, Draya carefully peeled the sodden bandage away from the mage's wound. Beside her, the Edifier sucked in a breath through her teeth. The size of the wound hadn't changed, but rather than a sickly gray, his entire calf was nearly solid black with the unnatural veining.

"You understand why coming here was our only recourse?" Nel asked. "We need to know how to treat whatever is happening to him."

She clucked her tongue, the pity clear in her eyes. "You might need more than an old librarian for that," she mused.

"Librarian?" Draya was confused. "Edifier, Conservancer, bartender. Who the abyss are you?"

"Lass – I'd imagine in all your years you are quite aware that a person can be more than one thing at a time." The woman continued before Draya could comment. "I am – either officially or unofficially – all three, and a few more besides. There is a reason Invranid is in the middle of nowhere. This small sleepy town is the best place to hide the Archive."

Draya's brow creased. She kept her expression neutral as she fought to slow her rapidly increasing heartbeat. "You cannot be referring to *the* Archive? The *Lost* Archive?"

"Well, not the whole thing," the Edifier clarified. "But I can assure you that at least this portion is certainly quite well accounted for."

"That's ridiculous," Draya scoffed. The idea was laughable. Unhinged, even. There was no way such an important repository could escape notice for so long this close to the Cimmrean Canal. She looked from Nyombe to Nel, but they remained stoic.

Yllari spoke up. "I suppose that does make sense." He closed his eyes and leaned his head back. "The 'lost' prefix was never exactly confirmed by the Coronet – I've never seen it in official writing, anyway." He smiled slightly, his eyes meeting Draya's in solidarity. "I am very impressed its continued existence escaped my knowledge, let alone our Archeologian here."

Draya felt her cheeks blush at the compliment. Of what she considered her many positive attributes, her scholarly competence was rarely appreciated.

Nel nodded. "Aside from the highest echelons of the Coronet, only the Aegii maintain records of the Archive's location. And even then –"

"Even then," Nyombe cut in, "I'm sure very few bother to retain the details. The Archive stopped being a priority some time ago. When it was first placed here – long before my time mind you – an Aegis under the guise of a common priest guarded the Archive's location. After a decade or two of that, one would check in once a month, then once a year. Finally, they just started assigning a layperson like me to the role." She stood and crossed to the back of the room. She swung open the doors of a supply cabinet and pulled out strips of clean linen and an amber vial. She returned and started redressing Yllari's wound, adding a few drops from the vial as she went. "It's why I had to do all this myself." She gestured to the workshop around them. "Without the aforementioned Aegis, there was no one to repair and restore our ceremonial objects. Broken bits and bobs no one felt right throwing away cluttered more space than the Archive itself. So, when none of my requests for aid were answered, I just...started doing it. Most townsfolk assumed I'd gotten permission and those who suspected otherwise kept quiet about it. What I can save, I restore. What I cannot, I consign to the depths of an underground river a league to the west." She finished dressing the wound and sat back on her heels.

"Was that...was that it?" Yllari's eyes went wide as he touched his leg. "I'm cured?" He lifted his shin off the ground without a wince of pain.

"What, this?" The Edifier shook the small vial in her hand. "Don't get yourself too excited. It's just a numbing agent. You still don't want to put much weight on that leg, but at least you'll be able to sleep without tossing and turning all night."

Visibly disappointed, Yllari rearranged his robes and let Draya help him to his feet. "Well, thank you regardless, Edifier Tayit."

"Just Nyombe is fine. And it's the least I can do," she answered. "And I mean that – there are jugs of this stuff in storage. We trade the Buckling Dark with our neighbors for tinctures."

Draya rubbed a hand across her forehead. "This is all well and good," she grumbled. "But what does the Archive have to do with Yllari's wound? Why does the sanctuary look like an amateur butchery? And I'll ask again – where is everyone?" She threw a glance back at the way they had come. The sight of all that blood and gore was still fresh in her mind.

The Edifier stood and turned to Nel. "Is she always this ornery?"

They shrugged. "I wouldn't know. We only just met a few days ago." They pressed their lips together in a thin line.

Nyombe tapped her chin thoughtfully. "A few days, hmm? And I assume the Aegis Commander General had been at their usual post on the Radiant Sea?"

"Yes, I was," Nel answered cautiously.

Nyombe chuckled as she pushed herself to her feet. "One Creeping Drought. One Aegis to the Brightbourne. One well-dressed boy I sincerely doubt is the Chosen One." Her hawk-like eyes narrowed in on Draya. "And one redhead with a temper."

Draya stiffened. "I don't have the faintest idea what you're implying. You'd have a temper too after the last few days we've seen."

The Edifier placed a patronizing hand on her shoulder. "Of course dear." She tapped the side of her nose. "I should have anticipated you lot stopping by." She suddenly turned and strode to the rug Draya had noticed earlier. She pulled it away, revealing a circular trap door secured with a locking mechanism.

Nel gave Draya a look she easily translated. She nodded, affirming her knowledge of its existence.

"And as for the...redecoration, well, it's a precaution," Nyombe continued. "Folk tradition teaches that the blood of livestock killed by an amalgam will protect a home from future attacks – muddy up its senses and hide the scent of the living. Let's just say I used what they left behind and hoped for the best." The woman pulled a large ring of iron keys from her belt and picked through them.

"So it's all animal remains?" Draya asked.

"I didn't say that," Nyombe answered vaguely. She found the key she wanted and slipped it confidently into the waiting keyhole. She turned it until there was a click, then looked up to Nel. "Help an old lass out?"

Accustomed to grunt work, Nel wrapped their gauntleted hands around the iron ring, spun the door halfway around, and then lifted it clear of the casement. The Edifier then moved to the hearth and pulled at a decorative bar of wood that traveled under the mantle. The false lintel came free, revealing itself to be the outside edge of a thin ladder twice the height of the old woman.

"Trick ladder? Really?" Draya remarked.

"The Coronet does not perform half measures. As I said, they once genuinely cared about the safety of the Archive. Watch your heads." The Edifier didn't wait for a reply before she spun the ladder, prompting Nel to dodge out of its path in surprise. She tipped one end into the hole in the floor and let it drop into the darkness. There was a muffled thud then two clicks as she secured the top rung in place just below the threshold. She almost started down but then padded her pockets and, finding them empty, grabbed a box of matches from the mantle. "Well let's go. The boy's wound isn't getting any better just standing here." Nyombe made her descent.

The pull from the secret passage was even stronger now. Draya waited to hear the older woman's feet hit the floor, then proceeded after her.

"I think I'll stay here," Yllari said. He was back on his feet and leaning against the center table again. "Our host may have numbed the wound, but as she said, not a cure. Best I steer clear of ladders for the time being."

"Wise decision!" The Edifier's voice boomed from below them.

Nel nodded. "Understood."

Draya paused and almost shot the mage a concerned look, but stopped herself at the last second. *He's not your responsibility,* she reminded herself. *This is just another job – stay professional.* She knew that wasn't true, but it was getting harder to convince herself to maintain distance from her new companions. She continued down, step after step, glad when she was finally below floor level and hidden from view. She didn't want them to see the emotions playing out on her face.

The bright flash of a struck match startled Draya as her boots hit the naked earth. The flame sizzled as Nyombe lit lanterns on either side of the ladder, illuminating the storeroom surrounding them. Dust and cobwebs shrouded a handful of wooden crates and overturned barrels. The far wall was lined with shelves from floor to ceiling, but all they contained were the remains of a pantry reserve. Jars of every type and size were gathered in haphazard groups, their dark contents indiscernible. Only one conspicuous square of shelves near the far right wall looked recently stocked. The preserves there were bright berry reds, dark beet purples, and pickled green, the glass containers sparkling clear.

Draya took a step further into the room, clearing the way just in time for Nel to land heavily behind her. "You said you were in possession of the Archive." Their apprehension reverberated in Draya's gut, souring her stomach.

"Indeed I did," the Edifier said. She faced the pair. "What do you think, Draya dear? Am I dumb enough to lure two well-trained warriors into a basement unarmed and alone, or am I telling the truth?"

<Clever woman.>

The Voice was back.

Draya wrinkled her nose but stayed silent. Focusing on the problem at hand, she turned to the wall behind them. The seam of a door practically glowed. She scanned the stones at waist height until she spotted a hidden latch tucked in the mortar. Draya stopped herself from reaching out, instead searching the floor and ceiling. She didn't see signs of any obvious traps, but it wasn't worth the risk. She turned to face the old woman.

"Go on, then." Nyombe waved her forward. "You'll be fine."

Deciding to trust the woman's words, she pressed a finger up and under the brick facade until she felt a small square of stone give way. With a loud clunk, the hidden door swung inwards on well-oiled hinges. The small room inside was impressively built, every space filled with an array of shelves and cubbies shaped to hold any manner of book, scroll, or tablet.

"See? As I said, the Coronet does not perform half measures. Excuse me." Nyombe's eyes beamed with satisfaction as she sidled between the pair.

Draya's heart sank as she and Nel exchanged identical looks.

The shelves were empty.

32

Well, not completely empty, Draya amended.

Barely a fourth of the wooden compartments contained anything at all, and no single shelf was full to capacity. The Edifier ran her fingers along a few spines at waist height and glanced reverently at a honeycombed wall to the left. There was but a single row of scrolls in what could have housed twenty times their number. Draya pursed her lips and tried to look pleased with the meager hoard. Nel nodded politely and followed her lead.

"Aye, yes. Here it is."

As Nyombe turned, Draya held her breath. She'd grown up on the legends of the Lost Archive and the secrets it contained. Even if the selection was small, the tomes left had to be the most desired – a distillation of knowledge, not a decimation.

At least she hoped that was the case.

The book in Nyombe's hands wasn't enormous, nor was the cover bejeweled or delicately embossed. It was simple and thin, more like a pamphlet than a tome, sloppily bound in rough leather hide. Even the title of the book was obscured, crookedly handwritten in heavy black ink across the front. Draya's performative smile only dimmed for a moment, but Nyombe noticed nonetheless. She clucked her tongue. "Don't tell me you're judging this wee book by its cover," she chided.

Draya begrudgingly accepted what was offered and peeled back the brown leather. The leaves inside were impressively thin, the vellum nearly transparent. The minuscule script that flooded the pages was a sharp contrast to the handwriting on the cover. She turned back and squinted at the title until she could make out the letters: *Lewedrin's Enchiridion of Fauna*. Draya's eyes went wide in disbelief. "Lewedrin? As in Cosmi Lewedrin?" She tried and failed to hide the excitement in her voice.

The Edifier answered with a satisfied grin.

Even more carefully than before, she leafed through the first few pages. Blocks of cramped handwriting were accompanied by perfectly preserved sketches of creatures large and small. Despite the lack of headings and dates, it was clear the author's journal started in the south and circumambulated northward.

"You know it?" Nel stretched their neck over Draya's shoulder, somehow managing to keep a respectable distance between them at the same time.

"Of course I know it." Draya couldn't peel her eyes away from the text long enough to cast them an incredulous look. She turned page after page without reading, as if the book could dissolve in her hands at any moment and she needed to absorb as much of it as she could. She was two-thirds of the way through before she stilled, her blood running cold. A rearing creature glared back at her from the center of the page. It had deep-set eyes, the horns of a goat, and the flattened snout of a warthog.

"What is it?" Nel looked between Draya and the page with a furrowed brow. "You recognize that creature, I can feel it."

Draya nodded and passed the book back to Nel, allowing them a better look. "In the Palace." When they gave her an odd look, she elaborated. "There was a stuffed one in some kind of trophy room. The Loatrin logograms beneath translated to "Beloved" – I think it was the Undying's pet." As ugly as it was, the taxidermied amalgam hadn't fazed her. Even when she ran her fingers through its coarse hair for the Sarcophilum, it was more an object than a once-living animal. But there was something viscerally terrifying about the way Lewedrin had captured the creature's likeness.

The Aegis ran a gloved finger gently down the page, stopping at a line of text that stood out in capital letters. "Elotragos," they read, lifting the book closer to one of the wall sconces for a better look. "This goat-hog hybrid is the rarest subspecies of amalgams so far recorded. It is believed to have an origin in Loatra, which would account for its elusivity. This particular memory was acquired from a young man named Whalen Fisher two days after his death." They looked up in surprise. "This Lewedrin – they possessed the Calling of Advocation?"

"A Death Witness, yes. A very proficient one," Nyombe answered. "It is said they could recover almost a full day of memory from the remains of the deceased, even days after decay had set in." She turned back to the meager library and pulled a much larger tome from its place on the shelf. "This might help as well."

Draya had to swing her arms out to catch the heavy weight of the book. The sage green cover was embossed with spiral knot work, the lambskin as supple and soft as it must have been when it was bound to its pages at least seventy-five years ago. The tome was in meticulous condition, well cared for with the reverence it deserved.

Draya smiled eagerly. *This is more like it.*

"It's an early history of Aiylonia," the Edifier continued, affirming the Archeologian's assumption. "If I recall correctly, in addition to contemporary reports on the amalgams, tidbits of Droughtbringer prophecies and the nature of the Undying One's entrapment are buried in there. I can't recall the precise chapters though."

Draya shrugged in an attempted bluff. "Why would you think we'd want that?"

Nyombe returned a withering look. "Just a hunch," she said dryly.

"You've read it yourself, then?" Nel asked, diffusing the awkward direction of the exchange.

"I'm a librarian dear. I need to know what is useful information to whoever arrives to use the Archive. I admit it's been some time since I did so and even longer since anyone has come looking, but this old brain still retains the most important details." She tapped her temple with her finger before stacking a much thinner hardback on top of the growing pile. "And this is its accompanying commentary and annotations. Caetra is a bore, but it might point you in a few right directions."

Draya cursed herself for being so starstruck. *Sarding amateur – get yourself together.* The history book was old enough to be nameless – likely recorded for posterity rather than recognition by one of the dead religious sects that once roamed the kingdom. But Lewedrin and Caetra – the only reason anyone even knew who they were was through the writings of later historians. They were quoted everywhere, but no one had found an original copy of the texts for decades.

Except that isn't true, Draya reminded herself. *The Order has kept these texts under lock and key for decades.* Knowing as much filled her with resentment. Rather than help construct a proper accounting of the last century, they'd hidden the texts away, and it was clear the Archive itself had seen better days. Her mind spiraled with questions for the Edifier, but she bit her tongue. None of the questions would help Yllari. They had no idea what would happen now that the infection had spread past his leg.

"May we remove these tomes from this..." Nel paused, searching for the right word. "...sacred alcove?"

Nyombe nodded. "Aye, but they must stay inside the Temple."

"Why's that? Some kind of old magic?" Draya asked despite herself. She'd already been devising a way to sneak the *Enchiridion* out of Invranid.

Nyombe gave her a sideways glance as if reading her ill intent. "Because I'm their caretaker and I said so."

Draya nodded but noted the lack of confirmation.

"Understandable," Nel said. She wasn't sure whether they sensed her machinations through the bonding or just understood her proclivities the old-fashioned way, but the Aegis gently pulled Draya back out into the outer room of the basement.

Nyombe gave her a final suspicious glare but then shook her head, her expression returning to the more neutral state of someone used to being listened to. "Go ahead now. Light's best up in the workshop. I normally sleep there myself, but I'll give you some space. I'll rest in the rectory off to the side. There is a reasonably comfortable rug under the desk."

Draya started for the ladder and then turned. "Where will we sleep?" she asked.

Nyombe eyed the stack of books they were holding. "Oh lass, I doubt you'll find the time for any of that now."

Nyombe's words rang true.

Searching the books for information was a tedious affair. The Enchiridion had no index. According to a note scribbled on the inside cover, the loose pages had been bound not by the author, but by a well-meaning apprentice before its placement in the Archive. Apparently, it was Lewedrin's actual field notes – the first draft of what he would later transcribe into the more polished final edition. The unnamed history was broken into sections, but the titles were flowery and abstract, referring to archaic anecdotes not even Draya had committed to memory. Only Caetra's Commentary had both a table of contents and an index, but at a certain point, it was impossible to know what words would be worth searching for. Working their way through the books was like picking needles out of long-decayed haystacks.

What they knew for sure was sparse: First, amalgam bites had a draining effect on the victim's life force. This prevented the wound from healing properly. Second, the above typically didn't matter – the placement of the bites was generally fatal, preventing anyone from studying a cure.

The candles were burning low when a few crucial words caught Draya's attention. She rubbed her blurry eyes and pulled a candle closer as she reread Lewedrin's tiny handwriting.

"You found something?" Nel asked, reading her change in posture. They settled a ribbon between pages of Caetra's Commentary.

"Not just something. I found the – oh sarding abyss!" She slammed a palm on the tabletop, making the candle flames bounce and flicker. "The cure calls for an entire tub of saltwater!"

A groan rose from the other side of the room as Yllari stirred in his sleep. He'd made a valiant effort to assist in the research, but it didn't take much persuading to coax him into the makeshift bed after an hour or so. Draya went silent, watching his chest rise and fall steadily. Assured he was still asleep, she continued in a lower voice. "Caetra was positive no one studied cures, right?"

"Right. He noted that there were never enough test cases to perform proper experiments." Nel looked towards Yllari themself, then moved to a seat closer to Draya.

"Exactly – people died too quickly." Draya turned the thin vellum page for the Aegis to see. After visiting the Archive, Nel had removed their armor, polished it clean of dirt and grime, and prayed in the neighboring rectory. It was strange seeing them like this, the natural silhouette of their broad shoulders freed from the bulk of their pauldrons. They almost appeared vulnerable except for the rigid state of their spine, stock straight as if they still wore their breastplate. Some people hid behind their attire. Nel embodied their armor, its essence protecting them even from its resting place across the room. They pulled in close enough for Draya to pick up the scents of incense smoke and earthy linseed oil that still clung to their tunic.

"But things were different this time," she continued. "The wounds were small, non-fatal on their own even though the draining effect would eventually claim their lives. The bites were from some kind of rodent hybrid that had infested one of the northern towns. They tried exterminating the creatures, but the villagers were still losing their life force. It was like the amalgams were merely the delivery method of the curse or disease or whatever. The actual source was something else." She pointed to a line of words scribed into the margins, half hidden in the book's sloppy binding. "But they found a cure, see?" She pulled at the creases, gently trying to reveal the text without ripping the delicate material.

Nel pulled a second candle closer. "It's an ingredient list – a cure?"

Draya nodded at the confirmation of her findings but then slumped back into her seat in defeat. "But it must be a Cresting Tide rite or something. We could get the rest of the materials from Nyombe, but that much water? We'd have better luck catching a tailwind with a gill net."

"Not necessarily."

Draya and Nel looked up to see Nyombe in the doorway to the rectory. She was dressed in a sleeping shift, a candlestick in one hand.

"There might be one place the Drought hasn't hit just yet."

33

"She was further away than I'd anticipated." Nel strode to the town's central green, Tabitha's bridle in one hand and the remains of her tether in the other.

Draya looked up from the overturned wagon at the sound of their voice. Something large had trampled the back axle, and one of the wheels lay in pieces a few strides away. She'd scratched out the remains of the Hawkers' Mark and had been salvaging what she could of the interior, but there wasn't much there to begin with. "I just assumed you abandoned us." She stood, dusting her hands off on her trousers.

Nel stopped short where the dusty street met dying grass. "How could you say that? I would never —"

"She's kidding, Nel." Yllari cut in from his perch on a low stone wall. He smiled at the mule. "Where was she?"

"She was nibbling remnants of clover half a league north." They gestured to the tiny scratches that looped around her legs. "She must have run through some thorn bushes, but no debilitating injuries. I suspect the thorns are what kept her hidden and safe – that or the amalgams prefer human prey to animal.

"Human prey," Draya repeated. "I can't say I like those two words up against each other like that."

"I'd be worried if you did," Yllari said lightly. "Either way, I'm glad the old girl is alright."

Nel led Tabitha to a hitch and checked the knot of their tether twice to be sure. "How are things here?"

Draya kicked at the remains of the wagon wheel. "Dreadful. We aren't getting anywhere in this pile of kindling, that's for sure."

"Which is rather unfortunate for me." Yllari dug his staff into the hard soil and pulled himself to his feet. The infection was seeping into his joints, weakening the knee above his wound. He was forced to lean into his healthy leg as wooden splints kept the joints rigid. "I can't even walk the length of the temple nave without assistance. Are we sure there's nothing else we can use in this sorrowful little hamlet?"

"Nyombe said the surviving townsfolk took anything in good repair with them the morning after the attack, and it would take a day or two to fix whatever bits and pieces they left behind." Draya threw the sack of odds and ends she'd scavenged over her shoulder. It was disappointingly light.

Nel nodded. "Unfortunate, but very sensible of the townsfolk."

"Nel, can I get your help with something over here?" Draya gestured vaguely at the wagon behind her.

"Of course," they said. "Whatever you need."

When the pair reached the back of the wagon, Draya dropped from the mage's sight line. Confused, Nel crouched beside her. "What do you think?" Draya asked, raising her voice to be sure Yllari could hear. "Can we use that?"

Nel frowned. They looked at the bare backboard and then back to Draya. She widened her eyes expectantly, suddenly concerned the Aegis might be too guileless to get the hint.

Holding eye contact, Nel mimicked her volume. "I'm not sure. We should take a closer look."

Draya nodded and leaned in close enough to feel the heat radiating off Nel's armor. Their time in the sun couldn't have been very comfortable if the metal still hadn't cooled. *Is that why Aegii all have the Calling of Will? So they can withstand living their entire lives in that ostentatious armor?* "We — I mean Yllari doesn't have a few days to wait," she whispered. "Nyombe says that black slime is spreading at increasing speed."

"It is a corruption of some type, possibly eldritch. And it is technically a very deep indigo."

Their correction was more informative than condescending, but it still challenged Draya's patience. "Excuse me, I forgot to bring my book of swatches along to compare shades."

Their lips pressed into a thin line. "Tabitha," they decided, ignoring her retort. "She can easily hold his weight."

"And we just...walk? What about our supplies?" Draya thrust a hand into the sack and rifled around.

"We can manage with what we can carry." Nel's eyes narrowed suspiciously as Draya pulled out a pair of iron bow shackles. "Where...where did you get those?"

"Why does it matter?" She banged the shackle against the backboard, hoping the sound sufficiently simulated prying iron from old wood.

"Did Edifier Tayit give those to you?" they pushed.

"What are you on about? Do you think I just took them from her workshop?" She dropped one shackle on top of the other and smiled at the satisfying clang. Nel's silence was telling. "Of course, I didn't," she said, annoyed that she had to explain herself. "One of the derelict carriages had a small skiff hooked up to the rear. Considering the circumstances, I didn't think they'd need to secure the sails anytime soon."

"That's rather callous of you, is it not?"

Draya bristled. "It's just the truth, isn't it?"

They shook their head. "Yes, I imagine so, but –"

"But what?" she interrupted, her voice rising defensively. "But it's *my* fault the skiff is useless? It's *my* fault the water is gone? Is that what you're trying to say?" Abandoning the charade, she stood abruptly and slammed the shackles against the backboard in frustration.

Nel rose to their full height. Any closer and their breastplate would be pressed against Draya's unarmored chest. It was meant to be an intimidating posture, but it had no effect on her. She was used to standing off against all manner of opponents. Despite her upbringing, despite her namesake, it was something she had to do time and time again to prove she belonged in the Guild. Compared to some of her less than reputable colleagues, Nel was a house cat.

"*I'm* not to blame for this," she said, pressing her finger against the polished gold plate. "*I'm* not the one who kept the truth of the prophecy a secret. *I'm* not the one who put up some stupid maze around a fragile prison cell inside a veritable goldmine hoping it wouldn't attract fortune seekers. For Rook's sake, *I'm* not the one who created this sarding curse to begin with!"

Nel's nostrils flared. "You are the Droughtbringer – you cannot deny your destiny any longer. Your actions were the catalyst for what has befallen the people of Aiylonia. Had you not entered the Palace; had you not been so eager to plunder its antiquities; had you simply made less selfish choices and followed a less unsavory profession –"

Draya heard enough. "First of all, I never asked to be part of your sarding prophecy. Your precious Coronet didn't even find me! How was I supposed to know I was the Dawn Harbinger?"

"Harbinger of Eternal Dust," the Aegis corrected. "Or the Desolate Dawn."

"Seriously? That's your response?" She glared up at them, vaguely aware of a growing ache where the cuff met the flesh of her wrist. "Whatever," she spat. "You want to question my choices? That's rich coming from you, *Aegis Commander General Sentinel*. At least I made choices. Your whole identity was manufactured by the Temple through indoctrination and isolation. I had a path laid out for me, and I *chose* not to follow it into a gilded cage. I've lived my own life, on my own terms."

"Yes," Nel said in a low voice. Their eyes went deadly cold. "And you can see what devastation that has wrought."

Their condemnation burned into Draya. She took a step back, unsure if she was seething with anger or drowning in guilt. Despite her words to the contrary, she knew her shoulders bore the weight of the Creeping Drought and its myriad horrors. It had only been a few days, and already the bodies were piling up around her. *What will happen in a week? In a month? In a year, will there even be anything left of Aiylonia at all?* She balled her fists at her sides, refusing to buckle in the face of such a dismal future. She was about to channel her frustrations into some truly cutting insults when her thoughts were interrupted.

<That isn't exactly how destiny works, is it? One cannot choose their fate; only what actions one takes when confronted by its realities.>

"ENOUGH!" Draya released her rage into the empty sky for lack of a better target. "Get out of my head!"

Nel glowered. "Unless you know a way to break our Bonding – or even less likely, my subdermal sigiling – I'm afraid we are stuck with one another."

"I'm not talking to you!" she barked. Draya pressed the heels of her palms into her temples.

"Draya?" Yllari asked. He'd been uncomfortably quiet during the shouting match, but now he shuffled towards the pair. "If not Nel – and presumably not me – who *are* you talking to?"

She looked up in alarm, suddenly aware of her outburst. "It's nothing." She lowered her hands from her head and grabbed the shackles.

Nel's shoulders relaxed, anger melting into concern. "Even without our Bonding, I would know that to be a lie."

Draya pushed past the Aegis, shoving the shackles into the sack. "Never mind. Let's get that map and the ritual supplies from Nyombe and get the abyss out of here. With any luck, we'll get to the pools before sundown." Nel clamped a gauntleted hand on her shoulder as she passed, stopping her in her tracks. "I said it's nothing. Let me go." She shrugged off their hand. She almost hoped they'd resist and give her an excuse to keep yelling, but their hand just fell away.

"Draya." Pain radiated from Yllari's eyes with every step. "A friend once told me that there is a murky place where the riddles of prophecy end and the stark truths of reality begin. I suspect we're treading water in that unknown now. Every piece of the puzzle matters – especially when it comes to you."

She squeezed her eyes shut. "I just told you – I don't want anything to do with any of this."

"Regrettably, I don't think that's an option anymore," he replied. "All things considered, I doubt it ever was."

The embers of Draya's anger winked out, leaving her feeling hollow. She sighed in defeat. "There has been a Voice in my head. I don't hear it often, but every once in a while, it's there."

Yllari leaned forward. "What kind of voice?"

"I don't know – an annoying one."

"Are you hearing it right now?" Nel asked.

"What?" Draya didn't trust their sudden gentleness. "No, I mean, it said something before, but it's silent again."

"What did it say?" Yllari asked.

"Something about choice and destiny." She narrowed her eyes at Nel. "That it was fate – not my choices – that brought us here."

They flinched at the rebuke.

"Interesting – that means the source of this Voice is aware of your present circumstances." Yllari pushed ahead. "When did they start talking to you?"

"After I escaped the treasury." She closed her eyes, trying to recall the moment in detail. Already it felt so long ago. "I was trapped. The tunnels I took into the labyrinth were flooding and I didn't know where to go. Just as I...as I was sure I was going to die in that tomb...the Voice spoke. 'This is not your end,' it said. And then, I don't know, I saw how to get out. It wasn't just instinct like it usually is. I literally saw a path leading me to safety. I followed it to a hidden door and a narrow staircase to the surface." Draya side-eyed Nel. "Where I was met with a blade to my face."

Yllari raised an eyebrow. "Really, Nel?"

They cleared their throat. "In my defense, I had watched Jierdan leave by that route not long before."

Yllari considered this. "And without him with her, you assumed the worst. Which wasn't exactly far off." He turned back to Draya. "This all happened after the Brightbourne dove into the Vault, correct?"

As soon as Draya nodded, something blossomed in Nel. "Do you think...?"

"It's possible." The mage shrugged.

"What's possible?" Draya looked between them. "That he's in my head? Are you saying your hallowed Brightbourne not only forced this sarding cuff on me, he invaded my mind too?" Draya seethed with renewed rage.

"The circumstances are unprecedented," Yllari replied. "There are no records of a Brightbourne transferring their Bonding to anyone – even another candidate for their role. I have no idea what the resulting effects might be."

"Great." Draya pulled away and began trudging back to the chapel. It wasn't Yllari's fault – it wasn't Nel's either – but she couldn't look at them right now. It was all too much. She was halfway to the doors when she heard heavy footfalls at her heels. She slowed her steps and Nel fell into pace beside her.

"I'm sorry," they said. "I was harsh. He is right. The Drought was fated to occur. The Coronet always warned us that it could come any time, but I guess...I guess I just never imagined it would be during my lifetime, let alone my tenure as Aegis to the Brightbourne."

Draya kept quiet, her eyes on the spiraling helix carved into the lintel above the entryway. She appreciated Nel's words, but they didn't ease the tumult of emotions waging war inside her.

"Can you ask him?" Their plea was quiet, almost shy.

"We don't know it's Jierdan," she said. "It doesn't even have a pitch of its own. It just sounds like me."

"Right, but – can you ask anyway?"

Draya stopped her march and turned to the Aegis. "And what if it is him?" she asked. "What would that mean?"

They looked past her towards the horizon. "I don't know."

Draya took an unsteady breath. "It may not answer, you know."

They nodded. "I understand."

Glad one of us does. "Fine." Draya closed her eyes and tried her best to center herself. She felt utterly ridiculous. "Um, strange Voice? I'm sorry I yelled. Can you – can you tell us who you are? Are you the Brightbourne Jierdan?" she asked at last. She repeated the question again and again in her mind. By the time Yllari and Tabitha caught up, Draya had given up.

The Voice, whoever or whatever it was, felt no compulsion to answer.

34

The mouth of the cave glimmered in the afternoon sun, thick points of crystal dripping like opalescent fangs from the ceiling. Further inside, the multi-faceted outcroppings hung so low they nearly touched the white stone stalagmites growing from the floor. It was brighter than a cavern had any right to be – countless garlands of burnished brass coins reflected the sun's rays into the corners and illuminated the beautiful space. Just outside, a neatly appointed cottage stood with the words 'Welcome to the Pools of Pearl' written in block letters above the ticket window. The blown glass shutters were closed tight, but a menu of services hung alongside. The cave entrance ahead was ineffectually blockaded by a gate in a low iron fence.

"Pearl?" Nel asked. "Edifier Tayit said it was filled with milk quartz."

Draya huffed. "Creative license, I suppose. You see that a lot with places like this."

"Not many 'm' or 'q' words to satisfy the heavy-handed alliteration, are there? Quarry of Quartz and Moat of Milk don't sound nearly as appealing." Despite his smile, Yllari's coughing fits had ground his voice down to a rasp.

Nel looked unconvinced.

Draya strode up to find that the twisted iron gate only came up to her waist. "Seems a little superfluous don't you think?" She shook the padlocked chain.

Yllari swung one unsteady leg over the mule's back. Before he could attempt the dismount on his own, Nel was at his side with an offered hand. Tabitha chuffed lightly but otherwise made no complaints as they both walked her to a patch of dying grass. As she leaned her head down to her meager meal, the Aegis swung the saddlebags of salt over their shoulder. "What are you doing?" Nel asked in disapproval.

Draya looked back, having already hopped over the fence at its lowest point. "Getting inside?"

Yllari leaned against Nel as the pair hobbled to the ticket window. The Aegis rapped a knuckle against the shutter. After a few moments of silence, they turned back to Draya. "It costs three copper per entrant."

"Five if you want to use the communal baths," Yllari added as he peered at the menu. "Not completely unreasonable for a pilgrim trap, I guess."

"If it still has water, it's worth a lot more." When Nel didn't move, Draya retreated a step in their direction. "Are you coming...?"

"We should check inside the cottage, in case the proprietor is only asleep," Nel said with a touch of concern.

Draya huffed out a breath. "There's an empty stable down the hill, it's quiet as the grave, and the window is shuttered. If there ever was a caretaker, they must have fled with one of the passing caravans already."

"Their absence doesn't invalidate the fee," they said.

She was about to make a retort when Yllari caught her attention with a subtle head shake. His face was gaunt, his eyes sunken and bruised. A deep unnatural purple rimmed his eyes and colored his lips. "I'll take care of it," he said as he reached into a pouch on his belt. The mage set a few coins on the window ledge.

Nel glanced one more time at the abandoned cottage, then led Yllari to the gate. Together, the pair were able to hoist him over without jarring his injury too much. The Aegis vaulted over after him and they started along a winding path carved into the rock floor. It gradually sloped downward and when the ground leveled out Draya realized the wide entrance was hidden from view.

Great, we lost the high ground. She hadn't noticed anyone tailing them, but her knowledge of amalgams was less than ideal. *And don't forget the brigands and opportunists that come hand in hand with tragedies and disasters,* she thought grimly. She tried to discern an alternate exit, but nothing manifested. She was resigning herself to discomfort when the path opened up into a cavernous grotto.

"It's like being inside a geode," Yllari whispered.

Draya agreed. All around them, veins of milky quartz sparkled like diamonds in eruptions of towering crystal. The brass garlands of reflected sunlight had followed them along the path, and now the rays bounced from facet to facet, bathing the space in filtered white light. In the center was a shallow depression filled with water so clear it was nearly invisible, the tranquil surface extending further and further into the darkness beyond.

Draya's tongue felt like sandpaper against her parched lips.

"I never thought I'd be this happy to see glorified bath water," Yllari said, voicing her thoughts.

Fighting her base instincts, Draya conscientiously looped her arm around Yllari's waist to take on his weight. Together they slowly moved to the water's edge and knelt beside it. Up close, the pool was clearly not a natural marvel. The large basin had been carved into the white rock floor, its sinuous veins of quartz sanded smooth along the bottom. Draya cupped some water in her hands. The temperature was so close to the surrounding air that she could barely feel it between her palms. From her experience with other therapeutic springs, she expected the rotten smell of sulfur or even damp clay. Instead, it was as odorless as it was clear. She took a tentative sip and looked to Yllari in surprise.

"Well?" he asked. "Will it bring me even closer to death?"

She gave him a chastising look. "I don't think so, but did you know that 'clear' was a flavor?" When he gave her a puzzled look, Draya grabbed Yllari's water skin and thrust it under the surface with her own.

He gulped it down as soon as she handed it back and managed a weak laugh. "It's probably the natural filtering of the rocks. But in any case, it would be delicious even if we weren't withering away from dehydration."

Her stomach soured. *Some of us are withering away from something worse.*

There was a thump behind them as Nel had unslung the saddlebags. They eyed the pool suspiciously. "I can't imagine this is enough salt."

In perfect synchronization, Draya reached up and accepted Nel's waiting waterskin. She'd already filled it and was handing it back before she'd recognized the exchange even occurred. By the look on Nel's face, they were just as confused by the unspoken exchange but didn't comment. Instead, they took slow sips of water and looked out over the pool.

Draya stood and searched the periphery of the cavern, patently ignoring the unsettling way she and Nel acted in tandem. "What are those?" She pointed to a series of alcoves cut into the walls to the left and right. The interiors of only a few were visible from her position, but those each housed a small pool perfectly sized for an individual bather. *Or a rather intimate couple,* Draya thought. She kept the observation to herself.

"Private baths," Yllari confirmed. "Of course – this is just the communal pool the sign mentioned. It's for simple ablutions, purification rites, that sort of thing. Those pools must be what pilgrims pay the real coin for."

Nel looked back to the bags of salt. After taking another long draw from their waterskin, they refilled it and hefted the saddlebags over their shoulder again. "Best we begin the ritual. We do not know how long it will take for the cure to work." They reached down to Yllari and helped him to his feet.

"If it works at all," Draya added. She refastened her waterskin to her belt and stood.

"We must pray it does," Nel answered.

"You do that, Aegis. I'll get moving instead." She started walking to the right. "That one," she said, pointing to the third alcove in.

"Smart choice." Nel sounded almost impressed as they reached the spot.

"Glad you approve," she replied dryly. Draya hoped her tone feigned enough disinterest in their opinion to squash the exchange. It was a good choice for several valid reasons – or at least it would have been if she'd made any choice at all. The space around the pool was a little larger than the closer ones, but more importantly, the entryway was about twice as wide. If anything hostile showed up, they'd have plenty of time to react and room to move. It wasn't as good as a back door, but it would have to do. It wasn't until she was already moving towards it that she recognized those strategic benefits, however. She'd already revealed too much when she confessed she was hearing a strange voice in her head. After a life fighting for her independence, she wasn't about to admit the lack of agency she seemed to have over her own body. The concern was disturbing enough – voicing it would only make things worse.

The alcove's interior was egg-shaped, its private bath tucked in the narrower end against the far wall. Short steps descended into the side of the pool closest to them, while a simple seat had been carved into the far side a few hands breadth below the water's surface. Unlit braziers flanked the entrance, but there was enough ambient light to see without them. Draya dropped her pack on a convenient bench and pulled out her flint. "Are we going to do this or not?"

Nel stiffened in response to her harsh tone, but they began the necessary preparations once Yllari was seated beside the pool. Lewedrin's description of the cure hadn't been overly detailed, instead written in a kind of shorthand that assumed the reader was already familiar with the standard ritual format. Nel and Yllari seemed to understand the basics well enough to explain the process to their impious companion, and as decided, Nel handed Draya a bundle of pungent herbs they'd gotten from Nyombe's temple. It was wrapped in marsh weed and heavy golden thread to form a wand shape, and she lit one end with the flint and steel. Once the top was fully engulfed, she blew out the flame and allowed the leaves and stems to smolder like an incense stick. The heavy smoke curled upwards, filling the space with the scent of sea lily and sharp samphire.

At the same time, Nel knelt at the edge of the pool and diligently emptied the contents of one bag of rock salt and then the other into the still water. When they signaled her with a nod, Draya passed the smoldering bundle to the Aegis. Head bowed in reverence, they held it between their bare palms as they repeated a prayer over and over in hushed tones. When the embers reached their fingers, Nel lowered their hands into the water. The spent leaves and stems sizzled and broke apart over the surface, revealing a second smaller bundle that Nel allowed to float on its own. The wrap of rice paper dissolved, and the petals of a pale blue lotus unfurled. Nel stood and finished the ritual by making the sign of the helix over their chest.

Draya bit back her cynicism. The burning wand was a lovely bit of showmanship, but it was no more magical than a street performer's prop work from what she could see. Her already unsteady faith in the rite's efficacy waned even further. Rather than dwell in doubt, she indulged in her professional curiosity. "The language of the prayer – was that Thalassan?" she asked Nel.

They looked pleasantly surprised. "You know it?"

"I wish I did," she admitted. "I recognized some of the words as cognates in Old Aiylonian. I always suspected they shared a common linguistic antecedent, but not even the Hawkers Guild has a sample I could study."

"That is good to hear," they said.

The relief in their voice surprised Draya. "Really? How is that good?"

Nel broke eye contact, instead looking down at the floating lotus. "It's the sacred language of the Tides. There is a reason education in Thalassan is prohibited when it comes to the uninitiated."

Draya scoffed. "Right. It's called gate keeping knowledge."

"That's not – no, that isn't the reason," Nel insisted, meeting her eyes again with open sincerity. "Language has power, and no language has more power than the holy words of the Order."

They honestly believe that. Before she could argue their naivety, there was a rustle of fabric behind her.

"It's time."

Draya turned to see Yllari shrugging his tattered and bloodied robes from his shoulders. His belt and sash were already draped on the bench beside him, his leather boots neatly placed beneath. She sucked in a breath through her teeth before she could stop herself. He stood bare-chested, his brown skin taunt over lean muscle, but that wasn't what gave Draya pause. The branches of purple-black veins enveloped his torso and rose threateningly over his ribs and up the chords of his neck. He still wore his ruined trousers, and through the ripped fabric Draya could already see ichor seeping out from the fresh bandages she'd replaced only two hours before.

"That bad, huh?" Yllari's smirk was interrupted by a sudden coughing fit.

Any of her criticisms died on her tongue as she and Nel helped Yllari to the steps. *It will either work or it won't*, she thought. She did her best to dismiss the hollow feeling in her core as a byproduct of Nel's concern, not her own.

"Don't look so glum," he said, throwing Nel a lopsided smile. "Remember Parascus?"

Nel maintained a stoic expression. "This isn't a gambling house, Yllari."

"We'd be having a much better time if it was." When Nel's expression only darkened, Yllari dropped his nonchalance. "You know what I mean. I'm not giving up yet. Neither should you." He gave Draya a nod. "Here goes nothing." The mage took the stairs one step at a time until his feet touched the bottom, submerging the lower two-thirds of his body into the pool.

Draya held her breath. There was no flash of light, no fizzing spray of water, no sudden physical reaction from Yllari himself. Draya sat back on her heels. She didn't know what she'd expected to happen, but she expected *something*. The mage closed his eyes and rested the back of his head against the far rim. She was about to ask how they'd know if the cure was taking effect when a splintering crash and a pained yelp disrupted the complete silence of the cave. Yllari's eyes shot open and the three froze in place.

"You thrice-damned cur!" A guttural voice echoed off the cavern walls. There was another fleshy thump followed by a further succession of whimpers. "Stay out of the water!"

The sounds came from the grotto's entrance, but the wall of the alcove blocked the source from view. Draya looked out across the communal pool to the alcoves at the other side. Had they taken a private pool to the left, they'd have been seen from that angle. As it was, they remained hidden in the shadows.

"This seems rather dangerous, don't you think?" a second nasally voice asked. "I told you the Cleansing would need more time to reach these caves. The quartz deposits –"

"Do you think this puddle is a threat to me?" the first voice barked. "I am Ghalloran! Favored Bastion to the Occidrious the Undying! The Infamous Butcher of Braehold!"

Draya shot a look at Nel. *Bastion?* she mouthed silently.

They gave her a quick nod, their eyes focused on the open entryway. Carefully, they reached over their head. Draya clenched her jaw as she waited for the inevitable clank of plate against plate, but it didn't come. The Aegis smoothly freed their sword and shield from their back with just a quiet swish.

That explains the diligent oiling, she admitted as she silently unsheathed her rapier from her hip.

"I would think not, my liege," the second voice continued. "But it is my sworn duty to act as your adviser; to be your emissary to Aiylonia's present age so that you may pave the way for the Emperor's return. You have only just been freed. We have no idea what effect –"

"Bah!" the Bastion scoffed, interrupting the nasal voice again. "That abyssal whelp just got lucky. It was the damn spear."

<Not a spear.>

"Not the time," Draya hissed under her breath. To her relief, Nel didn't seem to notice.

"Of course, Overseer. But consider the waergs. They do not have your abundant fortitude."

"They led us here, they can track down the survivor," the first barked. As if only just remembering the beasts were there, they shouted, "Go! Sniff out the dying bastard!"

Draya heard snuffling and the scramble of claws on stone. The waergs weren't advancing fast, but they would reach their alcove soon enough. Nel held up four fingers, indicating the number of amalgams under the Bastion's command. They both glanced over their shoulders to the pool, fearing the worst. But Yllari's eyes were closed again, his body relaxed and his breath steady. The eldritch veins had receded, leaving his face clear and unmarred.

It's working. Draya grabbed Nel's arm in excitement with her freed hand, completely forgetting the cuff around her wrist. The soft chime of metal on metal wasn't much, but it was enough.

"There! To the right!" the Bastion ordered. There was a renewed clatter of claws as the waergs converged and headed in their direction. "Come out, come out, wherever you are!"

Nel took a step forward and waved Draya behind their shield. She took another look at Yllari. There was so much corruption still inside of him. She spoke in a low voice. "If you heal, will you get your magic back?"

Yllari groggily opened his eyes again. "Maybe." His voice was slurred, almost as if he'd been drugged. Draya found herself jealous. "Yes. Yes, I think so. I can feel a little bit of it now...I just have to reach out and –"

"Yllari, stop. Reserve your strength." Nel's nostrils flared, but they didn't take their eyes off the alcove's entrance.

"That's going to take time we don't have," Draya said, inexplicably knowing her words rang true. She drew the cultist's dagger from her belt. "I'll buy us some." Before Nel could stop her – or she could change her mind – she took two steps past the threshold. The waergs spotted her immediately, the two in the front hurtling towards her, their wicked fangs on full display. She planted her feet and held the serrated blade out in front of her. All four of the beasts slid to a halt a mere long stride away, two in front and two behind. They growled and salivated but didn't advance. Draya smiled, glad her bluff paid off. "Good little beasties. Now stay."

The Bastion and her lackey stood further away, the former nearly shaking with rage at the turn of events. She was a hulking mass of muscle and leather armor, her skin more hide than human, and heavy jowls clenched around a pair of ivory tusks jutting up from her lower jaw. A mohawk of stiff dark bristles crested her scalp and ran down the back of her neck. The human at her side looked more annoyed than angry. His deep hood shrouded the upper half of his face in shadow, and he wore black and violet layered robes much like those Yllari wore.

"Call off your dogs!" she shouted. "Or I'll sic them on you instead!" She hoped the lie sounded more convincing to them than it did to her.

The boar-woman narrowed her eyes, considering the validity of the threat.

One down, she thought to herself.

"Improbable," the adviser declared.

Blood and bones. Draya fought the impulse to glance down at the snarling pack. "Do you want to make that wager?"

Bolstered by a confident shake of the adviser's head, the Bastion took a step forward. "Who are you hiding back there, waif?"

You just need to stall, she reminded herself. *They don't need to believe you, they just need to keep talking.* She flashed her most practiced smile, guaranteed to disarm a target if not completely win them over. "I'd love to say my armored escort is waiting in the wings, but that would make me a sarding idiot to come out here alone." She could feel Nel's sense of chivalry chafing at the remark. *I feel those eyes boring into my back,* she thought in their direction. *Don't you dare muck this up and prove me a liar.* She didn't exactly believe the bonding let them read her thoughts, but she hoped she at least relayed the sentiment.

"You're an idiot either way!" the Bastion barked. "Do you have any idea who I am? I am Ghalloran! Favored Bastion to Occidrious the Undying! The Infamous Butcher of –"

"Braehold, yes, I heard you the first time." It seemed the smile had a third unfortunate effect – inciting the target's pride. "First of all, your precious master is still trapped like a toddler in a well. Second of all, do you know how many armies have defeated Braehold since the Deluge? It's not much of an accomplishment."

Ghalloran's shoulders stiffened. She almost took a step forward when the adviser casually lifted his hand. "We know you are not alone," he said with confidence. "The waergs tracked a survivor to this cave. As you appear perfectly hale and hearty, our quarry must be nearby – I assume in the alcove behind you."

Draya coquettishly lowered her eyelids. "Perfect? You flatter me. Sallow-skinned, vaguely threatening toadies aren't usually my type, but if you want an excuse to get me alone back here you just have to ask." She gestured towards the alcove and took the opportunity to glance inside. Nel's eyes were wide with horror, but they managed to shake their head. Yllari needed more time.

She looked back towards the adviser. She couldn't see his eyes, but his clenched fists told her he didn't take kindly to her insinuation. *At least something is working – an angry man is a reckless man.* She turned her attention back to the Bastion. "So, you're a real-life, walking, talking infamous Bone General, huh?" She tilted her head to one side. "Did he make all of you pig-people, or did it just suit your particular disposition?"

Ghalloran glowered and the waergs grew more agitated in response. "The boar is a noble beast. It's an honor to bear its visage." Draya flinched as the furthest amalgam nipped at the tail of the one barely an arm's length away. The dagger might hold some sway over the creatures, but the hold was tenuous at best.

The Bastion must have noticed the reaction. What might pass as a wicked smile pulled at the corners of her jowls. She laughed and thumped a heavy hand on the adviser's back. His upper torso pitched forward, but he managed to keep his footing. "You're right Skellin – she's lying!" Emboldened, Ghalloran unspooled a long heavy whip from her belt. "Perhaps they just need a little motivation." She threw her arm out and a sharp crack split the air like thunder. "Attack you worthless curs!" the Bastion growled.

The waergs in the back surged forward, snapping ferociously at their pack mates. The two closest snarled in return. It was clear the effect of the dagger was no match to the unbridled ferocity of the boar-woman. Draya leaped back and extended the tip of her rapier as the pair stalked forward. Another crack of the whip echoed off the cave walls. "Nel? I think I've done all I can," she called anxiously.

In a sudden burst of speed, the one on the right pounced. Draya lifted her blade in defense, but before the waerg could bowl into her a flash of gold cut across her vision. Nel's shield caught the mass of fur and muscle in midair and forced the amalgam back. It whimpered and whined as it fell into the pack behind, pinning one to the ground and scattering the other two.

Good timing, she thought, then did her best to hide her relief. "What took you so long?"

Nel didn't even bother to glare this time. They took position on her right, their shield poised to protect her torso as well as their own as needed. "The majority of the eldritch corruption has receded. It is only the area around his initial injury that needs to heal."

So just a little bit longer.

One after the other, the unencumbered waergs attacked from both sides. The first homed in on Nel's right, the second on Draya's left. Unwilling to move their shield and leave their ward unprotected, Nel angled their broadsword downward and took the brunt of the attack against the flat of their blade. They leaned back to absorb the impact then sprang forward, throwing the waerg back and slashing out at its vulnerable belly. The golden blade easily sliced through the beast to its spine, nearly cutting it in half. Its body landed hard, black ichor spilling across the cavern floor. On the other side, the waerg lunged at Draya's exposed ankles. Unlike Nel, her rapier was too thin to deflect the head-on assault, forcing her to sidestep out from the safety of the shield. The waerg snapped uselessly at the empty air, and in its pause of confusion, Draya plunged the cultist's dagger down into the top of its spine. It collapsed in a heap, its eyes wild as the rest of its body lay paralyzed. Nel brought their sword swiftly down, severing the connection completely and putting the creature out of its misery.

The two uninjured waergs retreated to Ghalloran's side. "Who the sarding abyss are you?" the Bastion shouted.

The adviser stepped out from behind her. "That, my liege, is the

Aegis Commander General, which should mean their so-called Chosen One is nearby." Draya could practically see the wheels turning in his head. All of a sudden, he let out a disconcerting laugh that left her with a slimy feeling and the urge to wash off in the pool. He managed to look even more pompous. "But the boy isn't here, is he?"

Nel tensed. Draya knew she had to say something. "Of course, he's here. Where else would he be?"

Ghalloran looked between her adviser and Nel, nakedly confused.

Skellin crossed his arms over his chest. "An Aegis would never leave the side of their sworn charge. Which could only mean we owe this woman our thanks."

"What?" Ghalloran balked. "Why?"

"Traveling with a wayward Aegis. A coil of red hair. And if I had to guess, gray eyes, yes?"

Draya cringed. She'd been avoiding thinking about it, but since the Palace, the blue in her eyes had completely faded, leaving dark gray irises behind.

Skellin's smile broadened at her small but telling response. "My liege, we are in the company of no one else but your emancipator."

Ghalloran looked even more confused. "My what?"

Skellin took a calming breath. "The Harbinger herself, the Droughtbringer."

"Oh." Recognition dawned on the Bastion's face. "Does that mean – the boy Brightbourne is the one injured? The one we've tracked here?" She stepped forward, her beady eyes wide with excitement.

"If I understand the prophecies correctly, unlikely. But there is one way to find out." The adviser dropped his hands to his sides. A soft thrum radiated from his body, filling the grotto with its power. Draya watched as inky tendrils of shadow began to curl out from the sleeves of his robes. "Stand down, Droughtbringer. We are meant to be allies, not enemies."

"Not in this sarding lifetime, creep," Draya spat.

Ghalloran narrowed her eyes. "You'll come with us one way or another. There is nowhere for you to run."

"I'd beg to differ."

Draya's head swiveled. Yllari stood tall behind them. His eyes were bright and a smile played at the corners of his mouth. There was not a dark unnatural vein to be seen.

"Is that him?" Ghalloran asked the adviser.

To Draya's surprise, Skellin somehow managed to sound even more irritated. "No – I don't know who –"

"Now would be a good time to move," Yllari said before the adviser could continue his train of thought. He swept an arm out magnanimously, ushering the pair into the alcove.

She and Nel exchanged glances. Both knew their position wasn't ideal for combat, but at least they stood between a wall on one side and a pool of water on the other — a pool that was clearly anathema to the waergs. That had to be an advantage worth holding onto.

"Enough talk!" Ghalloran bellowed as she cracked her whip again. The tip flew farther than should have been possible, violently splintering a quartz stalagmite. The two remaining waergs howled, jumping forward and avoiding the shards. The Bastion moved closer and raised her arm to strike again.

"Do you trust me?" Yllari shouted over the din.

This time they didn't argue. Draya sprinted around the corner, Nel protecting her retreat from behind. The heavy claws of the two remaining waergs struck hard against the stone and the strange thrum of dark magic grew louder. But none of that mattered anymore. They had a way out.

Yllari's portal tore through the air in front of the private pool, a kaleidoscope of sparks and shimmering golden light. She was about to ask how he'd managed to create it when her eyes fell on a beam of sunlight she hadn't seen before. She traced the source to a hand mirror wedged into a crack in the wall. Despite its small size, the silvered glass was perfectly situated to capture and reflect the rays of light that bounced between the brass garlands.

Sarding genius. She caught Yllari's eye.

He grinned. "Ladies first."

There was a clash of metal behind them as Nel caught one of the snarling waergs against their shield. "We're out of time," they called over their shoulder.

Draya didn't bother to ask where they were going or what to expect on the other side. She knew the answer to Yllari's question. If it had been Nel, the answer would have been the same. As she threw herself into the swirling lights, she wondered what the price of that trust would be.

Kristen Kail Roberts

Looking for more?

The story continues in serial form with all new episodes of Droughtbringer each month. Join our community for exclusive access to early drafts and other special perks. As a subscriber, you'll not only find out what happens next — you can leave comments, ask questions, and potentially influence the story as we go on this daring adventure together.

Visit kristenkailroberts.com for more details.

Acknowledgments

From world-building to first drafts, from serial episodes to what you hold in your hands, coaxing Draya's story into existence has been no easy task. Without going into the details, when I became a new mom in 2022 I suddenly found myself in a very difficult place, mentally, physically, and socially. Two years later things have improved by leaps and bounds, but back then? Looking forward to my next writing session kept me moving from moment to moment, day to day. Paragraphs came out in drips and drabs, stuffed into every spare moment I could find to distract myself. Writing became more than a passion, more than a career — storytelling fueled my survival. I wouldn't go so far as to say it saved my life, but I'm not exactly sure where I'd be now without the trope-filled, nostalgic escapism Droughtbringer has given me.

There are, of course, so many people who have supported me throughout this process. I must extend special thanks to my community at the Mercury Cafe and Teahouse in Historic New Castle. The vast majority of Droughtbringer was crafted from my favorite table between the door and the bar, the work broken up by lattes and lunches, banter and snark. Dwayne, Caroline, Robin — you have given me refuge and a second home for which I will always be grateful. I can also thank Dwayne for introducing me to Jon, a fellow author who had just begun the process of building what has now grown into Arts Focus Delaware. Writing is inherently a lonely endeavor, but sharing and celebrating with others in the field has been invaluable. And speaking of other writers, thank you Jax for introducing me to the trope of the

Apocalypse Maiden. Falling down that research rabbit hole in no small way set the stage for what this story would become.

It cannot be emphasized enough that this version of the book wouldn't exist if not for the lovely humans who have suffered through multiple drafts of Draya's misadventures — Megan, Maranda, Eric E., Eric K., and Victoria. Your advice, encouragement, and tough love have meant more than you can imagine, providing motivation when I've needed it most. Last but not least, I have to thank my long-time partner Sam. He will insist he played no part in this, but I couldn't have made it happen without his support and encouragement.

Kristen Kail Roberts

About the Author

**Kristen Kail Roberts** has an obscure Buddhist history degree and former experience as a recipe blogger, event planner, and charitable fundraiser, among other seemingly unrelated things. Today, she writes adventure fantasy in the nooks and crannies of mom life and helps fellow authors as a developmental editor when time allows. She currently lives in Delaware with her partner of twenty years, two elder cats, and a toddler too clever for all of them combined.

Droughtbringer is the first piece of fiction published under her name.

Made in the USA
Middletown, DE
07 August 2025